# Amaranth

T0244849

# AMARANTH

A NOVEL

JEN BRAAKSMA

spark press

Copyright © 2024 Jen Braaksma

All rights reserved. No part of this publication may be reproduced, distributed, or transmitted in any form or by any means, including photocopying, recording, digital scanning, or other electronic or mechanical methods, without the prior written permission of the publisher, except in the case of brief quotations embodied in critical reviews and certain other noncommercial uses permitted by copyright law. For permission requests, please address SparkPress.

Published by SparkPress, a BookSparks imprint,
A division of SparkPoint Studio, LLC
Phoenix, Arizona, USA, 85007
www.gosparkpress.com

Published 2024
Printed in the United States of America
Print ISBN: 978-1-68463-244-2
E-ISBN: 978-1-68463-245-9
Library of Congress Control Number: 2023920113

Interior design by Tabitha Lahr

All company and/or product names may be trade names, logos, trademarks, and/or registered trademarks and are the property of their respective owners.

This is a work of fiction. Names, characters, places, and incidents either are the product of the author's imagination or are used fictitiously. Any resemblance to actual persons, living or dead, is entirely coincidental.

**NO AI TRAINING:** Without in any way limiting the author's [and publisher's] exclusive rights under copyright, any use of this publication to "train" generative artificial intelligence (AI) technologies to generate text is expressly prohibited. The author reserves all rights to license uses of this work for generative AI training and development of machine learning language models.

*To Abby and Megan*
*Best. Daughters. Ever.*

# CHAPTER 1

I'm nervous watching Holly clamber up the fraying rope ladder on the old play structure, concerned it'll break under her weight, but Holly insists she'll be safe.

"Please, Lyra?" she begs, her eyes wide with excitement. How could I say no? It's the first time since she arrived at the orphanage more than three months ago that I've seen her remotely close to happy. And a little five-year-old girl who lost both parents to the rampaging Hecate's Plague deserves at least a moment of happy.

I immediately regret my decision when she nearly slips. I rush forward, my heart in my throat, but she catches herself with a squeal of delight and carries on.

I shiver in the early April chill and pull my brown leather bomber jacket around me, clenching it tight in my fists. I hear Mama Jua's voice in my head—*"Relax, Lyra"*—and see her old, lined face crinkling into a smile. "You're too serious for someone so young," she always tells me.

"I have reason to be," I always reply.

"No seventeen-year-old has reason enough," she always insists.

But she was joking, I knew. She understood how hard it was to be on the run with my parents all these years. Twenty-one places in nine years. I'd never told anyone that before. Never could. Always too dangerous. You never knew who might rat you out to government agents. But when we arrived in Jamestown last fall, when I met my new neighbor, I knew Mama Jua was different. She didn't care that *I* was different. She never even asked *how* I was different.

"Oh, sweet child," Mama Jua said, and put her hand to my cheek. It was the only time someone other than my parents had touched me like that in nine years.

Until I met Holly, that is. Ever since she came to the orphanage where Mama Jua had dragged me to volunteer, I can't get enough of her squeezing, over-the-shoulder hugs. They're just like the hugs my little sister Ivy used to give me when we were kids, before everything began.

From the top of the slide, I hear Holly speaking to someone I can't see. "Wow, your cheeks are red like my mommy and papa's were," she says.

My head flies up and, in a single bound, I'm at the base of the play structure. I look up and see a little boy, not much older than Holly, huddled inside the mouth of the cold plastic slide. Even from this distance, I can see what Holly means. The boy's face is flaming with the telltale rash.

"Holly, get back!" I shout, terrified. Hecate's Plague isn't airborne, but one sneeze, one cough from this sick little boy and Holly will be as dead as he is about to be.

Holly glances down at me, at first confused, but she must see the fear in my eyes, and she scuttles away from the slide.

"Go get Mama Jua," I say, lifting her down from the splintering wooden platform. Mama Jua'll know what to do. She always does.

Holly races off across the park, across the street to the orphanage as I climb up. My heart is pounding; I know I can get close to the boy, I know I won't get sick because I never get sick, but still I hang back.

"What's your name?" I ask. I want to ask, why are you here? Where are your parents? But I know the answers. Because surely his parents are dead.

The little boy only whimpers like a frightened puppy.

I glance toward the shabby building across the street. *Hurry up*, I plead to Mama Jua, as the boy and I wait in awkward silence. I wish I knew what to do, what to say, but can't think of anything. At least nothing of comfort. There are no words to comfort a kid who is, with one-hundred percent certainty, going to die in no more than three days.

"Lyra!" I hear Alexis's voice ring out across the park and I groan. I wanted Holly to get Mama Jua, not the director of the orphanage. I'm afraid Alexis will play by the rules. She'll send this boy to a quarantine camp—and she may send Holly there, too, the way we're supposed to turn in anyone who came in close contact with a plague victim. But I won't let her. I'll tell her Holly never came near the boy, that there was no chance she could have been infected.

I jump from the play structure, readying for a fight when I see Mama Jua hurry along behind Alexis. I exhale with relief. It'll be okay, now.

"Where is he?" Alexis asks, and I point to the slide. "It's true?"

I nod. There is no mistaking Hecate's Plague.

Alexis's shoulders slump. She frowns, and I see the lines etched deeply into her skin. For a moment, I feel for her, for the thankless job she has trying to protect all these orphaned kids, until she says she'll call the health authorities. "They'll want to know who found him," she adds. "I'll have to name Holly."

"*No*," I snap, panicking. I whirl around toward the orphanage across the street, ready to bolt back to Holly, but Mama Jua comes over to me, and wraps her small arm around my waist. Her head barely reaches my shoulders—she's as short as I am tall—but still she feels like a pillar of strength beside me. *It'll be okay*, her squeeze tells me, and I relax because I believe her.

"Alexis, there's no need to call anyone," she says, "I will take care of the boy," Mama Jua says.

My eyes widen in fright. *She can't*, I think, and Alexis echoes my thoughts: "If you do, you'll die." She lowers her voice. "Ahimsa doesn't equate rebellion with being reckless," she whispers. "You of all people should know that."

Mama Jua's eyes flare with fury. "That is *exactly* what my daughter's group is about. It's about being reckless in the name of morality and decency and humanity. I will *not* stand by and let the government swallow up another innocent—another young child!—in its heartless quarantine camps. Isn't that why we risk our lives every day, Alexis? If we don't care for people with the plague, if we don't offer them dignity in death, then who will?"

"*We* can't, not anymore," Alexis insists. "You know as well as I do that we don't have any more protective equipment."

She's right. *No one* has any more HAZMAT suits or masks or anything, not even the remaining hospitals. Goddamn government, bleeding the country dry for *ten* years to support its inane and pointless Middle East war. And look at the results: hardly any hospitals, doctors, or supplies left to fight Hecate's Plague this time around. Only mass incarcerations and cremation in inhumane quarantine camps.

"So are we simply going to desert this boy to his cruel fate, throw him all alone into the anarchy of the camps?" Mama Jua argues. "He deserves more. He deserves better."

"Not at the cost of your life," Alexis says.

I tug Mama Jua closer to me. I feel the warmth of her touch, I smell the comforting scent of her lilac perfume. Alexis is right. We can't risk Mama Jua for the sake of this stranger.

Mama Jua is too important to Ahimsa, to the resistance. She's the heart of the struggle, and I think for a moment that I won't let her go. I'll hold onto her, physically block her path.

Mama Jua softens her tone. "We—all of us—have no choice but to die," she says. "We can only choose how we want to live."

No, no, no, I shake my head. It's not true, I want tell her. *I* won't die, I want to say. And then I imagine myself explaining: Remember how I said I was different? Well, that's because I can't die. I have these strange cells that always regenerate. They're called phoenix cells and they heal from *every* injury and illness, so you see? The plague can't kill *me*. Nothing can.

Which means, I realize with a start, that *I* should be staying with the boy. If I believe, like Mama Jua, that this boy shouldn't die isolated and alone in a heartless quarantine camp, and if I don't want to see Mama Jua die, then that's my only option.

"I'll stay with him," I volunteer.

"No," Mama Jua barks.

"You don't understand," I start to say, but Mama Jua cuts me off.

"You are young and have a full life ahead of you, one that I promise you will be filled with love and laughter. I am old and leave a good, long life behind me."

"But—" I try again.

"Holly needs you," Mama Jua says emphatically, and my eyes are automatically drawn to the crumbling house across the street. We're too far away to see through the front window, but I imagine Holly's little nose pressed up against the glass, watching us.

"Mama Jua, I can't let you—" Alexis speaks up, but Mama Jua cuts her, off, too.

"I am not asking your permission to love and care for a sick child," Mama Jua says softly. Then, with more ease than I expected from an old woman, Mama Jua climbs up to the wooden platform at the top of the slide. Gently, she pulls the boy from the slide. He resists at first, like I did when I first met her, but like me, she quickly wins him over, and he clambers down.

Mama Jua lowers herself to the ground, then bundles the boy into her arms. Instinctively, Alexis and I take two steps back.

"Let's take you home," she says to him and the boy melts into her embrace.

And I stand there, doing nothing.

I stand there and let her go.

"God willing, I'll be back," she says to me, and I believe her. I believe her because I want to believe her. There's never been a case of a caregiver *not* contracting the plague—it's why doctors and nurses aren't even allowed in quarantine camps—but today, as I watch Mama Jua walk away with a dying boy, I believe she will be the first to survive.

At least that's what I tell myself as I turn back toward the orphanage with Alexis, as I turn back toward Holly.

I believe that Mama Jua will be back and everything will be okay.

✦

But of course I was wrong. It's not okay. Mama Jua doesn't come back, and three days later, I'm telling Holly that Mama Jua is dead. Holly screams and cries and flails her little fists against my chest, and then tells me that I'm lying, that Mama Jua isn't dead because Holly told Mama Jua she wasn't allowed to die like her parents and she says Mama Jua agreed. And my heart breaks, as I wrap her in a big bear hug, because it's all my fault. I could have saved Mama Jua. I should have insisted that I take the boy. I should have planted myself in front of her and stopped her from walking away. I could have made her understand about my phoenix cells; I could have made her see I'm the only person to *ever* survive Hecate's Plague and then she'd still be alive today.

But I didn't. I let Mama Jua die.

Holly's sobs subside to a sniffle, and she climbs into my lap. She curls her head into my chest. "Why am I so bad?" she asks me.

"What?" I say, shocked. "You're *not* bad."

"Everybody leaves me," she says. "Mommy and Papa and Granny and Grampa and Mama Jua. They all went up to Heaven without me."

My throat tightens, and it takes me a minute to find my voice. "Oh, honey, they didn't want to leave you. They had no choice. But they all loved you."

"Are you going to leave me, too?" Holly murmurs.

My eyes sting, and I can't breathe. I can't get sick and I can't die, but I think about the countless towns I've lived in and our abrupt, furtive, middle-of-the night departures. I think about Jonah, my secret boyfriend from two towns ago, whom I had to desert without even saying goodbye, and I think about the look I imagined on his face when he realized I was never coming back, and I can't, can't, can't do that to Holly. I can't run again.

Then it hits me.

I *won't* run again.

Oh my God, I'm suddenly excited. I'm not going to run, no matter what my parents say about fleeing agents. I'm going to stay and help take care of Holly. I'll finally tell my parents about her—and Mama Jua and my time secretly volunteering for the orphanage—and I'll get them to come and meet Holly and they'll fall in love with her—and maybe they'll even adopt her—and then they'll see that we don't have to leave again, agents or no agents. They'll see we *can* stay, that we can make a good life for ourselves in Jamestown.

So when I finally answer Holly, there's laughter in my voice. "No, honey, I'm not going to leave you."

✦

I don't tell my parents right away, though. I decide I need to do one last thing before I confess all. I need to tell Mama Jua she was right. She'd always wanted me to come clean with my parents—"secrets are like death by a thousand pinpricks," she'd tried to warn me—but I wouldn't listen. I couldn't listen. Not then. Not when I was too afraid of my parents' reaction. But Mama Jua's death has opened my eyes, changed my perspective. It's given me courage, the strength to stand up to my parents' restrictive edicts. I'm almost eighteen; no longer will I let them rule my life. From now on, I make my *own* choices, and I need Mama Jua to know that. I need her to know she changed me. So I decide to go to her funeral. It's dangerous, I know. Funerals for plague victims are outlawed; only mass cremation by the government is allowed, so health authorities often scour cemeteries to round up mourners whom they feel are at risk of spreading the disease, but I decide it's worth the risk.

If I failed her in life, I won't fail her in death.

I sneak through the woods toward the small group of mourners huddled in the far corner of the overgrown cemetery. I stop in the dawn shadow of an ancient oak tree and I stare at the plain wooden coffin balancing on two rough planks over a hand-dug hole. I listen to the soft, solemn lilt of the mourners keeping their voices low. I catch a stray phrase, an isolated word. *Great loss . . . Saint . . .* Then a laugh. A great guffaw, and it's followed by a chuckle, and then a giggle. How *can* they? How can they laugh at her funeral?

"Because that's what I want," she would have said. I hear Mama Jua's voice in my head.

The cold morning air slices through me. I'm shaking, and I feel my chest tighten, my eyes burn, but I will *not* cry. I have no right to cry. Her family, the ones I've never met, the ones standing by the grave, they're the ones who are allowed to cry: her daughter, the famous Ahimsa founder, the one I assume is the woman in the thin gray coat, and the rich-looking couple dressed in black, and the tall, lean teenager. He must be the grandson, the one from New York City, the one Mama Jua kept trying to set me up with. "I have a boyfriend," I would lie, and Mama Jua would play along. "You can never have too many boyfriends," she'd say, and she'd laugh. Because she loved to laugh.

In the distance, I hear the shriek of a crow and it startles the mourners, too.

"Hurry up," hisses a short thin woman, and I'm surprised I recognize her voice. Alexis. My stomach roils in anger. What's she doing here? If health authorities do descend on the funeral, they'll not only throw her in the quarantine camp, they'll also throw in *every* kid she's been in contact with into the camp and leave them to die. Including Holly. *How* could Alexis risk Holly? Mama Jua would have understood Alexis not coming, so why is she here?

I want to lurch out of the shadows and lunge at Alexis, and I feel my foot slide forward through the melting patch of dirty snow, but the other mourners, about ten in all, suddenly seem to remember that they shouldn't be here either, and they rush to the coffin. I watch, as if from the wings of a poorly rehearsed play, as four people, two on either side of the casket, feed two thick ropes underneath it, then the grandson and the rich man in the black suit wiggle away the planks. The four people strain against the ropes as they lower Mama Jua into her grave.

I shut my eyes, squeeze my eyes, because I can't watch them bury Mama Jua. I hear the soft thud of dirt land on the top of the coffin as the mourners refill the shallow hole and I can't breathe. It's as if every shovelful of earth that buries Mama Jua suffocates me. I shift around the tree and sink again to the cold wet ground, burying my head in my hands. I tense every muscle I have in a desperate effort to stop myself from running to the grave and flinging away their shovels.

"*Don't do it!*" I want to cry. "*Don't bury her! She was my only friend! And I haven't told her what she meant to me! I haven't said goodbye!*"

But then I find my body weakening, my energy draining. What's the alternative? Mass cremation, the way health officials dispose of all the other plague victims? No, Mama Jua deserves to be buried. She deserves the dignity of a funeral.

I just didn't know funerals could hurt so much.

I listen as the mourners pay their final respects, a low murmur of indistinguishable voices. I think for a crazy minute that I should join them now, that I should share my pain with them, and allow them to share theirs with me. I should tell them that Mama Jua was my friend, the only friend I've had in nine years. I could cry about how much I'll miss her, how much I already want her back, and I think Mama Jua would have liked that. She would have wanted me to step out of the shadows, but I can't. I can't risk Alexis seeing me and I shouldn't have risked anybody else seeing me here, either. It was dangerous and foolish. If my mom finds out about any of it—me coming to the funeral, Holly, the orphanage—she'll kill me.

Ha. Funny.

Kill me.

As it is, I need to get back. I check my watch, worried. I have barely enough time to walk home, sneak into the house and into bed before Mom returns from her night shift at the truck stop. She will *freak* if she checks on me and I'm not there. And she will check on me. Guaranteed. She does it as routinely as a prison guard.

I wait for the mourners to weave their way through the crumbling gravestones to the gravel road where a few cars have been discreetly parked. I watch them climb in. I'm about to jog to the road, but suddenly, I can't leave. I haven't done what I came to do. I hate it, I don't want to do it, but I have to say goodbye.

Pivoting, I return to the mound that is now Mama Jua. I crouch beside the grave and pull a dried sprig of flowers from my pocket. I hold the deep, garnet-red amaranth petals in my palm, remembering when Mama Jua gave them to me last fall.

"They remind me of you," she said, clipping the velvety, tassel-like flowers from her garden and thrusting a bouquet into my hands. "They are beautiful and vibrant and strong. And," she added with a squeeze of my hand, "they thrive longer than most."

No one except my parents had ever given me a gift; I knew I would keep them forever. I pressed the flowers dry and tucked them away. But yesterday, when I heard Mama Jua would have a real funeral, I knew I had to give them back to her.

I lay the dried sprig on her grave, its red petals bright against the dark, damp earth. I shudder, my shoulders shaking as I start to cry, and then I can't stop.

"I'm sorry," I whisper, and I realize all at once that's the real reason I came—not to reveal my epiphany, not to say goodbye, but to apologize. I start gasping and crying and again I can't breathe. "I'm sorry I let you die."

*Like Ivy.*

Abruptly I stand and shake my head. *No. I will not think about Ivy.*

But I can't stop, not while everywhere I turn is a headstone, old markers of people who've been dead longer than they were alive, like Ivy: nine years dead to her six years alive.

A gust of wind whips my unruly black curls into my face and I fiercely swipe them away. I will not think about my little sister's small plague-ridden body disintegrating in a grave a half a dozen states away. I will not think about how I infected her. I will not think about how she's dead because of me.

Instead I will myself to think about Holly. About my promise to her.

I look back at the mound, at Mama Jua.

"She won't lose me, too," I vow.

I hop onto the road, the gravel crunching beneath my thrift store canvas shoes, and take a deep, crisp breath. A car comes up behind me—I shiver because it slows as it passes me, and I think for a second that it's a black agent car, but I know I'm being paranoid. I'm always paranoid, always skulking in the shadows, sticking to the shade. Well no more. That part of my life is done. I'm *not* going to live my life in fear of phantoms anymore. Instead, I'm stepping into light and laughter. This afternoon, in honor of Mama Jua, I'll make Holly laugh. It will sound like the squeak of a mouse and that always makes *me* laugh.

I take a short cut through a bare-branched forest—after nine lonely years on the run, I'm an expert at finding alternate routes—and I pass the rest of my walk home devising my strategy to make Holly laugh. Tickling is an old favorite, but that's too easy. Knock-knock jokes? Holly laughs at them all, but that's a cop-out because she doesn't always understand them. I'm thinking of making her do fairy tale voices—she loves Little Red Riding Hood's line, "My, what big ears you have, Grandma"—when I turn onto the decaying street where my parents and I live in a sad little bungalow. I kick at a chunk of loose pavement, and catch my toe.

"Goddamn it," I seethe, shaking out my throbbing foot. "Goddamn road." Goddamn *country*. Falling apart at the seams. It's not just health care that's been neglected all these years. How *is* it that the government can still get reelected? If the goddamn voters had turfed out the bastards long ago, we might actually have a functioning society.

I draw my jacket around me, hunched against the increasing wind. I hurry past Mama Jua's house. I don't want to see the sad, empty windows, the vacant front porch.

"Come for lemonade," she said, the first time she called to me last fall. Out of habit, out of caution, I avoided her. "Come for tea. Come for juice. Come for whiskey," she persisted. I smile now, remembering how Mama Jua twittered like a little sparrow when I strode up to her porch, expecting to call her bluff. But Mama Jua was Mama Jua and I can still taste the hot burning alcohol on my tongue.

Could my cells have saved her? Not from the boy in the park, but in the lab nine years ago? I would never tell my parents this, but I wonder sometimes what would have happened if we'd stayed. If the scientists had cloned my phoenix cells the way they wanted, if they had made their indestructible, un-killable army. Could that have stopped this futile war long ago? Could I have helped save the lives of thousands of soldiers and hundreds of thousands of civilians who were caught in the crossfire during all these years? Have I single-handedly doomed our country and our world by not sacrificing myself to their painful procedures all those years ago?

The question echoes in my head. I remember the last time I asked it.

The last time I was in a cemetery.

I was ten. It was the second anniversary of Ivy's death. We were nowhere near her grave—never again could we visit it since it was too close to our enemies in Washington—but we were in another cemetery, *pretending* someone else's tombstone was Ivy's tombstone. I looked out over the vast expanse of lawn, at the gray stones rising from the ground like rows of rotting teeth. Mom crouched slowly in front of the worn slab of marble, and lay down a bouquet of daisies, Ivy's favorite flower, as if her daughter were truly buried here. She looked far away, and she looked happier, her face softer, smoother.

My hand hovered over her shoulder. I was afraid to touch her, afraid I'd break her spell. But after two years of keeping my question to myself, afraid of the answer, I finally had to know. "Mommy?" I touched her sleeve and she jumped as if she'd been shot. I cringed, but I couldn't bear the torment any longer. "Could I have saved Ivy?" I asked. I remember not knowing what I wanted the answer to be. *Yes, you could have saved her and she'd still be with us but you didn't*, or *No, you couldn't have saved her and you'll always have to live with the grief and pain and loss.*

Mom shook her head and for once, the soft smile she used for Ivy turned my way. My insides collapsed with relief.

"No, honey," Mom said, and tried to explain the science, "to create a cure for the plague, doctors need antibodies from a person who fought the disease; but your body used your phoenix cells to heal itself—not antibodies—and your phoenix cells won't work on other people. Their immune systems attack them."

"Then how come they want to clone me?"

Mom sighed. "They thought they could replace *all* of someone's cells with cells like yours."

"But that's impossible . . . Then they'd be *me* instead of them." I shuddered at the image in my mind of rows upon rows of camo-clad ten-year-old look-alike soldiers.

That image still haunts me today. Even though I've learned that the science is capable of cloning only the protective part of my phoenix cells, I always imagine a desert battlefield strewn with my body, my face, repeated hundreds of times over.

"We won't let that happen, honey," Mom said that day, pulling me close. "That's why we're here."

I don't remember where "here" was then, and I don't care. I gave up trying to track our meanderings long ago. One minute we're in North Dakota and another we're in Pennsylvania. One day Rhode Island, the next day Florida. Today it's New York. For the past nine years that we've been on the run—since I was eight—I have most definitely been safe. And secure. And protected. I have *also* been lonely. And isolated. And alone. Since I was ten and begged my parents to let my new neighbor Piper stay for a sleepover and my parents refused in case she asked too many questions, I have been friendless. Since I was twelve and wanted to join the school's volleyball team, which would have meant filling out a medical consent form, and suspicion about us if we had *not*, I have been homeschooled. Since I was sixteen and had to abandon Jonah without a word when we up and moved in the middle of the night, I have been dateless.

I check my watch. I'm late, I'm late, I'm late. Mom usually gets off work early Friday mornings, so I hope she's late, too. I rush along our rundown neighborhood, up our rundown path of our shabby bungalow and creak open the door.

"Lyra Sage Harmon, where *have* you been?"

I almost jump out of my skin at the shriek of my mother's voice. I turn around, an excuse forming on my lips. *An early morning jog,* I'm thinking, since a run or a hike is the only time I'm allowed out from under Mom and Dad's hawk eyes. The excuse always works; it's how I've gotten away with volunteering at the shelter all these afternoons. But I wince as I face my mother's wrath; I've never gone outside this early, especially not without telling them.

I don't get as far as my first word before I see my mom ransacking our small linen closet and tugging out our patched-up backpacks. I see my dad in their bedroom at the end of the hall, pulling clothes out of the dresser drawers.

"No," I say because I know what this means. Another move.

"I saw them, Lyra," Mom says, as she rushes toward the bedroom, throwing the backpack at Dad. "The agents," she adds as if I don't already know who *them* is. The *them* that have destroyed my life. "On the highway on my way home from work," she continues.

I suck in a breath. The car on the road from the funeral.

But no, that's silly. There are no agents. There's no way they would have tracked us here. Our moves are much too spontaneous—even we don't know what town we're moving to until we get there. And since the only people I know in town are Mama Jua, Holly, and some kids in the orphanage, and Alexis, who knows nothing about me, there's no way *they* could have turned me in. No, Mom must be wrong. She's seeing things again, so I don't move. I remind myself I'm done running.

Sensing I haven't budged, Mom stops and glares at me. "Hurry *up*. It won't take them long to find us."

"I'm not going." The words burn on my lips, bubbling up from the lava of long-simmering anger and newly-added grief boiling within me. I match my mom's hard, determined stare.

Mom's lips purse into a thin *o*.

"This is not a negotiation, Lyra." Mom grips her hands on the back of the shabby couch. "We *have* to leave. They're too close."

Dad comes out of the bedroom, his hand resting lightly on top of Mom's tense shoulders. At one time, I thought their affection for each other was cute, but now it's offensive. In a household of three, it's always two against one.

"You *know* she's being paranoid," I say to Dad. "She sees boogeymen *everywhere*."

"Watch your tone, Lyra," Dad snaps.

My chin flies up as if I'd been slapped. Yes, Dad always sides with Mom, always demurs to her sightings, always picks up and moves without complaint, but he's always sympathetic to my frustrations. "Someday we'll settle down . . ." he'd say wistfully, drawing me into a bear hug.

Well, that someday is *now* for me.

I look hard at Dad, then at Mom. I see Mama Jua in my mind, see her at the shelter caring for those destitute kids. I see little Holly, and I see me reading to her, me teaching her to read. She'd snuggle into me and I'd put my arm around her and we'd take turns flipping the pages. Holly has lost two parents and a surrogate grandma in Mama Jua. She's not going to lose me, too. Not for some shadowy figures of my mom's overwrought imagination.

"There's a little girl," I say, and it all gushes out. Holly and the children's shelter and Mama Jua and how I am not, *not* going to run again.

My parents gape at me, open-mouthed. My mom's expression darkens, fury clouding her face. "Lyra, what have you *done*?"

"Done? *Done?*" My voice rises two octaves. "What I've *done* is carve out a life for myself, one you kept me from all these years. What I've *done* is make friends—people who care for me and love me—" And here I see a smear of hurt across my mom's face, but I don't care. I don't *care*. If she truly loved me, if Dad truly loved me, they would *not* have kept me prisoner for nine years. "What I've *done* is take back my own life, so, yeah, I'm *done*." I whirl toward the door and the whole cardboard bungalow shakes when I slam it.

*I'm done, I'm done, I'm done*. The anger, the lava beast within me, roils and churns. No more. I'm *not* going to be a pawn in anybody's game anymore—my parents' or the government's. Mama Jua taught me it's *my* life, *my* choice. I will *not* accept an eternity of scurrying like a sewer rat, nor will I let the government turn me into a goddamn lab rat.

Seething, I slip under the broken chain link fence at the end of our street. Another short cut, this one to the orphanage; I have to see Holly, to reassure her I'm not leaving. I half-expect my parents to come after me, but they know I'll make a scene and they hate a scene, what with their laying-low, pretending we don't exist philosophy and all, so I think I'm safe from them for a while. I dart across the empty, wasteland of a field, wetter and muddier from the early spring snow melt than the cemetery. My thin canvas shoes are soaked, but I don't care. I don't care about what's "safe" or what's "good for me" anymore. If I want to get my goddamn feet wet, then I'll get my goddamn feet wet.

I hear a train in the distance and I sprint toward the rusting railroad tracks that cut through the field. I jump onto the rails, the cold wind buffeting me. I feel my legs tremble from the vibrations on the iron rods, then I see the freight train round the curve in the distance, a roaring monster hurtling toward me.

"*Move!*" its shrill whistle shrieks.

I don't. I stand my ground, my feet spread apart, balancing on the rails, absorbing the shuddering tremors, and I scream into the gray air, a crazy, bitter laugh drowned by the thundering train. I feel my heart pump wildly and feel my skin prickle with goosebumps.

But I don't feel fear.

At the last second, I fling myself off the track as the train clatters past and I feel *alive.* I smooth back my wild black curls even as I hear my mom's exasperation in my head: "Good God, Lyra, why do you have a death wish?"

"I *don't,*" I constantly tell her. "I have a *life* wish. I want to *live*, to feel the rush and exhilaration of being *alive*—not placidly accept the stifling drone of my existence."

"That stifling drone of your existence has kept you *safe* these past nine years," my mom always snaps.

No fucking kidding.

I pick myself up, and swipe at the mud on my jacket. It's my prized possession. It's real leather with a real sheepskin collar and a real, hefty price tag I could never afford. Good thing I know how to shoplift; good thing I know how to lie. Mom actually believed me when I gushed over my incredible "find" at the thrift store. That was four towns ago—or five? No one's coming after me for it.

I feel calmer now, after my train-dodge. The lava beast recedes into its crevice in my stomach. It always does after I defy death, my favorite pastime. Base jumping with homemade parachutes was fun off the craggily cliffs in Utah (only six broken bones, all of which healed before I hobbled home) and rock climbing without ropes in the Appalachians was fun (rubbed my skin raw on all ten fingers, plus a concussion, all of which healed before I made it home) and motocross racing in northern California with Jonah was fun (cracked ribs, cut cheek, all of which healed before Jonah and I returned to his home). If death can never find me, I can damn well chase it.

I'm thinking more clearly now. As much as I would love to see Holly, I realize I need to make things right with my parents. It's the only way to convince them to stay. I slog through the field back toward our neighborhood, toward the neighborhood Mama Jua will never return to. I think about her dead in her grave, and instinctively I take a deep breath, as if my own unending supply of air can revive her. Once, I tried to calculate how many breaths I might take before I somehow, someday expire. I read that an average person who lives till eighty will breathe about 672 million times. Mama Jua was seventy-five. How many breaths was that for her? How many more than that do I have in me? A billion? A trillion? A googol—ten to the one-hundredth power? Am I really immortal? Will I truly be here in a hundred years? A thousand? I age, obviously. I'm not frozen as an eight-year-old kid. The doctors—before they turned on us—told my parents they suspect I'll age normally until I'm about forty or so. That's when normal people's cells start to deteriorate—descending into old age. But they think I'll keep aging at the rate I do now, which would make me live to a thousand.

Yay. I'll be a thousand-year-old forty-year-old.

Forever.

The thought terrifies me. What am I going to do on my own for centuries? My parents will die—*everyone* I've ever encountered will die and I'll still be, what, running from place to place, an ephemeral ghost on the fringes of society?

My stomach squeezes in fear, the fear I live with every day, every minute of my forever life. Why can't my parents see that? Why can't they put aside their concerns for my safety just *once* to see that the real villain is a meaningless, purposeless, restless, existence that I have to put up with forever?

Hot tears sting my eyes and I impatiently brush them away. I'm supposed to be invincible, not melting into a blubbering mess. It's a cruel irony that my phoenix cells will fix any physical symptom. I may feel pain, but it's temporary and I have the comforting assurance it will always pass. *Why, God, in your malicious sense of humor, would you not grant me the same powers for my mind? Why make me immortal, then allow me to suffer interminably?*

No.

Something's got to change.

It will change.

*I* will change it. And my parents will just have to understand. They'll have to accept that, as always, Mom's being paranoid—like when we were in Michigan where we fled in the middle of the night because she saw a glint of a black vehicle on the highway outside of town. There *are* others who drive black cars—or the car could have been dark gray or midnight blue. Government agents may now drive tangerine and lemon sherbet-colored cars for all we know—but Mom insisted we pack up immediately. She wouldn't even let me go back for my special illustrated edition of fairy tales that I forgot in our frantic dash.

I sigh as I crawl underneath the fence, careful not to tear my jacket. I know my parents mean well. I know they love me. I understand they gave up their whole lives—their careers and friends and families—to keep me safe. I know their intention is not to stifle me so they'll have to understand about Holly. I'll make them understand.

I squelch across the ditch. My feet are sodden. And cold. I shiver in the gray chill. Maybe I shouldn't have ventured into the field.

I scramble onto the crumbling road. I refocus and rehearse how I'm going to convince my parents to stay. Rational and reasonable, that's what I have to be. Keep the lava beast locked up. Don't lose your temper.

I repeat to myself: *Once you meet Holly . . .*

Again: *Once you meet Holly . . .*

Once more: *Once you meet Hol—*

I round the corner to my house.

And stop dead in my tracks.

The street is full of sleek, shiny new cars.

Black cars.

Agent cars.

Like the one that passed me by the cemetery.

My stomach lurches and a streak of fear, as sharp as electricity, jolts through me.

*Oh my God, oh my God, oh my God* . . . Mom was right . . .

Why did I think we could stay? Why did I think we'd be safe? I stand, frozen, as coils of guilt and shame snake themselves around me. Agents dressed in black swarm the street, like giant ants scouring for crumbs. I see a pair of burly agents emerge from our house. They drag my mom and dad out, their hands cuffed behind their backs.

"*Mom!*" I instinctively screech and instantly I clamp my mouth shut.

Too late.

The agents' heads swivel like robots toward me. In a nanosecond, they've drawn their guns; in a millisecond they're after me, the footfalls of giant elephants pounding on the cracked pavement.

"Run, Lyra!" Mom screams at me, her arms twisted behind her back, her face contorted with concern.

I will never question my mom again.

I run.

# CHAPTER 2

I pound down the street, my heels slamming into the pavement, my heart rising in my throat. I run, I sprint, I fly. *Faster, faster, faster!* I want to look back to convince myself I'm losing the agents, but I'm afraid the glance will slow me down. I pump my arms. *Go, go, go!*

Suddenly I feel as if I've smashed headfirst into an imaginary brick wall. Go *where?* I slow down, wobbling, as if I've been knocked off balance. Where do I run? To the police? Funny. They'd fling me over to the agents before I could spit out my name. To the neighbors peeking out their windows, peering at me as I run for my life? Just as funny. No one in their right mind would go up against the authorities to help me. I whip my head back, thinking crazily that my mom will have the answers for me, that she'll tell me what to do, but I see only the swarm of black-coated agents drawing nearer, the clomp of their boots drumming louder.

*Goddamn it,* I seethe. My breath comes out wheezing, ragged. I'm a fast runner; I've had lots of practice, but I'm terrified I won't be able to outlast my pursuers. Why didn't Mom and Dad ever tell me what to do if agents came for us? Why didn't they teach me an escape plan? We had fire drills and lockdown practices in case of emergencies at my old school when I was little and since then, my whole *life* has been an emergency yet my parents never bothered to prepare me?

"Goddamn you!" I scream into pale morning air, but I don't know if I mean the agents or my parents or both. Thanks to them, *all* of them, I'm on my own.

So I go where lately I've always gone when I'm on my own. To Mama Jua's. I wish she were there, rocking on her porch, her frayed quilt wrapped around her legs, waiting for me to drop by. *She'd* know what to do; she'd help me get away and then she'd help me get my parents back where I swear I will apologize to my mom and reassure her I'll never talk back to her again. I don't know how Mama Jua would have saved them, but she was magic, that woman. She'd wave her walking stick and—*poof!*—my parents would be home and this time I'd listen to my mom when she says we have to leave and I'd pack immediately. I'd convince Mom to let me say goodbye to Mama Jua, and then Mama Jua would wave us off like we're going on a fun little road trip, and then later, after a few weeks, maybe, I'd come back to see Holly—just for a visit, of course, and I'd be very careful not to be spotted by agents—and then my life would be . . .

Normal.

All of a sudden I want *my* normal back. All of a sudden, my nomad existence with my parents seems pretty darn good. I had parents who loved me, even if they isolated me, and a roof over my head, even if it changed all the time, and the ability to go out on my own, even if it wasn't with other people, and now I've lost it all. No parents, no home, no freedom. And it's all my fault. It's all because I was so blind and so stupid and so selfish, that I never appreciated what I had. Instead, I thought I knew best, and when I didn't get my way, I threw petulant, childish temper tantrums, like a kid who's denied candy. If only I had listened to my parents, if only I hadn't run off, then my parents would be snug and safe, driving into the sunset in our beat-up old station wagon.

If only I could turn back the clock, I swear I'd be a better daughter.

The footsteps grow louder; they vibrate in my head. The agents are gaining on me. I don't know that I can make it to Mama Jua's. But when I round a corner and I see her house, my heart surges because maybe I can get there after all, and then I can barge through the front door (why she always left it unlocked, especially in this neighborhood is still beyond me) and then I can sneak out the back. If I can get to the fields, I can hide inside the old drainage pipe near the tracks until they call off the search and then—

And then *what*?

The same uncertainty again wallops me. What am I supposed to do after I shake off the agents? Go to the orphanage, the only other place I really know in town, and count on Alexis to help? Trust the woman who lied to her colleagues about going to Mama Jua's funeral? Or trust that I don't inadvertently lead the agents there and endanger Holly? Shit, that won't work. So where? Track down Mama Jua's Ahimsa friends and ask them to hide me the way they hide plague victims?

But Mom's voice reverberates in my head. *Trust no one, Lyra.* My family's motto. My conditioning. Even if Ahimsa is a secret resistance group opposed to the government, I can't trust them to help *me*. If they learn that federal agents are after me, they might believe I'll endanger their operations and turn me over before that happens.

I slow down. Mama Jua's house is almost within reach. All I have to do is cross the street.

Or . . .

Or . . . I let them catch me. I let them catch me after all these years and the military will finally have what they want—me, my phoenix cells—and then they'll let my parents go because Mom and Dad are of no use to them, and then I'll have saved my parents and I'll have made up for what I did to them.

I step into the street, almost at a walk.

Mama Jua's? Or the agents?

Save myself or save my parents?

Momentum propels me forward. I'm halfway across the rutted road, still undecided, when I hear the *crack* of a gun. The sound is like the *pop* of a firework, but the pain is like its flame. The bullet tears through my left shoulder, violently spinning me around, crashing me to the ground.

I scream as the white-hot pain licks my shoulder, my arm, my back, and I forget that it will be momentary, that soon I will heal, that a bullet wound means nothing to me. I grasp at my limp left arm, my right hand covered in blood. I grimace, my eyes squeezed shut, my mouth clamped tight. Pressure builds in my lungs from trapped air, but I can't exhale.

*Run, Lyra!* I hear my mom and I swear she's beside me, she's so loud in my head, so I pick myself up and I stagger forward. It's a flesh wound. It's no big deal. I head toward Mama Jua's sagging porch. If I can just get inside, then I'll be fine.

*Then you'll be alone.*

The voice, my own, unnerves me.

*Pick your poison,* it tells me. *On the run on your own? Or with the agents and your parents?*

I stumble to my knees, the pain dragging me down.

No, not the pain. *Don't lie, Lyra. You don't want to be alone.*

Fucking conscience. Go away.

But it's too late. Strong, thick hands pinch me under the arms and pull me to my feet.

I've been caught.

*You let yourself get caught.*

To save my parents.

*To save yourself.*

Is that what I'm doing? Saving myself?

Is that such a bad thing?

Two agents, as thick as tree trunks, grasp me on either side, and I become deadweight in their arms because I'm not going to make their job easier. But they show no mercy and drag me, as if I truly am a rag doll, back toward my house. They ignore that I'm injured—do they *know* about my phoenix cells or are they naturally heartless bastards?

A black car cruises slowly past us. Inside, in the back seat, I see my parents' pale faces. The windows are up but I see my dad's lips, hear his muffled cries. "Lyra!" He looks murderous, a papa bear trying to protect his cub, but my mom . . . My mom stares at me silently, her eyes heavy with disappointment.

Her pained look skewers me more than the bullet wound did.

"As if I *meant* to let you down," I want to shout at her, the familiar anger bubbling inside. "I didn't *know*!"

*You should have known*, Mom's glare tells me. *You should have known better.*

The car passes by, turns a corner and drives out of sight and only then do I realize this is all wrong. The agents were supposed to take me to my parents and then they'd let them go and then Mom and Dad would find a way to rescue me and then we'd all be okay again.

"Where are you taking them?" I screech, my voice rising an octave. I sound like—I *am*—a shrieking child crying for her mommy. I wriggle, I writhe, trying to twist my way free. The movements reopen my starting-to-heal bullet wound, sending a shot of pain through my side. I feel warm blood seep onto my skin.

The only response is a tightened grip on my right forearm as the agent's meaty fingers dig into my skin.

We arrive back at my house as the line of black cars start to peel away. Another agent, made only of bulk and muscle, wrenches my arms behind my back—another lash of pain from my shoulder—and slaps metal handcuffs on me.

"You know I'm *shot*, right?" I snap at him, my left side burning. "You don't think first aid would be a better option?"

He says nothing. They all say nothing, not even to each other. It's as if they're robots, programmed to carry out their function without regard to, well, me.

The agent at my side, the tree trunk, opens the back door to the last black car and shoves me inside. I wince as my shoulder bangs on the seat. He climbs in beside me and the one who handcuffed me gets behind the wheel. We squeal onto the street.

"What, no seatbelts?" I say. "Not concerned for my safety?"

I'm flippant, I'm sassy, because I have to be, right? It's what all the heroes do in the movies. They stay in control. They talk back. They prove they're not cowed, not concerned, not frightened.

Never let them see you sweat.

But I am sweating and cowed and frightened as fucking hell. Mom warned me about what the scientists will do to me. To get at my phoenix cells and the secrets of their immortality, they'll cut me open and slice me up and stitch me back together like Frankenstein's monster.

*God help me. Somebody help me.*

I catch a twitch of a muscle at the corner of the agent's mouth and I think maybe he is human, after all. Maybe *he* will help me.

"You know they're going to imprison me for life?" I ask. I don't tell him how long that life will actually be.

He doesn't reply.

"You know I've done nothing wrong?" Do I sound confident? Convincing? In control? I twist on the smooth leather to better look at him, to make him look at me, but he stares straight ahead. "You know my parents are innocent, too?"

I see him press his lips together, but otherwise he remains stone-faced.

"Where are you taking me?"

Silence.

My stomach churns in anger and frustration. His silence is getting under my skin and I want to explode. I want to scream and fight and kick and *hurt* him until he answers me.

"Tell me, dammit!" I shout and then I *do* lunge because I lose control. They've taken my parents and they've kidnapped me and I'm helpless and I can't *stand* it. I fling myself onto the agent and kick at him and screech and bite like a feral child. The agent is taken aback; for a moment, he shrinks into his seat as I attack, but he's well trained. Within seconds, he's shoved me off him, knocked me back against my seat, my hands still handcuffed behind me, and pins me there with his arm across my chest. I squirm against his grasp, but his arm is like steel rod trapping me in place.

I puff and wheeze from my exertion, pain again shooting through my shoulder, and I let slip a weak little moan. I suck back the sound. No. I will *not* let him hear me whimper. I'm trembling now, and I can feel my lips quiver, but I will not let him see me cry.

The agent remains expressionless; he drops his arm, the cocky bastard, as if he knows I won't attack again. He's right. The fight drains out of me, and I slump into the seat. I'm scared now, more scared that I've ever felt in my life. I think back to the train, when I was on the tracks, the freight cars bearing down on me and I felt no fear. It didn't matter if I jumped off in time; the consequences, while painful, would have been short-lived. But now? How long will this nightmare last? A month? A year? Forever? How long will it take them to create to their un-killable super soldiers? How often will they have to slice and dice me before they succeed? And what about my parents? Where are they? What will the agents do to them? They don't have phoenix cells—only me, I'm the only freak in the family, the only freak in the whole world—so why hold them prisoner? What good are they to the government?

And when will I see them? What will they say to me? What will *I* say to them? *Sorry I messed up your well-laid plans? Sorry I threw away nine years of your sacrifice?* Sorry is what you say when you forget to take out the garbage or when you bump someone by accident. How can that be enough for what I've done to them?

The agents drive me to a makeshift airfield on the outskirts of town where a sleek gray helicopter, its blades spinning slowly, perches in the yellow-brown grass. The agent beside me pulls me out of the car, but his grip is gentle, softer than before. Because he's showing a faint hint of humanity? Or because he knows I have nowhere to run. I scan the area, but I'm trapped. The helicopter is ringed by the black cars from my street—minus the one my parents were in. A platoon of agents stands guard, guns and rifles drawn as if they expect an assault any minute. Maybe they do. Maybe they think that desperate citizens, enraged by the government's stunning neglect, will overrun them, strip the multi-million-dollar military machine for parts, and sell them so they can afford to buy food, clothing, medicine.

I wish.

Instead, the surrounding fields remain deserted, the agents pointing their guns at nothing more menacing than rustling grass.

I'm dragged to the gleaming helicopter and lifted inside.

"Uncuff her," the pilot says, turning around from the front. She wears green combats—she's military, not a federal agent—but I don't know whether that's better or worse for me. My bodyguard obeys without question. He pulls out a small key, clicks open the cuffs and releases my wrists. In a jackrabbit flash, I'm throwing myself out the open door, but I barely get my butt off the seat before the agent lazily reels me in. He leans across me, snaps the cuffs around my right wrist, then wrenches my arm over my head and snaps the other side to the cross bar over the door.

Damn.

He slams shut the door, snaps a seatbelt around my waist, then buckles himself in beside me.

"For safety," he growls.

Ha, ha.

The helicopter roars to life. I hear the whip of the blades cutting the air, their whine growing louder as they spin faster. With a jolt, we're airborne and I grip the crossbar tight in my right hand. We lift up, up, up, then, banking left, we fly over the city. I stare through the window, awed. I never knew just how small everything looks from the air, like the tiny village Ivy and I used to play with. We pass over my gray neighborhood and the forest I'd jog through—I thought it was so much bigger—and there, around the bend, is the cemetery with Mama Jua. I can see the dark patch that is her grave. Was she buried just this morning? It seems like a lifetime ago.

I can't look anymore. I lean my head back wearily and close my eyes. I can't watch my life, the one I was trying to build, slip away. Like Holly. She's going to think I've abandoned her when I don't show up this afternoon or tomorrow or the day after or the day after or the day after, and that guts me. I want to beg the agents to tell Holly they took me, so she knows that I didn't want to leave her, that I had no choice, that it's not my fault.

But it is my fault. It's my fault I listened to Mama Jua and got involved with the orphanage and met Holly. Mom and Dad warned me about connections. *"Keep your distance, Lyra."* Otherwise it's harder when you leave.

Because we were always going to leave.

I see that now. We were either going to leave my parents' way, like thieves in the night, or the agents' way, like dangerous criminals. I was never going to get my dream; I was never going to be able to make a life for myself.

*Goddamn you, Mama Jua, for convincing me otherwise.*

The old woman's wrinkled face appears in my mind as I rip into her.

*I was fine before I met you—well, if not fine, at least I was managing. But you had to go and sell me a bill of goods and you let me buy into it, hook, line and sinker. You manipulated me into thinking I could have it all—secrecy and security and friendships—but it was never possible, was it? A life with purpose, with meaning, with stability, that was all a pipe dream, an illusion for me. My parents knew that. They'd been teaching me my place in this world since I was 8 years old. But you thought you knew better. You came along with your* sweet child *and* dear me *and caresses on my cheeks and within months, you ruined me.*

*Goddamn you.*

Goddamn me.

*How* could I have been so stupid? How could I have bought Mama Jua's lies? Was I that desperate? Am I that weak?

*Yes.*

*Fuck you,* I tell the voice, I tell myself. I am not that weak.

I stretch my left arm, feeling my shoulder tingle. It's tender, still sore, but it's healing. Still, I feel awkward about it, embarrassed, knowing my body is healing in front of other people. I've never had that happen, never had someone watch as my cells make me whole—not even Jonah after I crashed my dirt bike and he ran for help despite my objections that I was (would be) fine. I feel, I don't know . . . exposed, somehow. Like I'm naked and the agent is watching me change. But that's silly. My phoenix cells don't make me vulnerable, they make me strong. That's why the military scientists want me, because I can make everybody stronger.

But the burden of that strength is weighing me down. I feel a dull heaviness inside, a sadness I can't shake, and all I want to do now is curl up into the ball and make the world go away. But I know now I'll never get what I want, so I force myself to look out the window at my receding life.

Lesson learned, Mom and Dad. I finally get it. My life will never be my own.

# CHAPTER 3

Just over an hour later, the helicopter lands in an open field close to a campus of low-slung buildings. No one tells me, but I assume we're in Washington, at the lab my parents always warned me about. It's my nightmare. While most little kids had the bogeyman and monsters under their beds to scare them at night, I had federal agents and military labs to terrorize me. Mom always told me they'd do terrible, painful tests if I were ever caught and I always pictured myself helplessly strapped to a bed like in a horror movie, with monsters in white lab coats coming at me with butcher knives.

I thought I'd long since outgrown spooky bedtime stories, but here, now, in broad daylight, when I'm seventeen years old, I shake with that same childhood fear, as the pilot cuts the engine. Now here I am, the lamb to the slaughter.

The agent releases my handcuffs from the bar of the helicopter, re-cuffs my wrists behind my back. I roll my fully-healed shoulder as he nudges me out the door, and all I sense is a little itch from the new skin. I walk upright under the whirring blades, not bothering to duck—if the blades chop my head off, I'd just grow another one, like an alien, right?—and then I'm forced to march, handcuffed again, across the wet field. My eyes scan the horizon, looking for my parents. I need them to tell me everything will be okay. I need Dad to sling his arm around my shoulder and squeeze me hard and I need Mom to rest her hand on my cheek and tell me not to worry. Are they here, too, or did the agents keep them in Jamestown?

I'm led to a bunker-like building and prodded inside, into a long, bleak, narrow corridor.

"What, no blindfold?" I quip, trying to project that smug confidence I think I should possess, but most definitely don't. *See? You can't get to me*. A lie, I know, but I desperately try to cling to the illusion anyway.

My agent stares, stone-faced, straight ahead. Is he for real? Does he even have a brain? A conscience? Does he know that what he's doing is morally, ethically and in all other ways wrong?

A short, trim man with midnight-black skin and tight gray curly hair approaches us from the end of the hall and he looks like he's practically skipping.

"Ms. Harmon," he calls, his hand outstretched to shake mine. I glare at him. Really? I rattle my handcuffs behind my back.

He frowns, like the cuffs are unexpected. "No need for those," he waves his arm dismissively in my general direction. The agent pulls a key from his pocket, unlocks them and releases me. I bring my hands up, rubbing the welts on my wrists.

"Oh, let me see," the Black man says, grabbing my arms. His hands are soft, but his grip is firm. He stares at my skin as if it glitters gold. "My, my, my," he says. "It's almost as if I can *see* your cells creating the collagen necessary for the foundation of your new tissue, it's happening so fast."

I yank back my hand, my skin prickling in disgust.

"Dr. Simon Moto," he says, introducing himself gallantly, again holding out his hand. "Director of Cell Research."

"Director of Torture, you mean?" I retort, ignoring his outstretched hand.

Moto laughs as if I wasn't serious. "Oh, Ms. Harmon, you've got that wrong. You don't know how excited we are to have you here. After all these years . . ."

I scowl. All those years on the run . . . all those lost years of school and friends and a stable home. All because he kept his agents hunting me, all because of him.

"Come, come," he says to me, then waves away the agent like he was a pesky fly.

"That's all the thanks he gets for dragging me here?" I say. A flicker of a smile crosses my agent's face—and I smile a little, too.

Moto ignores me. Instead, he hurries me down the long corridor.

"I have so much to show you," he says.

My eyes scan the walls for doors, cameras, anything that might help my parents get to me, or me to them. I've got to find a way. I'm not going to be stuck in this hellhole forever.

At a set of double doors at the end of the hall, Moto swipes his access badge and leads me through.

I stop, surprised. It's a different world in here. All of the walls, the lights, the doors, the labs look sleek and new, all shiny chrome and gleaming white. We're on a viewing platform, overlooking an expansive basement lab set up with workstations and lab benches, clean rooms, and storage shelves. Dozens of scientists and technicians in white lab coats and masks scurry around like mice in a maze.

Or rats in a cage.

"This is all because of you, my dear," Moto exclaims happily.

"Because of me?" I repeat lamely.

"The sample cells Dr. Hendricks took from you nine years ago."

I don't understand. Dr. Hendricks was the doctor who helped us get away; my parents always said he saved us. They told me that after he identified my phoenix cells, he discovered what the military scientists really wanted to do with me. He learned they were going to strip Mom and Dad of their parental rights and make me a ward of the state. Dr. Hendricks warned them that if they tried to fight it, the government would tie up the case in court for years and by then it would be too late because they'd already have their hands on me. He told my parents we had to run. Hide. *Right then.* So we slipped away that night.

So why would he have taken my cells? And if he did, why would the agents still be after me? Why would my parents have kept us on the run for nearly a decade if the scientists already had what they wanted? It doesn't make sense. None of it makes sense.

Moto takes me through a side door, down three flights of stairs and into an anteroom. He hands me a white cloth, like a hospital gown, paper booties for my feet, a hair net and a paper face mask. "Put these on—we need to keep the environment sterile."

"From what? Me infecting me?"

Moto laughs as if I'm the funniest comedian in the world, then he ushers me to cover up.

I think I won't, of course. Mom and Dad would kill me for cooperating. It's the thing they hammered into me again and again. But against my better judgment, I'm intrigued. All of these people work here because of *me*? They all know about me, about my phoenix cells? I convince myself my parents would be okay with what I'm doing because I have to do this to survive. To learn the lay of the land. The more I learn about this place, the more I may be able to find a way out.

Hesitantly, I garb up.

Moto pushes open an airlock, and we pass through a decontamination room. Through the airlock on the other side, we emerge onto the lab floor.

"Ladies and gentleman," Moto calls out excitedly, his voice slightly muffled by the mask. "I have an important announcement. After so many years, and so many unanswered questions, I am proud to finally introduce you to our *raison d'être,* Lyra Harmon!"

I hear audible gasps, and a few squeals. Applause breaks out and I feel like I've just been crowned Homecoming Queen.

"I don't understand," I stammer. For nine years, I've lived in the shadows, on the edges of society. No one knew who I was, what I was. But here in this bunker, among strangers, I'm being celebrated.

Moto motions me over to a workbench in the middle of the room, and all eyes follow me as I shuffle after him. I can feel my cheeks flush under my paper mask, but for once, I don't feel like the freak I am. No, I feel like they're admiring me. I know I haven't done anything to deserve it, and that I should probably dread it, but I kind of like their attention.

Moto pulls out a glass dish and sets it up under a microscope. He urges me to look in. "What you're seeing is a normal, healthy living cell," Moto explains. "The basic building blocks of all living organisms."

Curious, I peer at it. The cell looks the shape of a fried egg with an oval-ish clear part and a darker "yolk." Despite myself, I'm fascinated. I've never seen a real cell before. When you're homeschooled on the run, there isn't much time, money or resources for lab equipment.

Moto switches out the plate. I'm looking at the same shape, but here the darker nucleus takes up more than half the area.

"These are yours," he says, like a proud papa.

I look up at him. "Why—?" I begin, but I'm not even sure what I'm about to ask. A million questions rush to my mind. *Why do you still have them? Why are they so different? Why can't they die? Why can't I die?*

"Have you ever heard about HeLa cells?" Moto asks, as if I'm in kindergarten.

I feel my spine stiffen, and suddenly I'm brought back to where I am. Trapped in the very lab my parents tried to save me from.

"I had the best science teacher," I reply coldly. My dad taught me all about HeLa cells. He thought I'd be interested: they're an immortal cell line. They were taken from a Black woman, Henrietta Lacks—without her consent—decades and decades ago when she was being treated for cancer, and to the scientists' surprise, they were able to keep growing the cells in their labs. But HeLa cells are not like my phoenix cells, because they didn't cure Henrietta. In fact, they killed her. Henrietta died of cancer at the age of thirty-one.

"The best science teacher? Excellent," he says, either ignoring the ice in my tone or unaware of it. "Then you know that normal human cells die after a set number of cell divisions. But HeLa cells never died, so researchers created a cell line that still exists to this day. The cells are still used in medical research—their value has been incalculable ever since they were discovered."

"Not to Henrietta Lacks," I say.

Moto's eyes crinkle in delight. "So you do know your science history. You're quite right. HeLa cells were cancerous. But they're also unique. You know what telomeres are? They're the caps at the end of each strand of DNA that protect our chromosomes. Think of them like the plastic tips at the end of a shoelace. Usually, a telomere shortens every time a cell divides, and when it gets too short, the cell dies. But not HeLa. Its telomeres remain the same length no matter how many times the cell divides."

"Which means it will never die."

"Precisely," Moto says, pleased. "Yours are similar, and so we've used them to create another immortal cell line—"

"Wait, what?" I demand. They have a line of my cells? They keep duplicating them, the cells with *my* DNA, the cells that make me . . . *me?* In my mind I see the image that's haunted me throughout my childhood, the one of the battlefield strewn with soldiers who all wear my face, and I feel dirty, suddenly, violated. It makes me want to throw up.

"Yes," he says, "A line of cells that never die, like HeLa. We thought about calling it LyHa, you know, the first two letters of your first and last name, like Henrietta Lacks, but that's much too close, much too confusing. I'm sorry to say we weren't very creative in the end, so we've just called it LH-1."

I stare at him, shocked, then stare around at the lab, suddenly wanting to trash all the beakers, break all the microscopes, and burn all my cells, all the ones not in my body because these scientists have no right, *no right*, to do research on *me* without my permission. Who do these people think they *are*?

Moto seems oblivious to my distress. "We know that your cells, like HeLa, are immortal, and we know they're very resistant to mutation, but what we still haven't figured out is how they keep regenerating *inside* your body, and in a way that isn't fatal to you. That's why we need you. The original source. There's only so much we can do, staring at a bunch of cells in a culture dish. We need to see how they act in your body."

I am shaking. How can he talk so cavalierly about *my* cells, *my* body?

"*Why*?" I whisper.

Moto looks over at me, like he's seeing me for the first time. "Why what?"

"Why do you need to understand how my cells work in my body? They're *my* cells in *my* body."

"They're essential to science," Moto says.

"*Science?*" I repeat. "Really? Cloning me to create an army of indestructible super soldiers is science? Not politics, not greed?"

Moto's eyes flash with unconcealed anger. "It's your duty, Lyra," he hisses.

"It's my duty to revoke all my basic human rights for the sake of war? No thank you."

My knees feel weak. I feel like I'm going to collapse. I want to run, I want to scream. I want to find my mom and dad and tell them they were right to run, right to hide, right to keep me as far away from here as possible. I want to tell them I'm sorry for ever doubting them, and for refusing to go with them this morning. I think again about windows and doors and cameras. I think about the spy movies I love to watch, where someone is always being rescued, or devising clever ways to break out and I want that to be me. I want someone to rescue me, or tell me how I can escape because I can't stay here—not for a day, not for a year, not for forever.

Moto looks at me long and hard, then he snaps his head away from me. His demeanor changes. He no longer pays me any attention. "Take her blood," he orders a technician.

"No, you won't," I say, and turn to leave. "You can't do this to me."

Moto walks away. The technician, the size of a linebacker, grabs my by the arm, but I shake him off. "It's not right," I shout. The technician seizes me again and clamps his bear-paw sized hand around my arm.

"You're hurting me," I cry, but he doesn't let go. "Stop," I say, and try to wriggle out of his grasp, but he's too strong. He drags me across the lab as dozens of people look on, no longer cheering. "Help me," I yell at them, but they turn away. "You *cowards!*" I scream. "I'm a real person!"

But I am invisible to them.

The technician shoves me into a small room off to the side that looks like a doctor's office. He throws me onto the examining table, where the white paper covering the mattress crinkles under me. I jump up and lunge toward the door, but the goon easily holds me back. Another technician comes in, a woman, and she strips me of the paper gown and mask I'd been wearing over my clothes. I writhe, I fight, I scream, but I can't get loose.

"Tie her down," the woman says, exasperated.

"No!" I kick at the technician and flail at the woman, but it's no use. In a minute, they have me pinned to the bed. The woman buckles thick leather straps across my chest, my arms, my legs.

And suddenly, I am living my nightmare.

# CHAPTER 4

Moto calls it my "quarters"—as in, "take Ms. Harmon to her quarters, please,"—and the guards call it my bedroom, but I call it my prison cell. They've stuffed me in a small barracks-like room with a metal cot, a tall, double-wide steel locker, and a wooden night table. Since we're in the basement, there are no windows and the only door, locked from the outside, leads into the lab. There's no bathroom, either.

"Knock if you have to go and we'll escort you," the guard told me when she shoved me in here.

I'd rather shit all over the floor than let them escort me to the goddamn bathroom.

I'm wearing the hospital gown they forced me into, but somebody has left a change of clothes on the thin mattress. They're blue hospital scrubs, thicker than what I have on, but I refuse to touch them. I won't be caught dead wearing anything they pick out for me. Ha ha. Since I can't die, I guess I win.

I flop onto the bed, aching. I'm not used to bodily discomfort, but maybe that's because my body has never sustained such prolonged abuse. I massage my arm where they pricked me with dozens of needles, some the size of the Space Needle, and I stretch my legs where they continuously zapped me with electric currents. I constantly resisted—at one point a nurse dared me to keep struggling so she had an excuse to break my fingers and watch them heal with her own eyes—but when restraints wouldn't stop me, they started drugging me. I still feel groggy, but more than that, I feel abused and molested. I feel sullied, dirty, naked. It terrifies me to think about what they did to me when I was unconscious. I wish I could shower and wash off this place, but I'll be damned if I ask a guard to take me.

I shiver, but I don't know if it's from the cold or from fear. I'm petrified about what will happen to me. If this is only Friday, Day 1, what will they subject me to on Day 1,000? Or maybe they'll have discovered all my cells' secrets by then—maybe even sooner—and maybe they'll have cloned their super soldiers and taken over the world and then they'll let me go.

Maybe.

But I can't count on it. I can't live every day pinning my hopes on the researchers' benevolent nature, not if those days are anything like today.

Reluctantly, I drag the thin cotton blanket off my bed and wrap it around my shoulders. I don't want to use anything of theirs, but the cold is seeping into my bones and I have no choice.

The story of my fucking life.

I have no choice. Never have, never will.

Look at what happens when I do try to exert my own will, when I try to make my own choice. I chose to defy my parents; I chose to stay in Jamestown and I got us caught. I've become the lab rat my parents have been trying to protect me from all these years and my parents . . . Where *are* my parents? No one will tell me a goddamn thing. When I ask, when I demand, and I scream and shout for answers, they ignore me as if I were . . .

. . . as if I *weren't* human.

The irony.

They are so hell bent on creating their new and improved humans from my cells, that they forget I *am* one. A human. I'm more than a collection of my phoenix cells. I'm more than a collection of organs and muscles and tissues. I am real person with real feelings and a real family.

*They're* the ones who aren't human, I think bitterly. They're the ones who have no compassion, no empathy, no shame. Especially Moto. Does he honestly believe that what he's doing to me is ethical? That it's okay to treat me like a slab of meat? Does he think he's immune from morality? That he doesn't belong in the world of right and wrong?

But then, *is* there a world of right and wrong?

I used to think so, but now I'm not sure.

I feel jittery, anxious. I scramble off the bed and start pacing, but I just go around in a tight circle. I feel like the walls are closing in on me. I feel like I'm suffocating, like I'm trapped in a coffin, buried alive.

*Mom!* I want to scream. *Dad! Come and get me!* Why haven't they come yet? Why haven't they escaped from wherever they were being held and mounted a rescue mission yet?

Maybe they're waiting for the cover of darkness.

Is it dark? Is it night? I don't know. Without windows, without a watch, I have no way of knowing. And since I don't know how long I was drugged for, I don't even know what day it is. Maybe it's not even Friday anymore. Maybe it's not Day 1. Maybe it's already Day 30. Maybe I've been here a month and don't even know it.

Oh God, that petrifies me. It's one thing if they take my body, but now they're stealing my mind.

I have to know. I have to know what day it is. What time it is.

I'm about to knock on the door, to ask a guard, but then I stop.

*No.* I will not ask them for anything.

I return to the bed and try to plot out a timeline. We were captured early Friday morning; the helicopter ride didn't take long, so it was probably mid-morning by the time I met Moto. And then the blood tests and the electric shocks and then—

And then I was unconscious.

Goddamn it.

Is this the way it's always going to be? Every day? Or night? Never knowing which way is up?

I hear a key in the lock and I tense. What do they want now?

The door opens and an older man hustles in carrying a shopping bag. He's short and round and has a neatly trimmed white beard that reminds me of Santa Claus. He's bald, and his pink scalp shines in the bright fluorescent overhead light. He wears a white lab coat and jiggles a set of keys in his hand.

A scientist.

I sit up straight on the bed, pressing my back into the frame as he closes the door.

"Lyra," he says excitedly. "How nice to see you again."

I glare at him, wary, guarded. I've never seen him before—have I? Maybe he does look familiar. Was he in the lab with Moto this morning--or last month or whenever I first went in there?

"I'm Dr. Hendricks," he says.

I bolt upright. Hendricks? *The* Hendricks?

Dr. Hendricks laughs at my spark of recognition. "Yes, I'm the doctor who first discovered your phoenix cells when you were eight years old."

I'm shocked. Dr. Hendricks is here . . . this is good. This is very good. He helped me and my parents nine years ago; maybe he'll help me now.

"You've come to get me out?" I ask eagerly.

Dr. Hendricks raises his finger to his lips and shushes me. "Of course not," he says loudly, but then he nods anxiously.

I'm thrilled, I'm elated. I'm going to get out. *Thank God, thank God, thank God.* I scramble off the bed and step toward the door.

Dr. Hendricks holds up his hands. "Wait a minute," he whispers. "It's not so easy."

Shit.

I sit on the bed, feeling deflated. I should know better than to let my imagination get away from me.

"Here," Dr. Hendricks hands me the bag.

I take it, look inside and see my clothes, my shoes, my jacket. I breathe out, relieved.

"How did you . . . ?" I start but Dr. Hendricks cuts me off.

"I'll turn around, you change quickly," he says quietly, and faces the door. "My eyes are closed, too," he adds.

I don't care. At this point, the whole lab can watch me change if it means I can get out of here. I shrug out of the hospital gown and whip on my jeans and shirt. I tie up my shoes and put on my jacket. Finally, I feel like me again.

"Done," I say, and Dr. Hendricks turns to face me. He smiles, but it's sad, and my stomach lurches.

"What is it?" I ask. I know, I sense, something is wrong.

"It's your parents," he tells me. He sits heavily on the end of the bed and motions for me to do the same.

My skin crawls. "What about them?" I start to panic. "Are they okay? Are they hurt?"

Dr. Hendricks looks directly at me. He doesn't drop his gaze. "It's bad, Lyra, I'm not going to lie to you. They've contracted Hecate's Plague. Both of them."

I feel like I'm going to faint. No, no, that can't be. They're fine. They were fine this morning.

But people can be fine for up to seven days after they're infected before symptoms appear.

I feel dizzy and I grip the edge of the mattress to steady myself.

"Where were they sent?" I ask in a small voice. Are there quarantine camps around here? There must be. They're everywhere across the country. Or were they kept in Jamestown? God, I hope they're close. I want to see them. I need to see them. Maybe I could convince the soldiers guarding the camps that I won't get sick and they'll let me go in and talk to my parents.

"They're here, Lyra." Dr. Hendricks answers with a thin smile. "They're in an isolation chamber in another part of the facility."

"Here? In this lab?" Oh my God, that's even better. I spring off the bed and jump to the door, like I've been given a second chance at life. They're here, in this center, not rotting in some death camp in New York. I really can see them. I have to tell them I'm sorry. I have to tell them I didn't mean to run off and have us get caught.

I have to have them forgive me.

Because I can't have my mom's sour, disappointed glance at me as she was being whisked away in the car by the agents be my last glimpse of her or have our last conversation be our fight. I can't live the rest of my unnaturally long life knowing my last words to my parents were an angry, "I'm done." I'm *not* done, I want to tell them. I'm not done with us or our family or running and hiding if that's the way it has to be. And I know now that *is* the way it has to be. I get it. I've learned my lesson. They need to know that. They need to know I'll listen to them, that I'll never question them again.

But Dr. Hendricks shakes his head. "I'm sorry Lyra. It's too dangerous"

"But why? I'm immune from the plague, *you* know that."

"You may not be immune, Lyra," Dr. Hendricks cautions.

"Fine, whatever, but if I get sick I'll get better almost instantly, so it's the same thing. Let me see my parents."

Again, Dr. Hendricks shakes his head. "I wish I could, but that'll arouse suspicion if I take you there."

A wave of sadness crashes over me. I'll never see my parents again. They'll never know how much I love them.

*I'm done.* My last words to them echo in my head like a death knell.

"Don't despair, my dear girl," Dr. Hendricks says, "because I think I can save them."

My eyes fly up to his face and I see his expression brighten.

"You have a cure?" I ask eagerly. Could this be true? Oh my God, could he really save my parents?

"Not yet," Dr. Hendricks replies, dampening my hopes. "But I'm close. I'm ridiculously close. I've been trying to find a cure for the past decade—it's my obsession, I assure you—and now I've created a serum that attacks the virus, but it doesn't yet kill it. I need one more element."

"What?"

"Antibodies."

"Antibodies?"

He nods. "You know what they are?"

I know what they are. They're part of the immune system. They're like a tracking device. They hone in on a virus or bacteria, lock onto it, and tag it so the immune system's cells know what to destroy. What I don't understand is why Dr. Hendricks is here now talking to me about them.

"Each antibody targets a specific antigen—a marker on the foreign object," Dr. Hendricks explains. "The human body can produce about ten billion different antibodies, each capable of binding to a distinct antigen. The problem with Hecate's Plague, though, is that none of those antibodies binds to the virus. That means the immune system can't lock on and destroy the virus on its own."

"Which is why it kills everyone," I say. I get it. I understand biology. What I don't understand is how this will this help my parents.

"Hecate's Plague kills everyone except you, of course," Hendricks says, smiling.

"So that's it? I have antibodies and you need my blood?" Even as I ask the question, I know it's not right. My parents would have made a deal of some sort to give Dr. Hendricks access to my blood or something. They wouldn't have kept me hidden if they knew I could help so many people.

"No," Dr. Hendricks says, "You don't have the antibodies. Your phoenix cells have a different structure altogether. They're what fought off your plague virus, not a traditional antibody. And I've tried, believe me, I've tried, to adapt your cells to make a cure, but so far I can't get it to work."

"Then how are you supposed to get antibodies?" I feel like this conversation is spinning in circles. *Get back to my parents*, I want to shout at him.

"Everyone always dies within three days, right?"

I nod. Yes. No one has ever lived longer than three days once they get sick. It's like one day you cough, the next day you're bedridden, and the day after that you're dead.

"Except I've just learned about a girl who's still living after *seven* days. I suspect she may have antibodies. I suspect her body may be trying to fight off the virus."

"So you get her blood and finish your serum and you cure my parents? All in less than three days?"

"Yes," Dr. Hendricks says. "The serum won't take long to complete once I get the antibodies. The only problem is, the girl is already in a quarantine camp."

"So? Go in and get her out."

"I can't. I've tried. Health officials won't budge. They're too scared that if she comes out, she'll spread the disease."

"So go in and get her blood."

"They won't let me in," Dr. Hendricks says ruefully. "No, not true," he corrects himself. "They'll let me in, all right. They'll let anyone in. What officials won't do is let anyone *out*. You know they're so paranoid about the spread of the disease that not even doctors or nurses are allowed in to help."

"But you have all the right gear," I argue. "The alien suits . . ."

"HAZMAT suits," Dr. Hendricks smiles. "Yes, we have the most sophisticated protective clothing, but the government doesn't care," he explains. His voice is bitter. "The officials made it very clear: even if we go into the quarantine camp all garbed up, the soldiers will shoot to kill when we come out."

"That's ludicrous," I protest.

"That's the government."

"But you've got to do *something*," I say. My parents need that blood. It's their only hope of surviving.

"I can't do anything more, at least not in three days." He pauses and looks at me. "But you can."

"*Me?*" Is he insane? How am I supposed to get some girl's blood?

"You're the only one who can, Lyra. You're the only one on the whole *planet* who can get into and out of the quarantine camp and *not* spread the plague."

"You want me to sneak in and out of a death camp?" I throw up my arms in frustration. No way is that possible.

"Not sneak in," Dr. Hendricks shakes his head. "You can just walk in, remember. But you will have to sneak out."

Fuck. Now I know he's insane and now I'm angry. How could he do this to me? How could he dangle my parents' lives in front of me, then rip them away like that? How could he build me up, raise my hopes, then leave me with this bullshit? Sneaking out of a quarantine camp . . . impossible. I've seen the camps in Jamestown, and I know it's the same across the country. Armed soldiers guard them 24-7 to make sure no one escapes to spread the plague. And if they try, they're killed. Yeah, I know *I* won't die, but if they shoot me, they'll just toss me right back into the camp and that won't help my parents.

"Please Lyra," Dr. Hendricks pleads. "Getting this blood is our only shot at a cure, and you're the only one who can get it."

"So how exactly am I supposed to sneak out?" I say sarcastically.

"It won't be as hard as it sounds," Dr. Hendricks says confidently. "You watch the soldiers' rotations, then find a back door and, at their shift change, when they're most distracted, you leave."

I sneer at him. "Just like that. I'm going to open the back door and stroll out of a quarantine camp while the soldiers' backs are turned."

"Lyra, there's more psychology here than you think. These soldiers don't want to be guarding the camps. It's a terrible duty, and it's boring as hell. It's so rare that anyone tries to escape, that they basically sit and do nothing all day. Their reflexes won't be sharp. They'll be slow to react. All of that will buy you time."

"You're a fucking lunatic," I tell him.

"I'm a *desperate* lunatic," Hendricks grimaces. "Look, I know it's dangerous, but here's the reality. If I don't get that girl's blood, your parents die."

*Fuck.*

I don't have a choice.

But then, I never have a choice.

I flop on the bed.

"Good," Hendricks says. "Now let's talk about the plan."

He tells me about the girl, Yasmine Smith, and what she looks like. He gives me the address of the quarantine camp and directions about how to get there. He pulls a syringe out of his coat pocket and gives me a crash course on drawing blood.

"Once you fill up the vial, look for the first opportunity to leave," he finishes. "I'll be waiting for you in my black van. You give me the blood, I race back to the lab, finish the serum and administer it to your parents."

"And after that?" I glower at him. This is so messed up. This whole fucking mission. I concede Hendricks's plan is the best one we've got, but it's still screwed up. Sneaking out of a quarantine camp because the government won't allow a doctor inside ... What kind of fucked up country do we live in?

Hendricks looks at me, confused.

"After my parents are well? Are you going to turn me back over to Moto?"

Hendricks laughs and it's full and hearty. "No, no, no, my dear girl, of course not. I'll do everything I can to ensure you and your family stay safely hidden again."

Really? Can that actually happen? Can this nightmare truly come to an end?

"It's late," Hendricks says, checking his watch. "This is the best time to get you out of the lab since hardly anyone works Friday night."

Friday. It's still Friday. Good. I haven't lost any days.

"Great," I say. "Then there won't be anyone to arouse suspicion when you take me to see my parents first."

Hendricks startles. "I told you it's impossible."

"Then it's impossible for me to help you."

I'm playing hardball, I know, and I'm frightened. What if Hendricks is right and me getting this girl's blood is my parents' only hope and I squander it because I'm too stubborn? But I *have* to see them, so I hold my breath, praying Hendricks doesn't call my bluff.

Hendricks looks me over, and I meet his gaze, trying to seem defiantly confident. My heart is pounding, though and I'm afraid Hendricks will say no and then I will have not only lost my chance to see my parents, I will have also lost my chance to escape.

Hendricks closes his eyes and shakes his head, his shoulders drooping. "Fine," he agrees reluctantly. He then looks at his watch, tapping it impatiently. "I'll make the arrangements and be back for you in an hour."

*Yay!* I think, emboldened by my success. Hendricks leaves quickly and I pace back and forth, excited now, instead of anxious. I'm going be *doing* something. I'm going to see my parents and I'm going to get out of here and I'm going to save them.

When Hendricks returns, his face looks grim and my stomach rises into my throat because at first I think he's going to tell me it's too late, that my mom and dad have already died, but all he does is beckon me out of the room.

I'm worried that the guard outside my door will stop us, but he stares straight ahead as we pass—I guess he assumes Hendricks is leading me to a late-night experiment.

Hendricks takes me on a winding path through a labyrinth of halls—there's no way I'd have ever found my way out of this maze on my own—until we come to a narrow door at the end of a narrow white hall. Hendricks swipes his badge to open the door and ushers me through.

I hesitate. Suddenly I'm scared. Suddenly I've changed my mind. I decide I don't want to see my parents. I don't want to see them pale and sick, to see Hecate's red flames, the rash that looks like fire, lashed across their skin. I want to see them whole and well and healthy. Strong. In control. In charge. I want to walk into that room and have them leap to their feet and pump Hendricks's hand in gratitude for rescuing us, then rush into the hall and we'd all scurry out of here.

"Lyra?" Hendricks whispers.

I bite my lip and cross the threshold. I step into an anteroom, a small space with a window that looks into the isolation chamber. I grip my hands together to keep them from shaking as I approach the glass.

My parents are there. On the other side. Each lying in a bed next to the other. Their eyes are closed and I want to pound on the window and tell them to wake up, I'm here, we've got to go, we've got to get out of here, but I see the telltale rash, the red flames that lick their faces. My stomach churns, nauseated. I can't look at them anymore. I can't see them so sick and helpless, not my mom who's always in control or my dad who's always strong. I can't stay and watch them die.

So I run. It's what I do best, anyway—running. I push past Hendricks back into the hall, and I gulp for air, even though there seems to be no air to gulp. The hallway seems smaller, narrower, like a compactor closing in on me.

I hear the soft click of the door latch as Hendricks follows me out.

"I'm sorry, Lyra," he says quietly.

So am I. Sorry I asked to see them and sorry for wishing I hadn't seen them. Their appearance shouldn't have surprised me. I've seen plague victims before like the little boy in the park. And the news is always warning us about Hecate's mark, what it looks like, and who we should turn in. But seeing it on my parents' still faces makes me tremble and I feel like I've been reduced to a child, a six-year-old pleading for her mommy and daddy to wake up.

"We've got to go, Lyra," Hendricks takes my shoulder, steering me back down the hall and I let him. "Once you're out of here, remember to lay low until morning before you enter the quarantine camp." His practical instructions bring me back to myself. Yes. Quarantine camp. Blood. Antibodies. Cure. "You'll be less obvious that way."

I shake off the image of my parents. I lock it away in another part of my brain, the one stuffed with memories of Ivy and home and our life before we ran. Everything that hurts to think about.

The lab is almost deserted, as Hendricks predicted, and the guards we do run into don't look at us twice. Finally, we make it to an elevator and up to the main floor. When we reach the entrance, though, we run smack into Moto.

"George!" he says, surprised. Then he looks at me and his eyes narrow. "What are you doing with Ms. Harmon?" he asks suspiciously. Then he makes a show of checking his watch. "At midnight?"

My heart hammers and I pray Hendricks has an excuse. Or was he too confident, thinking no one would question him?

Hendricks frowns. "It's important," he says curtly, then tries to skirt around Moto.

"George," Moto blocks him. His lips curl into a sneer. "You're not in charge anymore, and I haven't authorized you to work with Ms. Harmon."

Hendricks's face reddens in anger. He clenches his teeth, then, slowly, with great control, he responds. "Lyra is vital to finishing my cure. We can have a vaccine ready in a matter of days. We can stop Hecate's Plague and—"

Moto holds up his hand, as if addressing a wayward child. He sighs, exasperated. He seems to have forgotten I'm here at all. "George, George, George, this is why you lost the directorship—you just can't see the big picture. We're not here to stop just one scourge, we're here to beat all of them—cancer, heart disease, strokes, diabetes, you name it. And we can *only* do that with Ms. Harmon's cells safely under our scrutiny at all times, so kindly escort her back to her quarters. You are free to petition for time with Ms. Harmon like any other scientist at the lab."

My own blood starts to boil. I dig my nails into my palms, even as Dr. Hendricks rests a firm hand on my shoulder.

Hendricks shakes his head sadly. "No, Simon, you can't stop any scourge without Ms. Harmon's cooperation. You'll never get all your answers by drugging her. Lyra is more than a collection of cells; she's a real person with a rich history and you'll need to understand all of it if you expect your experiments to succeed. Treating her so inhumanely as you did this afternoon will only alienate her further."

I see a spark of worry in Moto's eyes—it disappears in a flash—but it was there. This is good. Hendricks is winning.

"And how, precisely, do you propose we ensure Ms. Harmon's cooperation?" he says sarcastically.

"Offer her something in return, which is *precisely*—" he mocks Moto's tone, "what I am doing now."

"At midnight?" Moto sneers.

There's a split second of awkward silence as I sense Hendricks faltering. Moto, too, senses it and I think he's about to go in for the kill, but I quickly jump in.

"Stars," I say.

Moto turns to me, as if he's forgotten I was here. "Stars?" he repeats, his voice dripping with scorn.

"I want to see the stars."

*My* stars in the night sky.

I want to see the constellation Lyra. *My* constellation.

I remember when Dad first told me that was what I was named after. We were camping in our backyard, just him and me, when I was about five, the two of us stretched out on our sleeping bags peering up at the twinkling stars in the night sky.

"There," Daddy pointed to the stars. "Do you see that bright one?"

"The one like a spotlight?"

"Yes," Daddy said. "That's yours."

"Daddy," I swatted him playfully.

"No, I'm serious, sweetheart. It's called Vega, one of the brightest stars in the sky and it's part of a pattern that looks like a diamond. Do you know what the name of that constellation is, the name of the pattern?"

I shake my head.

"Lyra," he says.

My eyes widened. "Really? Like, named after *me*?"

Daddy laughed. "I *think* the constellation came first, but yes, like you," he said, still smiling. "So it's all yours. All you have to do is reach up and grab it."

That's what I'm going to goddamn do. I'm going to get the hell out of this lab and reach up and grab my stars.

"I'm a stargazer," I tell Moto. "And my . . . quarters—" I'm as sarcastic as he is "—don't provide me a window so I can watch the night sky. Dr. Hendricks offered to take me outside so I can see them."

Moto raises and eyebrow, unconvinced. "And what, Ms. Harmon, did you promise in return?"

"My full cooperation," I say and smile sweetly. "For every night of stargazing, you get one day of trouble-free testing and any answer about my life you'd like."

"See, Simon?" Dr. Hendricks laughs heartily. "There's more to being a scientist than just science. You have to understand people."

Hendricks pushes me past Moto with assured authority. "Good night, Simon," he waves behind him.

We burst outside and I breathe in a lungful of crisp, cold April air. I'm shaking over the confrontation with Moto as much from anger as from fear.

"Quick thinking, Lyra," Hendricks chuckles. "Stars . . . I like that."

"You were the director?" I ask. If only he'd still been in charge, this would have gone a lot better for me.

Hendricks presses his lips together. When he speaks, his voice is tight. "Until recently," he says. "But the generals felt I was too focused on curing the plague rather than creating their clone army." He pauses, then adds with a wry smile. "They were right, of course. But they were also getting impatient, seeing that I was neither succeeding with the serum nor their super soldiers, so they promoted Simon Moto."

"Oh." I feel badly for Dr. Hendricks. He's fighting an impossible battle and I admire him for standing up to Moto and the heartless generals—and for standing up *for* me.

Hendricks leads me to a back field where it seems as if we really will stretch out to watch the sky. I notice a few guards patrolling the grounds, but no one else comes near us.

He points to the edge of the field, behind which is a thick forest. "There's a barbed wire fence about a hundred meters back," he explains. "It's not electrified like the others around here because too many animals crash into it. I've cut a hole, big enough for you to crawl through. Here." He hands me a flashlight. "It might be tricky to find, but you'll have to do your best. Once you get past the fence, keep walking straight until you hit the road. You have the directions from there?"

I nod, patting the paper in my jacket pocket.

"I'm sorry it'll be such a long walk, but you can't risk transportation, remember. No hitchhiking."

"I got it," I say impatiently. We've already been over this. I know what will happen if I get caught. I'm not going to jeopardize my parents' lives.

"Good." He nods, but he seems nervous, like he's the one about to run into the deep, dark night. "Remember, I can only guarantee you about a half-hour's head start. Then, the agents *will* be after you again."

"I know." There's nothing new there. Agents are always after me. Always and forever. At least next time they get close, I'll actually listen to my parents when they say it's time to run. I turn to leave, but Hendricks stops me.

"There's one more thing, Lyra."

"What?"

"You have to knock me out."

"Sorry?" I'm sure I didn't hear him right.

"It's the only way I can retain my credibility, although I'm bound to get an earful from Simon," he exhales. "It has to seem like you attacked me to get away, otherwise, they'll drag me in for interrogation and then I can't get the blood from you and finish the serum."

I nod, I get it, but I've never attacked anyone before . . .

"Find a rock over there," Hendricks points to the ground near the forest. "Look for one the size of a baseball. Something you can grip, but still has enough heft."

I walk hesitantly to the rocks, scanning the ground with the flashlight. What am I doing? Running around in the middle of the night, knocking out scientists with rocks, escaping secret military labs . . . whose life *is* this?

Feeling like I'm in some surreal nightmare, I pick up a smooth, heavy rock and return to Hendricks.

"What if I don't hit you hard enough?"

"Then I'll scream and the guards will come running, and I'll have to immediately tell them you attacked me. That won't leave you much lead time."

I swallow. I don't know that I can do this. Am I strong enough to deliver a stunning blow to Hendricks's head? It's not exactly something I've practiced at home.

"What if I hit you too hard?"

"Lyra, so much is riding on this. We're all counting on you. Your parents are counting on you."

I inhale. I exhale.

Hendricks turns his back to me.

I raise my arm.

I smack the rock down hard on his head. I hear a small crunch and my stomach churns. Hendricks collapses to the ground, but I don't stick around to check whether I actually knocked him out or cracked his skull or killed him.

Instead, I run.

# CHAPTER 5

I don't know what I expected. When Hendricks told me to infiltrate the quarantine camp, I pictured me sneaking, ninja-like, over a high barbed-wire fence into a muddy field of ripped canvas tents inhabited by the walking dead. Instead, I'm slinking into an eerily normal suburb on the outskirts of Washington. I cut through a small park with a brown-green lawn and a set of squeaking swings swaying in the early morning breeze and I pass cookie cutter houses, sandwiched together on wide lanes and expansive cul-de-sacs. They look worn, faded, tired from the harsh winter and harsher economy, but they still look *normal.* A swept flagstone path, a repainted mailbox, a sprig of yellow spring daffodils tentatively poking out of a small front garden . . . But I don't understand how anything can look normal. I'm desperately swimming upside down in this goddamn snow-globe of a world, shaken up by the agents who captured us and again by Hendricks helping me escape, so how come everything around me looks so . . . so . . . ordinary?

I weave through the quiet neighborhood, still sleepy at this barely dawn Saturday morning. I feel like eyes are following me from every window of every house I pass, and my skin prickles at the thought that someone will turn me in, but I have to ignore it. For the sake of my parents, I have to push on.

I can't believe it was only yesterday, only twenty-four hours ago, that I was also slithering through the early morning light on my way home from Mama Jua's funeral. God, that seems like a lifetime ago. Jamestown seems like a lifetime ago. My *life* seems like a lifetime ago.

I hear the growl of an engine, and I snap my head around, terrified it's an agent barreling down on me in a black car, terrified he will recapture me before I can get Yasmine's blood. If they do, my parents are dead. If I screw up in any way—if I'm not sneaky enough or stealthy enough or smart enough to get in and get out of that quarantine camp with the miracle blood—I kill my parents.

No pressure.

But the car, a rusted green hatchback, whizzes by me without slowing, and I can breathe again. So far, no one's found me.

Yet.

I inhale slowly and hunch into my leather jacket against the cold, against the fear. I take a moment to re-check Hendricks's directions. I'm almost there.

A few minutes later, I round a corner and stop, half-hidden behind a gnarled sumac bush to gather my courage. In front of me is the quarantine camp, a regular neighborhood high school surrounded by a small army of combat soldiers, rifles at the ready. So much for Hendricks's theory that they'll be bored and lazy. The building itself is set far back from the road, rising on a grassy knoll, surrounded by a moat of damp green sports fields. Large, fenced area, lots of room inside the building—perfect for housing the living dead.

I feel the black plastic syringe case inside my jacket pocket. I'm all set. All I have to do is walk up to the soldiers, cough, and I'm in.

But I don't go.

I can't seem to make my feet move toward the soldiers. For half my life, I've been on the run from them so how can I now saunter casually up to them and say, "Hey there, put me in a prison, why don't you?" I know I have to; I know it's the only way to save my parents, but damn, I hate the idea of being trapped. Isn't that what my parents were trying to protect me from all these years? It feels wrong, somehow, like a betrayal of their sacrifice for me to turn myself in—even if it's only temporary.

And even if it's for the greater good.

I try logic, coercion, and threats on myself, reminding my stubborn body to *move* or else. I try pep talks and platitudes—*you can do it, Lyra; this will all be over soon*—but still I stand frozen. What is *wrong* with me? Every second I waste is a second of my parents' life ebbing away. Why am I hesitating?

Because I'm a fucking coward. A train-dodging, dare-devil, adrenaline-junkie coward. I am fearless, I always bragged. I am super girl. I can leap through the air and stop speeding bullets. I am bold and brave.

I am a lying, delusional chicken.

I am terrified of going into the quarantine camp. What if I go in and can't get back out? What if I go in, get out but get caught and turned over to the agents? Will they still deliver Yasmine's blood to Hendricks and he'll cure my parents? What if I go in, get out but I lose the vial of blood? What if the case slips from my pocket, cracks open, and shatters?

I stand behind the bush, hating, loathing myself more with each passing second. *Do it for Mom and Dad*, I berate myself. *They'd do it for you.*

Then I hear the rumble of vehicles, and a moment later a tarp-covered army truck rolls up to the military checkpoint in front of the school. Raging close behind it are more than a dozen cars and pick-up trucks squealing to a stop. Loads of protesters pour out of the cars with the whoop of a war cry and try to ambush the quarantine truck, but a line of soldiers steps between them, rifles raised.

At first I'm startled by this display until I remember Hendricks's warning. "Be prepared for skirmishes," he said.

"Skirmishes?"

"From protesters."

"Protesters?" I asked, as if I have never heard of such a thing. As if I didn't know about Ahimsa and their work to covertly fight the government, so I don't I let slip any of Mama Jua's secrets.

Dr. Hendricks sighed. "That's what you get for state-run news," he muttered. "Yes, protesters. Groups of usually angry, violent youth who try to block the quarantine trucks that do the unscheduled sweeps of different neighborhoods day and night."

Then I actually *was* surprised. "There are people trying to stop the government?" I asked. The idea seemed unreal, and I felt like Hendricks was playing a game of truth and lies. *Three things I said were true; one is a lie. Guess which one.*

Protests are illegal. Protests are banned. That happened years ago, not long after the war started, not long after mass protests broke out across the country, not long after a group of violent activists stormed the White House in a failed attempt at a coup.

"Damn fools," Hendricks snorted. "They try to stop the army trucks from bringing sick people to the camps. They want to free the healthy ones, the ones who simply got caught up in the dragnet, who may have been around plague victims but who aren't yet sick themselves, but ultimately they'll get more people killed. Honest to God, if the sick get loose . . ."

"You *agree* with the quarantine camps?" I asked, astonished.

"Of course not," Hendricks replied impatiently. "It's draconian and barbarian to lock up people who do not yet show symptoms of the disease. We are literally handing them a death sentence. But we have to segregate the sick. Without a cure, Lyra, that's the only way we can stop the spread of the plague."

Now I watch as the protesters storm toward the soldiers, who instantly lock their rifles on them.

"Get back, all of you!" shouts one soldier. "If you get closer, you'll be in there with them!" He cocks his head back toward the school.

A couple of soldiers remove the barricade from the end of the driveway and allow the quarantine truck through, but that doesn't stop the protesters.

"Save our families!" they chant. There are dozens of them, more than fifty people, maybe. Most, like Hendricks said, are young—teenagers or in their early twenties, but a few look like grizzled, wizened men and no-nonsense older badass women.

"Go home!" the soldier roars.

But the protesters don't listen, and I watch, awed at their defiance because I know they're risking death. Hendricks told me the soldiers often use the protestors' proximity to the camps as an excuse to claim they have been infected.

"It's more efficient to make that claim and shoot them or throw them into the camp rather than jail," Hendricks snorted. "You know, to avoid that whole nasty business of a trial and justice and all."

I wonder why the protesters would risk death. They're not going to take down the government, not with a few dozen of people yelling outside a quarantine camp, so why fight? What does it get them? I think of Mama Jua and her Ahimsa friends taking the risk of secretly ferrying plague patients away from the government—that makes sense to me because they're actually accomplishing something—but to stand in front of soldiers with guns, with no victory in sight?

It seems stupid, yet still I admire them. They're *doing* something. They're out here, standing up for what's right, visible for all to see.

And what am I doing to fight the government that has me, personally, in its crosshairs? Skulking in the shadows, hiding in corners . . .

Taking the coward's way out.

But what else can I do? Those protesters don't risk what I risk. Even if they offer up their lives as the ultimate sacrifice, their suffering will be soon over. Mine, on the other hand, will last forever. But it's more than that. It's more than what happens to me. It's what they'll *do* to me that will affect the rest of the world. Can I really, in good conscience, allow a deranged government who will kill hundreds of thousands of its own innocent civilians, to take over the world? To declare war on all of its enemies and win because it will have super soldiers cloned from my cells? No, my parents were right. I have to stay hidden.

So how then, among all this sound and fury, am I to quietly slip inside the quarantine fence?

I decide, in the end, that the protest can help me. The soldiers are so focused on containing the protesters that they won't look too carefully at a girl who voluntarily wanders in.

I take a deep breath—my 136 millionth of an infinite number—and I run across the street, unnoticed. I come at the gate from the side, away from the protesters, where a soldier, on high alert, raises his rifle to my chest.

I want to laugh. He looks like a scared little kid playing with guns. Maybe in a war zone, he'd look fierce, but here, on a suburban street, guarding the most dangerous place on earth where his own death is but a sneeze away, he seems to shrink into himself.

*Go ahead*, I dare him, *shoot me. See where that gets you.*

But I don't relish another bullet wound, nor do I want to draw attention to myself, so I meekly put my hands in the air. "I'm infected," I say.

The soldier doesn't blink; instead he ushers me through the gate and I wonder how many other people have done that.

How many other people have voluntarily walked through the doors of a quarantine camp as a way to protect their loved ones? I'm doing it to save my parents—but maybe so are the others? Maybe they turn themselves in, afraid that if they don't, the quarantine patrols will scoop up their healthy family members, too?

The thought of their sacrifice saddens me, so I try to push it all out of my mind. I try to block out the screams and chants of the protesters, as I walk up the long driveway to the school's entrance. When I arrive, the driver of the quarantine truck and her partner, dressed in yellow alien HAZMAT suits, are helping unload the last of the living and dying, the unlucky ones who were rounded up and ratted out by neighbors, friends, and secret government informants.

For a moment I watch them, wondering. What must they be thinking as they walk, shuffle and stumble up the stone path toward the front door, knowing they will all be dead in a matter of days? Are they taking a last gulp of fresh air? Do they look up at the sky one last time? Have they accepted their fate, happy to have some peace at last? Maybe their whole family has already died so they're okay not to be alone anymore?

I try to imagine. What would I think if I knew I was about to die? Would I fear it? Would I rail against it? Would I think it's unfair and unjust because I'm just a kid, that seventeen is too young to die? Would I regret what I've done in my life? What I haven't done? Would I mourn for the experiences I never got? University? A wedding? Children of my own?

But I can't. I can't imagine what it would be like to die because I can't die. I can't imagine what it would be like to miss life because I never lived. Wishing I could have grown up, gone to college, gotten married, had children? Those experiences, even the *daydreams* of those experiences, are as foreign to me as dying.

Which means I won't die when I go in there. Which means I will get out somehow. Which means I've got to push on.

The aliens, the soldiers in the HAZMAT suits, barely glance at me before they shoo me toward the entrance with the others who are all laden with duffle bags and backpacks and suitcases. I'm the only one who showed up empty-handed and I'm afraid that will make me suspicious, but no one seems to notice. No one seems to care. No one asks my name or where I'm from or who my parents are. It makes me wonder if the government even knows who goes into these camps, which makes me question if they know who comes out. Are the families even notified when their loved ones die? Or do victims just disappear into a black void?

I frown at the yellow soldiers, the goons of the government. Do they understand what they're doing? Do they care? Do they actually believe they're keeping the country safe? Or are they just following orders?

"Food rations come once a day at 8 a.m.," the soldier says in a raspy voice warped by her mask. "We'll bring pillows and blankets for new patients."

Patients. That's funny. Don't you have to be under the care of doctors or nurses to be a patient?

"Anybody who's still healthy will be expected to carry the deceased to the parking lot in the back every morning. Body bags will be in your supplies. Bring out all infected bedding and clothing. It will all be burned."

I shudder, because the way she says it sounds like she's just talking about textiles, but we all know she means the bodies as well. The people. Soon to be these people.

I look around at the group of about twenty or so. At least half of them, the tottering grandpa and the young mom and the middle-aged adults are sick for real, the red-flame rash across their sallow skin, a dead giveaway. Their eyes are glassy, and sweat builds on their brows, their noses red and raw, and I wonder if any of them will see tomorrow. The rest of them, on the other hand, look healthy and whole, as yet untouched by Hecate's cursed mark. I realize they may already be infected, since the virus can take up to seven days to incubate before symptoms, including the rash, start to show, but what if they're not? What if they just got caught up in the dragnet? How long can they last in the quarantine camp before they do catch the plague? I heard the story of a man in California camp who lived for almost a month. He isolated himself and refused to go near anyone, anything, or any part of the camp that was contagious, including the food rations. It worked. He never caught the disease. Instead, he starved to death.

Was that really a better way to go? Long, drawn out suffering instead of three quick days? His family said he told them that if he was going to die, he'd die on his own terms. Would I choose to do that? Would I say *fuck you* to the government, *you're not going to kill me?*

And then a thought shakes me to my very core: would I be able to? I mean, would I literally be able to starve myself? *Could* I die? All bodies need fuel; what if I didn't provide my astounding, amazing, unreal phoenix cells any nourishment? How would they heal?

Oh my God, is that possible? After all these years of thinking I'm immortal, am I not?

My head swims with the possibility as the world slants, but it's only for a minute. No, I'm sure Hendricks would have looked into that. That's kind of fundamental. If I could simply starve myself and kill myself off so easily, would the military have been chasing me for as long as they have been? But why did I never think about it before? We've never had much money, being on the run, and sure there are days when I've gone hungry, but never for real, never for good.

But the thought lingers. Could I? If I can't get the blood or Hendricks can't make the cure, if my parents die and I'm locked up alone forever in that fucking basement lab, *could* I control my own destiny? Could I kill myself?

Would I?

I feel unnerved, unsettled, and already I regret coming.

A commotion starts up around me. A man in his late twenties, maybe early thirties, a stocky blond-haired man with a trimmed blond beard suddenly breaks from our ragged little pack and tears toward the gate, screaming.

"I'm not sick! Let me out! You can't do this!" Rage, unadulterated fury, drives him forward.

We all turn to watch the scene unfold and I wonder what the other healthy people are thinking. *You crazy fool?* Or, *Good on you, I'll follow*? Or, *I wish I was that brave*?

The drama doesn't last long. The man is not even halfway to the gate when the guard who ushered me through raises his rifle and shoots him like a rabid dog.

The crack of the gunshot pierces the still morning, but more, it pierces the stoicism I'd seen on the victims' faces. The mom with the baby yelps and hugs her child closer; the teetering grandpa slips to the ground. All of our mouths, mine included, hang open. All of us stare at the stocky blond man bleeding into the ground.

*Get up,* I want to scream at him. Get up and get back here. But he doesn't get up. Only *I* could have gotten up from that shot through the heart. And why would he want to come back here? Did he choose his way to die the way the starving man in California did? Did he know that's what would happen to him? Was he prepared to die? Was it suicide by guard or did he truly believe he could escape? Did he truly believe there was such a thing as fairness?

The soldiers say nothing. The ones in the HAZMAT suit walk casually over to him, lift him up and toss him like garbage into the back of the truck, one more body ready for disposal.

God, the heartlessness.

The rest of us also say nothing and the chant of the protesters dies. Then again, what is there to say? *You bastards? You didn't have to kill him?* But wait, you *are* killing him by bringing him here.

Robotically, we resume our path to the entrance. Dead men walking. Dead women walking. Dead babies who will never learn how to walk.

Thinking of the stages in a kid's life, I realize something: this is my first time in high school.

And then I laugh, a mad, little cackle. All those days, weeks, months, years, dreaming, begging, wishing I could go to high school like all the other kids my age, all that time, desperate to be a part of the club, and here I am, finally. My high school debut.

Fucking phoenix cells.

We step through the big oak doors into the school's front foyer, and I want to pretend I'm a transfer student, here just to finish out the year so I can walk across the stage in a cap and gown with my parents smiling and crying in the audience as I collect my diploma—honors, of course—but I'm brutally pulled back into reality by the absolute, utmost, revolting stench. The smell overwhelms me. The air is thick with piss and vomit, sweat and shit. I gag, like my fellow new arrivals, and bring my arm up to cover my nose and mouth,

"Won't do you much good," says a stout woman sitting in a cracked leather office chair in the middle of the foyer. "I'd say you'll get used to it, but I haven't yet and I'm goin' on five days here."

She swivels her large behind out of the chair and comes over to us. "'Name's Norma. I'm your welcoming committee."

"You're in charge?" someone asks. A middle-aged mom with a kid in tow.

"Honey, there ain't nobody in charge. Just tryin' to be friendly, 'cause in the short time I got left on this here God's green Earth, I see no reason not to be." She smiles widely, and her whole, unblemished, rash-free face, lights up. Like she's *happy* to be here. "'Course," she continues, "most people don' share my idea. So I'm here to warn you, too. Stay away from the Black fellas down the blue hall there. That ain't because they're Black—that's because they're mean sons o'bitches. Them white boys you'll find lordin' over the cafeteria ain't any better. It ain't about color 'round here, tho' I suspect you won't believe me, seeing as we all seem to divide up by color. It's them Arabs in the library you gotta really watch out for—and I mean *watch out* for them as in protect 'em. They've been gettin' their asses kicked almost every day, as if they're the reason we're all here. War or no war, it don't matter. They're Americans, just like us, and even if they ain't, it don't matter, neither. We're all God's creatures. Take care of each other, okay?"

She looks around at all of us, and, even though we stay silent, Norma breathes out, apparently satisfied. "The beddin' is in the gym and food rations will be here in a couple of hours. You get one packet per person per day. I dare you to take mo' than your share and you'll see what I mean about those mean dudes—Black and white. You gotta be here, tho', cause ain't nobody gonna wait on you. If you ain't here, you ain't eatin'. If you're too sick to come, you don' eat. 'S the only way we can be sure no one's hoardin'."

"How many people are here?" the middle-aged mom asks, like she's calculating what she needs to do for her kid.

Norma shrugs. "Who knows? Maybe three hundred? Four hundred? People come, people go. Every day it's different—it's a short-term hotel, if you know what I mean."

I swallow hard. Three hundred plague victims. Four hundred plague victims. And that's just one quarantine camp out of thousands around the country. And that's just right now. How many people have passed through here in the six months they've been open? How many more before it's over?

I look around, as if Yasmine will magically appear at my side, but I see only the new "patients" drifting away. Most of them follow Norma down the hall toward the gym, while the girl with the baby and the mom with the kid head toward the library straight ahead. Should I go with Norma? Would a teen girl who's sick but not as sick as she's supposed to be hang out in the gym? The library? In another part of the school?

I decide to hurry after Norma. If the bedding is in the gym, and most people are sick, then that's probably where most people are. I hope my guess is right because now that I'm in, I really, really want to get out.

When Norma pulls open the doors to the gym, I almost flee. The gym looks like a bomb of blankets, clothing, garbage, and shit went off. The wretched stench is worse: disease and decay permeate my nose and seep into my skin, my pores. Hundreds of people are lying prone on their thin mattresses, some surrounded by family or friends, some alone, their eyes closed, their chests unmoving. Are they sleeping? Are they dead? *Get them out of here,* I want to shout, but there's no one to shout at. Who will get them out of here? The nursing staff? The janitors? There's no one but us. No orderlies to take care of the bodies, no nurses to take care of the sick, no janitors to clean up the puke that slips onto the floor or the shit that runs from the sheets.

Suddenly I think Norma is the bravest person I've met. How can she remain so cheerful, so friendly, so helpful amidst this horror?

As if she hears my thoughts, Norma throws a glance at us newbies over her shoulder. "It's a lot to take in fo' sure," she says, "but you'd be surprised just how many good folks there are. Mor'n the thugs, let me tell you. People are good, y'know? People are decent."

Is she right? Are people good? Decent? Except for Mama Jua and my parents, I'd have to argue the opposite. Exhibit

A: the ghostly agents chasing my family and me for nine years. Exhibit B: the government and military responsible for a deadly and futile war in the Middle East. Exhibit C: the government's inhumane treatment of plague victims. If there are good and decent people out there, I've never seen them.

I then realize that I can't judge because I've never really known regular people living their regular lives. Am I that naive about the world? Have I been that sheltered, that protected, that I don't even know if the average, every day person is good and decent?

Norma waves her hand, as if releasing us, and the little group fans apart, each looking to stake his or her own space.

"Norma?" I ask.

The stout woman turns around, her smile still radiant. "Yes, my lovey?"

"I'm looking for a . . . um . . . friend," I say. Friend. The word hangs off my tongue as if it doesn't belong, but I press on. "Yasmine Smith? Do you know her?"

Norma's eyes soften as she cocks her head. "I'm sorry, hon, I don't know the name. What's she look like?"

I think back to Hendricks's description and only now do I realize how little I have to go on. Why didn't I at least insist on seeing a picture of her? "She's tall, brown skin, and usually wears a head scarf."

Norma's eyes shine with hope. "She's Muslim? Check the library. Some Muslims stay there. Others you can find near the girls' change room," she nods her head toward a corner of the gym. "When'd she get here?"

Without thinking, I answer, "Last Friday."

A heavy silence falls between us. "Was yo' friend sick when she came?"

I nod. Shitty luck for Yasmine, but good for us, I think, because that's how Hendricks learned about Yasmine and realized she'd survived longer than anybody. He heard she got picked up from her house, along with her healthy little brother, more than a week ago after her neighbor caught sight of her rash and turned her in.

Good and decent people, my ass.

But Norma doesn't know what I know, that yes, Yasmine is sick, but she's still alive, so instead Norma frowns. Worry lines etch deep into her forehead and I think maybe she wasn't always this cheerful.

"Lovey," Norma says slowly, her voice gentle, soothing, calm, "Your friend ain't here. You know that, right? Ain't nobody lasts longer than three days once they catch the plague."

I'm about to protest that no, she's got it all wrong, that I know Yasmine is still here, still alive—she calls her parents every day from her smuggled cell phone and Hendricks said they just talked to her yesterday, a whole *week* after she'd been brought here. I want to tell her that Yasmine may have antibodies in her blood and if Norma just helps me find her, then I can get the blood to the scientist who can create a cure and then I'll tell Norma we'll come back for her, first thing after my parents, and then she can go and help as many people as she wants with all the time she'll still have on God's green Earth.

Instead, I say, "Oh," like I'd forgotten that detail. And before I know it, Norma throws her arms around me and hugs me tightly. I tense, my body stiff against her embrace because I'm not used to kindness, despite Mama Jua's efforts, but Norma doesn't seem to notice.

"You are a blessing, Lovey," Norma says, pulling away. She squeezes my hand, then walks away, leaving me wholly confused. Why does she think I'm a blessing? Because she thinks I'm so devoted to finding my friend? Because she wants to believe I'm a good and decent person? If only she knew what I'd done to my parents, if only she knew how I'd endangered them, how I'm now killing them.

God, I just want this all to be over. I want to get Yasmine's blood, get out, get my parents and—

*And what?*

What happens to us after Hendricks cures my parents? He lets all three of us escape and we go back on the run? Does my life pick up where we left off in Jamestown? Fleeing from one city to the next? Living the life I so desperately wanted to be rid of? But what other choice do I have? My parents were right all along. I tried it my way and look where it got us.

I shrug, despondent, because nothing is ever going to change. Once we get through this plague episode and I grovel for my parents' forgiveness for my colossally poor judgment, we'll resume our lives.

*At least you'll have a life to resume, so shut it, Lyra.*

I scan the gym, I see a group of women in headscarves in the corner. I weave my way through the rotting mass of humanity on the floor around me, but I slow down as I get closer. My stomach contracts with nerves. These people are complete strangers; I don't want to go up to them and ask them about Yasmine. It was one thing to ask Norma, a lady who already stepped up to a leadership role of her own accord, but what if they ignore me? What if they scoff or laugh at me for trying to find a dead girl? What if they're nice and helpful and good and decent, like Norma says, but they don't know Yasmine either? Hendricks should have arranged all of this better. He should have had her parents call her and tell her where to meet me. I'm the one on a time crunch here; was a little pre-planning too much to ask?

Obviously.

Sulking, I approach the group. A lady in a plain black hijab sees me coming, her eyes wary, like I expected.

*I hate this, I hate this, I hate this.* "Hi," I say brightly—too brightly, I think. "I'm looking for Yasmine Smith?"

The woman in black confers with the others around her, then shakes her head. Unlike Norma, she has no follow-up questions, no suggestions so now I'm worse off than before because before Norma gave me two leads and now I'm down to one. I scurry away, feeling blood rush to my face, although I don't know why. Did I embarrass myself? Had I done something wrong in asking about Yasmine?

*Goddamn you, Mom. Making me hide from the world.* How the hell am I supposed to know how to interact with people if I've never had to interact with people? And Mama Jua and Holly don't count. *They* came up to me. They wanted to know me, not the other way around.

I head to the library, which turns out to be a large, carpeted room completely void of books, although the heavy wooden bookshelves remain standing. I wonder if the school board packed up all the books when schools were shut down last fall or if the multitudes of quarantine victims destroyed them.

I force myself to ask the people inside about Yasmine, but they don't know her either. *Try the cafeteria*, they suggest, but I don't want to because Norma said the white thugs hang out there.

In the hall, I stop another woman wearing a hijab, and ask her if she knows someone named Yasmine.

"Jaz? I don't know if it's the same person," she says, "because she doesn't wear a head scarf, but check the vault in the main office."

Vault? Don't only banks have vaults? I scurry to the main office, annoyed, frustrated. I feel like I'm on a wild goose chase. I'm supposed to be looking for a girl named Yasmine who wears a headscarf but now I find myself hunting a girl named Jaz who doesn't.

The office is wrecked. Desks and chairs are overturned, and the floor is littered with torn paper and shards of glass from shattered interior windows. Still, it's a refuge; the stench doesn't seem as overpowering in here and there are no people.

"Yasmine?" I call out, looking for a vault. I wind my way through a narrow hall and in front of me is a thick, heavy metal door standing partially open.

The vault.

"Yasmine?" I peek inside, feeling nervous, scared. What if one of the thugs is hiding in here?

Instead, I see a girl about my age, with long black hair and brown skin, marked with the flame-like rash, but I notice it's faint, not angry, not burning, like most victims. She's pressed into a corner, below empty metal shelves. What did the school keep in here? Money? What else would they have of value that they'd need a vault for? A young boy's head rests in the girl's lap, his eyes closed. He, too, is marked with Hecate's curse, but his rash is deeper, redder, harsher than the girl's. When I step inside, she hugs the boy to her, wary.

"You'd better be Yasmine Smith," I say because I'm tired and irritated and overwhelmed.

"Who the hell are you?" She tries to make her voice sound tough, but she coughs on the last word.

I sigh, exasperated. "Just tell me if you're Yasmine Smith."

She glares at me for a minute, then slowly, she nods. "My friends call me Jaz."

Jaz. A nickname. Would have been good to know. I glower, irritated at Hendricks. "You're not wearing a headscarf," I snap.

Jaz sticks her chin in the air, defiant. "Who the hell are you?"

"Hendricks said you wear a headscarf. I was looking for someone in a headscarf."

"Well, Hendricks can go to hell, whoever he is. I'll wear whatever I want."

Then I laugh because, yes, Hendricks *can* go to hell. I feel my anger dissipate a little, my frustration ebb away.

"I'm Lyra," I say, "Your uncle works as a security guard at a military lab?"

Jaz frowns, obviously suspicious I know about her.

I take a deep breath. This is going badly. “Sorry. Let me start again. I’m Lyra and I’m here to help.”

She raises a skeptical eyebrow at me, so I try to explain. “Your uncle at the research lab knows this guy, Hendricks, a microbiologist who’s trying to find a cure for the plague.”

At this, Jaz’s head flies up, her eyes flash with hope, as if she’s jumped to a conclusion a million steps ahead of me.

“He told Hendricks that you got sick *last* Friday, but eight days later, you’re still alive.”

Jaz nods, then gives me a wry grin. “I’ve had a fever for days and I throw up all the time, but I just don’t seem to die.”

*I just don’t seem to die.* A shiver tingles down my back. It’s my thought, my line, and it’s strange to hear it coming out of someone else’s mouth. Is Jaz like me? Does she have phoenix cells, too? Hendricks told my parents there may be other people born with my genetic mutation, only maybe no one knows about them. A thrill runs through me, thinking that maybe I’m not the only freak of nature, that maybe this girl could understand me, understand everything I’ve been through. Maybe we’re mutant twins and we were meant to find each other.

Then my heart sinks, because Jaz can’t have phoenix cells. She’d have gotten better already, like I did nine years ago. And if she has phoenix cells, if they’re what’s keeping her alive, then her body, like mine, doesn’t have antibodies to the virus, which means Hendricks can’t finish the cure, which means my parents will die, so I tell myself Jaz *can’t* have phoenix cells.

“Hendricks thinks you may have antibodies in your blood, that your body may be fighting off the virus. If that’s true, you’re the only one.”

Jaz stares at me, her eyes wide with hope. “You mean I’ll get better?”

I wish I could say yes. Hendricks warned me not to promise her that. Even with antibodies, he said, she may not be strong enough to beat the disease. Dying slower is not the same thing as living longer.

I crouch down so we're face to face. Jaz drops her eyes to the boy in her lap. Her twelve-year-old brother, I presume. Mohammed. The kid who wasn't sick when the military rounded them up. Now, though, all color has leached from his face. His dark hair is matted with sweat, with sickness, with death.

"When did he get sick?" I ask.

"Yesterday," Jaz replies. "But if he's like me, he'll be okay," she says stubbornly.

"Yeah," I say, because what do I know? Maybe it's true. Maybe Mohammed has the same blood, the same antibodies as Jaz. I wonder if I should take samples of both their blood back to Hendricks. But I only have one vial. Jaz it is.

"If I can get your blood back to Dr. Hendricks, he can check for antibodies and then he can create a cure."

Jaz's face lights up—almost as bright as Norma's—until she processes what I'm saying.

"How can you get my blood back to the doctor? You're in here with me. Prisoners until death."

"I have . . . immunity," I say.

"You *do*?" Jaz's eyes widen.

"In a way," I shift uncomfortably. "But it's not the right kind of immunity to make a cure, not like the antibodies you may have."

Jaz shakes her head, the light fading from her eyes. "It doesn't matter if you don't get sick. You'll never get out of here alive. No guard will let you walk out."

"Guess I'll have to sneak out."

"You'll be killed."

"I'll take my chances," I say.

She looks at me. "You're brave."

No, I'm really not. I'm not brave for coming in here, not when I know I'll survive. Bravery means fear and risk and nobility and sacrifice and I most definitely possess none of those traits. I don't fear death and I'm not noble because the only lives I care about are my parents—and that's the only reason I'm here.

"Look, will you let me take some blood or not?" My words come out harsher than I mean, and I try to soften my tone. "Please?" I pull out the black syringe case from my coat pocket.

Jaz smiles. "For the opportunity to be the savior of humankind? Why not?" She rolls up her sleeve and holds out her arm.

"I've never done this before," I warn. "I'm not a nurse."

"What can you do, kill me?" she says, and laughs.

I prepare the needle and vial the way Hendricks showed me. I tie a tourniquet above Jaz's elbow and press on her skin to find the vein. My hand trembles and I shake it out to steady it. I have to do this right. I can't mess up.

If I do, my parents die.

I jab the needle into her skin and hold the vial close. I've stopped breathing as I wait for the blood to flow. Finally, a stream of dark red liquid starts to fill the vial. I breathe out. Almost done.

When the vial is full, I remove the needle, cork the plastic tube and return them to the black case.

I beam. I did it. I got in and I got Jaz's blood.

Now all I have to do is get out.

# CHAPTER 6

I slide the black syringe case, now more valuable than gold, back into my coat pocket. I bounce to my feet, taking one last look at the sleeping boy. Is he sleeping? For Jaz's sake, I'll go with yes.

"Thanks," I say. I pause. That doesn't seem enough, not when I can get out of here and she's still stuck. "Hang in, there, okay?" I try to be encouraging. "As soon as Dr. Hendricks has the cure, he'll come back for you. It won't be long."

It can't be. Hendricks has to finish the serum by tomorrow, Sunday, for my parents to survive.

I start to walk out when Jaz calls me back. "Wait, where are you going?"

I spin around, confused. "Back to Hendricks, obviously."

"You can't leave now," Jaz protests. "It's broad daylight. The guards will see you and kill you."

I smile indulgently. Of course she doesn't know that they won't kill me, but she does have a point about being shot. I can't afford the delay—and I'm afraid what the guards will do if they see I'm still alive. Shoot me again? Drag me back inside? Think I'm dead and try to burn me? Still, I don't have a choice. I have to risk it. I have to get Jaz's blood back to Hendricks *now*.

"I'll have to take my chances," I tell her. I mean to sound warm, caring, like I appreciate her concern, but instead Jaz snaps at me.

"No, you won't."

I raise my eyebrow defiantly. "Excuse me?"

Jaz eases her brother's head off her lap, tucks a pillow under it and stands to confront me. She's taller than me, but she doesn't intimidate me. Besides, she's weak, sick with plague symptoms. She can't stop me.

"Wait till after dark," she says. "We'll come up with a plan to sneak you out."

"After dark?" I laugh. That's hours away. Hours that Hendricks needs to finish the cure. Hours my parents may not have.

"You don't have a choice, Lyra," Jaz insists.

"Yeah, yeah I do," I snap. I whirl around and march out, but Jaz's hands grab my arm. I try to shake her off, but she's stronger than she looks. Even through my leather jacket, I feel her fingers dig into me. "Let go," I hiss and with a violent shake, I release her grip. I've stalked about three paces out of the vault, down the hall, when Jaz's clipped voice stops me.

"It's not all about *you*, Lyra." There's an accusation in her tone, but underneath I also hear a plea. I allow myself to face her, and she continues. "I need that cure—maybe not for me, but for Mo." She tosses her head toward her little brother. "He shouldn't be here; I'm the one who got sick and he got dragged here because he was home with me. It's not fair to him. Or my family. I talk to them every day and they're beside themselves. Mom says it's all her fault because she had to take a job out of town and was gone. Dad works in the Health Department—isn't that ironic? He's an IT guy, not a doctor or a nurse or even a policy wonk. He's just a cog in a big, fucked-up machine, but they won't let him come home because they can't afford any more of their employees to catch the plague. *He* is riddled with guilt, he says, because he put his job before his family. I've prayed to Allah every day that He won't take me before Mo because I can't stand the thought of Mo being here by himself. and you know what? Every day I've woken up. Every day when I shouldn't have, I opened my eyes. I wasn't getting better, I knew, and each day I feel weaker and weaker, but then you show up with wild stories about antibodies and cures. So you think I'm going to let you walk out of here into the line of fire with *my* blood? The blood you say is our only hope to cure Hecate's Plague? Are you crazy?"

I'm rooted to the floor, but the roiling lava beast inside my chest roars awake. I want to scream, "how *dare* you call me out? Do you *know* what risks I've had to take to get here? Do you understand how high the stakes are for me if I'm caught? Forget Hecate's Plague—the world will be in worse trouble if the military figures out how to clone me and our sadistic government ends up in charge. Don't you *see?* It's not about me. It's about what the military will do to me that you should be worried about. So don't lecture me about being *selfish*. I've given up any semblance of a *life* to protect all of you, just like my parents, so don't you *dare* think—"

*Think what?*

My whirling mind jolts to a stop.

*Think that this is only about you and your parents, Lyra? Isn't it? Aren't you here only because your parents are sick? Would you have come otherwise?*

That's not a fair question, I argue with myself. The scientists wouldn't have let me go.

*Isn't it? If Hendricks had come to you and said, go get Yasmine's blood because it'll cure the plague for everyone else, what would you have said?*

Fuck you. Get my parents out of jail and then maybe we'll talk.

Suddenly, I feel like I've been punched in the gut. Oh my God, it's true. It is all about me. I try to remember when I last thought about the plight of a plague victim—someone other than Mama Jua—and I can't. They're just numbers, statistics we see on the news. Another thousand people died today.

But Jaz isn't a statistic. Not yet, anyway. And neither is her brother Mo. Nor is Norma a statistic. Or the frightened mom with her baby who will never see her child grow up. And the blond-haired man who wasn't even sick. They're not statistics. They're real people, like Holly's parents, people with real families who will feel real pain, like Holly felt when they died.

I am such a bitch.

It was all about me. It is all about me.

And I'm the lucky one who will live.

I feel the heat rising to my face, and I drop my eyes, embarrassed. All this time, all these years, I've been thinking I'm special—why else would we have to live on the run?—but I'm not, am I? I may have phoenix cells, but what good will they do anybody? They won't help people; they won't cure people. Jaz is the real hero. It's her blood that may have the antibodies. She'll be the one to cure the plague. I'm just the fucking delivery girl.

My eyes start to sting and I blink hard to stop the tears, but that makes me feel worse because now I'm not only not special, I'm now so thin-skinned that I can't deal with the fact that I'm not special.

"Lyra," I hear Jaz's voice as if it's an echo. "Lyra, please wait until dark."

I nod. Yes, I'll wait till after dark to make my escape. Hendricks won't like it—he'll have to wait so much longer for me—but Jaz is right. For my parents' sake, for her sake, for her brother's sake, I need to maximize my chances of getting that vial to Hendricks.

I turn and slink down the hallway, a lump of self-pity, self-loathing forming in my stomach. Who did I think I was? The savior of the world? Stupid, Lyra, stupid.

"Lyra," Jaz calls after me. I don't respond. She got what she wanted. "Lyra, wait." She catches up to me, her breathing ragged. She coughs, then coughs again, then doubles over from violent coughing fit. When she finally straightens, her face is drained of color. Her eyes shine from her fever. "You got plans today?" She smiles.

I look at her, frowning. I don't understand.

"What I mean, is, we have hours to kill before nightfall. Wanna have some fun?"

My frown deepens, but Jaz's smile widens. "Think about, it, Lyra. We have the run of the school—with no teachers, no principals, no parents, *no one in charge*."

"So?"

"So?" Jaz dances on her feet impatiently. "Haven't you ever wanted to break your school rules? Well, now's our chance. Let's run through the halls and kick in some lockers and break some windows and vandalize a classroom."

I stare at her, as if she's gone crazy. Maybe she has. Does the plague do that to you? Fry your brain?

"Seriously, Lyra, you can't tell me you've never thought about taking revenge on a bad teacher or a piss-ass principal. Well, now you can. At least symbolically. Let this hellhole stand in for your real high school and let the fun begin."

My heart drops like a stone as Jaz's eyes dance.

Real high school.

Funny.

"Come on, Lyra, what do you have to lose? You'll be out of here tonight and I'll be out of here soon, too, one way or another. Nobody gives a shit—it's not like we're going to get into trouble."

Breaking school rules is the furthest thing from trouble

in my world. "It's not that," I say. "It's . . ." I'm ashamed to admit I never went to high school, that I don't have bad teacher experiences, unless you count the fights with my dad over Calculus and I never met a piss-ass principal or any other kind. It makes me feel like I truly don't belong to this world. Like I truly am a freak.

"What, you're telling me you had perfect classes with perfect teachers and perfect friends?" Jaz laughs. Then she sees my face. "Oh, no, it's something else . . . I'm sorry Lyra, I was just joking—"

I cut her off. "I didn't have perfect classes or perfect teachers or perfect friends," I snap, "because I didn't *have* classes or teachers or friends."

Jaz looks at me, her face filled with pity, and I hate her, suddenly. I hate her pity and I hate her high school and I hate her fucking idea to break school rules. I'm about to stalk away, but Jaz grabs my arm again, gentler, this time.

"Tell me," she says.

"Tell you what?" That I'm a freak of nature who's been hunted for nine years by the military which believes my phoenix cells can save the world, but my parents believe will destroy it? Tell her that I've been living in solitary confinement for nine years, never allowed out into the real world, no matter how good my behavior? Tell her that my parents kept me isolated out of love even as they suffocated me with their fears?

"I was home schooled," I finally say.

"Oh," Jaz says but I know she senses there's more to the story. Still, she doesn't press me. "Well, in that case, I'd better show you how it's done."

"Show me how *what's* done?"

"Breaking the school rules, of course. If you never had them, you don't know how to break them. Come, Lyra," she links her arms through mine, and drags me toward the main part of the office. "We have a lot of work to do."

"What about your brother?"

"He'll be ok. He's safe here, tucked away from the others. Only a few of us know about the vault."

"How do *you* know about the vault?"

"Didn't I tell you? Jaz laughs and pulls me out the door. "This is my high school."

# CHAPTER 7

"I'll show you my locker first," Jaz says, animated. She leads me through the front foyer and upstairs to the second floor. We pass handfuls of healthy-looking victims, young and old, clustered in small groups sprawled in the halls, and if it weren't for their gray hair or wrinkled faces or tiny hands or toddler squeals, I imagine this may be what lunchtime looks like on a regular school day. Just a bunch of people hanging out.

Jaz guides me to the end of one hall, littered with papers and ripped textbooks, where all the lockers are painted a sunshine-yellow. I like that it's bright, almost cheerful, despite the chips in the paint and the dirt on the walls. Jaz flings open a locker on the right. Inside is a mess of notebooks and lined paper, crumpled and shoved into the bottom. The door is wallpapered with pictures.

I step closer, studying the collage. I recognize Jaz in almost all of them—she is wearing headscarves, beautiful, colored, patterned hijabs—and she's surrounded either by girls with wide smiles or her family. I see her little brother Mo in a couple of them, his complexion ruddy and flushed, and I see a young man—her older brother Youssef, I presume. I'm surprised by her parents, though. Her mom, a woman with light mocha skin, is tiny and short—nothing like Jaz's stature—whereas her dad is a tall, thin white man covered with freckles and topped with a mop of reddish-orange hair.

"My dad's Irish," Jaz explains, when she sees me looking. "Mom's family is from Algeria, but that was generations ago. Still, she wanted to keep her heritage close, which is why me and my brothers have Arabic names."

Youssef, Yasmine, Mohammed. I remember Hendricks telling me about the three kids.

"'Course it backfired on her," Jaz continues, "You think we were going to be saddled with foreign-sounding names with a fucking Middle-East war dragging on? So we Anglicized our names. Joseph, Jaz, and Mo."

I'm fascinated. It never occurred to me that people would have to—would want to—change their names to fit in. I remember a bunch of kids from all different backgrounds at my elementary school and I never thought to question their names, but was I the only one who didn't? Or did things get much worse in the schools after I was yanked out? Suddenly I feel like I've been asleep for almost a decade, like I've been in a coma, and only now that I'm waking up do I see how the world has changed. I bristle at that notion, considering I follow the news, state-run as it is. I'm not ignorant, or blind to what's going on around me. It's not like I haven't taken an interest in world events.

But I haven't been a part of them. I haven't been a part of society, of school, of cliques. So no, I guess I don't know what it's like to want to change your name.

I only know what it's like to want to change your life.

"Why are you wearing a head scarf in all these pictures, then?" I ask. "Wouldn't that draw more attention than an Arabic name?"

"Yeah, it did," Jaz shrugs. "But by the time I got to high school, I decided to hell with all of the losers. I was done hiding who I am. I'm proud to be Muslim, so I took back my identity."

*Lucky her that she had an identity to take back*, I think bitterly.

"Your mom's not wearing a head scarf," I point out. "Is she Muslim?"

"Yep, but she chose not to wear one. It's not mandatory, you know. Muslim women don't have to cover their heads."

"So why don't you wear one now?"

Jaz's shifts uncomfortably. "It's easier," she mumbles.

"Easier?"

"The guys here . . ." she says. Then she takes a deep breath. "Let's just say the teachers kept the bullies in line at school."

I think of Norma's warning about the "mean sons o'bitches" in the blue hall and cafeteria.

"It's safer to blend in here," she finishes quietly. "I'd rather die of the plague than a beating—or worse."

Wow. I've never thought about those kinds of threats before—and not just because I can't die. I understand the threat of violence and the fear it provokes. I've lived with it for half my life. But somehow Jaz's situation seems more . . . raw. Personal. Frightening. That seems strange, I think, considering the agents have been after me all these years. But it's not out of hate. I mean, the agents hunt me down because they're ordered to, not because they have something against me. They don't actually see me as a person, even. Just a target, a goal. I don't threaten them because they know I can't hurt them. But Jaz's tormentors? They're afraid of her, of what she represents—a world where they may no longer hold the upper hand. If they fight, they'll fight dirty. At least that's what Mom told me years ago about narrow-minded bigots when she talked about her experiences in the military. She had to be tough, I remember her saying, because she joined before mandatory conscription, before men and women made up equal ranks in the armed forces. She had to be tougher than the men because most of the brainless nitwits—her words—feared they'd be shown up by a girl, so they tried to push her down. Mom wasn't the only woman in uniform, she said, but she was the only one in her platoon.

"So why did you do it?" I once asked her. I couldn't see why anyone would voluntarily subject themselves to that kind of punishment. Weren't you supposed to like your job? If you were always being attacked, why stay when you didn't have to?

"Because no man was going to tell me what I can and can't do," she replied, her voice fiery. "You can't let them get away with such reprehensible behavior."

*Yes, yes you can*, I remember thinking. Let them get away with it so you can stay home with us. Let them be horrible if it means you don't have to go away for months at a time. Why did *she* have to be the one to change the world? Let someone else do it. But she wouldn't hear of it, no, not her, the hero, the martyr. She claimed she did it to fight the system, to prove that women are as strong and fierce as men, but I understood the real reason. She just wanted to show off. She wanted to be best, to beat everyone else, and to hell with anyone else, including her family. That's why she'd abandon us for months at a time on deployment or rush to duty in the middle of events like my ballet recital.

"I'm trying to give you a better world to grow up in, honey," she'd often say whenever I'd call her out on her absences.

Yeah, look how well that's turning out for me. Mom and her fucking crusade to change the world is why we're in the mess we're in. If she hadn't joined the military intent on proving herself, then she wouldn't have served overseas in the first tour of the war, and she wouldn't have come back with the private who got bit by the camel spider carrying Hecate's Plague and we wouldn't have been living on the base when the virus spread and I wouldn't have contracted it and I wouldn't have infected Ivy and she wouldn't have died and we wouldn't have learned about my phoenix cells and we wouldn't have been on the run . . .

I start to spiral down my familiar rabbit hole of blame and recrimination when Jaz's light voice pulls me back.

"These girls here," Jaz says, proudly pointing to a picture of four giddy girls all mugging for the camera. "They're my posse."

I feel an unexpected stab of jealousy when I look at the friends, their arms draped around each other easily, confidently, like they know they all belong together. That damn green-eyed monster shares my soul with the angry lava beast. It's the one who constantly pops up whenever I see a group of kids hanging out at the local burger joint or straggling out of a movie theatre. The one who reared its ugly head when I spied on Jonah last summer having a blast at the beach with his friends. It started earlier in the day when he and I met down by the cliffs.

"Come meet the gang today," he pleaded. "You'll like them."

"I can't," I said. "Mom needs me to do chores at home."

"On such a beautiful day?"

And it *was* beautiful. The sun was hot and dry, the sky a crystal-jewel blue, the ocean waves a frothy white.

"Tell your mom to give you a pass for today," he said, leaning over to kiss me. I remember we were on a secluded cliff, as high as the water was deep, and we were both soaked to the bone. Jonah had brought me up here to show me the view, but then he told me how this was a popular jumping spot so I dared him to jump and he said no way, he's not crazy, but I said I was and I took a flying leap and I heard Jonah suck in a breath and then I was airborne and my stomach rose to my throat and I screamed into the wind, and I plummeted to the water below and I splashed in hard, going down, down, down and I let myself sink until I thought my lungs would explode and then I kicked up with all my might and resurfaced with a huge, satisfying gulp of air.

"Woohoo!" I whooped into the air, still charged with adrenaline. The water was cold from the rain the night before, and my t-shirt and shorts clung to me like a second skin, but I didn't care. I felt *alive*.

"Jump!" I cried to Jonah, the small figure on the cliff, and he did. He howled all the way down, his arms, flailing like a windmill until he crashed into the water and came up spluttering.

"Fun, eh?" I said.

Wet, sopping, we clambered back up the cliff, often slipping and catching ourselves—Jonah's arms were scraped raw, as were mine, but I made sure he didn't notice my arms healing in no time.

"Lyra, you're *crazy*!" he laughed, pulling me to him, and I remember not wanting him to let me go. I liked the feel of his arms around me, his skin touching mine. Our romance was forbidden, I knew; Mom would kill me if she learned I'd been hanging out with a local, but I couldn't help myself. He was just so hot. "My friends will never believe I jumped the cliff," he went on. "They've been calling me chicken shit for years because I was too sane to jump, but then you come along . . ."

I remember pulling back—I didn't want to, but I had to. "You can't tell your friends," I said. "At least not about me being here. Remember? Part of our deal?"

"But *why*?"

That question again.

"Look," I answered brusquely, "those are the ground rules, whether you like it or not. If you tell anyone about me, I'll never see you again."

Jonah shrugged. "You're a mystery, all right."

"Isn't that what all the boys want?" I said, needing to change the subject and trying to sound coy. As if I knew the first goddamn thing boys wanted.

Jonah smiled mischievously. "Come on, Lyra, you know what all teen boys want." He drew me to him, and starting kissing my neck. God, it felt good, but I had to stop him.

"Jonah . . ."

He backed off, his hands up in the air in mock surrender. "Okay, okay, I was just fooling around." He ran his hands through his wet brown curls. "But seriously, rules or no rules, mom or no mom, chores or no chores, I still think you should come to the beach this afternoon."

I did, but not with him. I watched him, though. I watched Jonah and his friends laugh and swim and tackle each other in the sand and waves. I watched as a thin blond chick—Barbie, I called her—dug her wretchedly manicured claws into Jonah's back as she massaged his shoulders, and I wanted to gouge her eyes out. "*Don't touch my boyfriend,*" I wanted to scream at her. But how could I? How could I lay claim to him when I wouldn't even allow him to acknowledge my existence? Imagine what would happen if I strolled down to the sand and introduced myself. "Hi, I'm Lyra, Jonah's phantom girlfriend. What? He didn't tell you he had a girlfriend? Why Jonah, why ever would you pretend I don't exist?"

It sucked, watching Jonah with his friends. I hated them. I hated their easy laughter, their carefree smiles, and I hated that Jonah joined in. I hated that Jonah looked happy without me, that he could have fun when I wasn't around. I hated that Jonah wanted to be there with them and not with me. I wished he hadn't gone with his friends. I wished he didn't *have* friends to go with.

That's what I feel now, looking at Jaz's friends. I wish she didn't have any.

"Where are they now?" I ask and I try to sound polite, but the whole time I'm thinking *gone, I hope they're gone*. Because if they are, then I can be Jaz's new friend and in this hellhole I can be her only friend.

"Jenn's parents sent her to live with her cousins in England right after the schools closed last fall," she says, and I shake my head, trying to get rid of the fucking voice inside, and try to concentrate on Jaz, but I don't want to know about them. I know I asked, but I don't want to hear how fun her posse is and how tight they are.

Too late. She keeps going.

". . . and Tracey and I hung out until about a month ago when her mom refused to let her leave the house. And Chris . . ." Sadness creeps into Jaz's voice. "Chris just disappeared. We don't know if she's still alive."

I see the pain, the worry cross Jaz's face and I feel my own burn with shame that I wished for these girls to be gone. Is this what kind of friend I'd be? Mean and possessive? Unwilling, unable to share someone's attention? Am I that needy? That pathetic?

That lonely?

I don't answer—I won't answer—my own questions. Instead, I change the topic. I have to talk about something else. "Why is all your stuff still here? Didn't they let you take it when they closed the schools?"

Jaz smiles wryly. "My parents refused to let anything from the school cross our threshold, in case it was contaminated. Ironic, don't you think?"

"How did you get sick?" I ask. I've wanted to know the answer since Hendricks told me about Jaz. I mean, shouldn't it be simple to avoid the plague? The virus isn't airborne. It's passed by contact with bodily fluids, or touching contaminated surfaces. So, avoid contagious people and places, and ride out the epidemic. Like her friend Tracey is doing.

Jaz sighs, and closes her locker. She links her arm through me—like we're friends?—and leads me down the hall.

"I got sick because I'm stupid. Because I thought I was invincible. Because I thought it wouldn't happen to me."

"What did you do?"

"I went to the park."

"That's it?" I don't know what I expected Jaz to say—that she was tenderly caring for an aging relative and knowingly sacrificed herself to help? That she couldn't keep herself from a boy as hot as Jonah had been? —but I didn't expect it would be something so mundane. Obviously I'd heard warnings about staying away from public places, but for me, staying away from public places is second nature, so I never gave it much thought.

"Yeah," Jaz explains. "My parents told me to stay inside, and more importantly, not to let Mo outside. But do you know how hard it is to keep a twelve-year-old kid cooped up all day every day?"

I think about when I was twelve, when my parents would release me on my own recognizance. Yeah, I understand how hard it is to keep a twelve-year-old kid cooped up all day.

"So I told Mo we could go to the park, but I had to check it out first. I'd make sure it was deserted, and I'd bring towels and spray to wipe down the swings and slide and stuff. Only, the park wasn't deserted. There was a nanny with some kids, all healthy, or so it seemed, but I knew better, so I turned around to go home. One kid knocked into me and sneezed. The next day, I started puking."

"The next day?" I ask, surprised. "Usually the incubation period is seven days."

"'Usually' isn't the same thing as 'always'," Jaz answers wryly.

"But maybe that's why you're still alive," I say. I had been focused on her dumb, shitty luck but I'm suddenly excited. "Maybe it shows your body was trying to fight the virus right away. Maybe you *do* have antibodies." I press my hand to the black case in my pocket, convinced for sure now that I'll be able save my parents.

"Maybe," Jaz says wearily. Then she steers me through a set of double doors into another part of the school. It's frigid in here; the air is as cold as outside, maybe even colder. There's obviously no heat and no electricity. "Transformers blew, or something," Jaz explains. "At least that's what I heard, but no electrician was about to set foot in here to fix it."

I start to wrap my leather jacket more tightly around me, until I realize that Jaz, wearing only a hoodie, is shivering. I shrug out of my jacket and offer it to her. She shakes her head, but I insist. I'm not the one who's sick.

"Just don't run off with it," I joke, pointing to the pocket with the vial of blood. "It's worth a fortune."

Jaz slips her bone-thin arms into the sleeves, and her expression relaxes as she gets warm.

"Why are we here?" I ask.

"Because . . ." she walks another few steps and stops in front of a classroom door. "I want to introduce you to the torture chamber."

I look at the door. It's a regular wooden door with a glass window in the upper half. Through it, I see a normal classroom, with rows of scratched, wooden desks. Unlike the main office, which has been trashed, this room looks intact. Maybe because this wing is too cold for people to hang out in.

"Physics," Jaz says, smiling.

I peer through the window and now I see lab benches lining the room and a sink in the corner.

"You don't like physics?"

"Lyra, *no one* likes physics."

"I like physics," I say. And I do. I love learning about matter and energy traveling through space and time. It's such a mind warp to think about things like black holes and wormholes in space. It makes me feel like there's more to our world, this life, than the petty, nihilistic, violent tendencies of humans. It also gives me hope. Hope that time isn't linear. Hope that time will turn in on itself and become my friend, instead of my immortal enemy.

"Yeah, well, you didn't have Mr. Brown," Jaz sneers.

"True," I say. "I didn't have Mr. Brown. You didn't like Mr. Brown?"

"Mr. Brown was a twit. An incompetent twit at that. He couldn't teach his way out of a wet paper bag."

"So why are we here in front of Mr. Twit's door . . . ?"

Jaz offers me a mischievous smile. "Number one: to kick it in."

I smile. I'm liking this. "Go for it."

Jaz backs up, two giant steps, lifts her right heel and slams it into the door. The wood splinters with a loud crack and the door swings open.

"Kick in door," I say, laughing. "Check."

Jaz walks ahead into the classroom, but for a moment I hesitate. Like walking through the entrance to the school, I've daydreamed a million times what it would be like to stroll into a regular classroom and drop my books onto a desk—not because I have any actual knowledge but because my dad used to describe for me his high school days. I'd be coming in with a group of friends, of course, my own posse, as tight as Jaz's, and we'd be laughing about our last class, history, where the teacher let us play cards the whole period because she didn't feel like teaching that day, which would remind us of geography, where *that* teacher would often digress into stories of his life and only in the last five minutes would he say, okay, kids, we've gotta push on now. But in physics, we knew not to mess around. We wouldn't have a twit like Jaz's Mr. Brown, no, we'd have a smart, serious teacher, who expected the best of us and always got it. I'd slide into my seat and get out my pen and open my book and then class would start, and I'd listen and take notes and when it came time for labs, I'd partner up with my best friend and we'd go to a lab table and we'd work on our experiment until the bell and then, packing up, we'd moan when the teacher would announce a boatload of homework, but we knew we'd do it because the teacher made us want to get better.

But the reality is a sad perversion of my imagination. The room is cold, dark, empty. Abandoned. A pile of books is askew on the corner of the teacher's desk up front and chemistry beakers sit empty in glass cabinets against the wall. There's a date more than six months old—October 3—written in dusty chalk on the board and a list of assignments stapled to the bulletin board next to it. It's as if the teacher, the incompetent Mr. Brown, will stroll back through the doors at any minute and resume his lesson.

Suspended animation.

The story of my life.

I move, like a ghost, between the rows of desks, trying to decide which one would be mine if I'd been in this class. I know the stereotypes—the keeners take the front rows, the slackers take the back, the daydreamers sit by the window and the cynics sit by the door. What would I be? Where I would fit in? I love science, so would I be a keener? But keeners are often the geeks and nerds—would I be one of those because I do okay at school? Or maybe I do okay at "my" school because my parents go easy on me. Or maybe they don't actually know how to teach, so the work they gave me seemed easy, but maybe I would have failed in a real school. I wouldn't be a slacker—or would I? If I had friends to distract me, and sports and clubs, would I not care about schoolwork? Is it only because schoolwork is *all* I had that I focused on it? I am a cynic—life on the run will do that to you—but would I have been a cynic had I lived a normal life? I spend all my time daydreaming of what a real life would be like, so maybe I'd be one of those spaced out kids? Or not, because I'd *have* a real life so I wouldn't have anything to fantasize about?

I turn slowly in a circle, an odd sense of panic rising up my throat. Where would I belong? Who would I be? I always thought if I could go to a real school, I'd find my answers. Everyone else at school finds their place and I know a school masquerading as a quarantine camp is not a real high school experience, but still I feel shaky, because I don't know *where* I'd sit.

"Where's your desk?" I ask Jaz because maybe if I know where she sat, I'd know where I'd sit, because we'd be friends. We're getting along now; she asked me to come on her destructive adventure with her, so she must like me. So she'd like me in regular school. I'd be a part of her posse; it would be the five Musketeers, instead of the four of them, because if Jaz liked me then the others would, too. Tracey and Jenn and the missing Chris . . . We'd all hang out and we'd all be friends and then I'd know my place. I'd know where I belong.

Jaz points to a desk near the back. Aha! I knew it. A slacker—sort of. But not too far back, so she didn't totally diss school. But then she taps another desk near the front, and another one smack dab in the middle.

I frown, not understanding.

"Mr. Brown believed in seating plans," she explains. "He'd constantly mix us up so we'd have to work with different people. Said it built character, having to learn how to get along with all sorts of different people who you may not otherwise talk to." Jaz shrugs, like she is reluctantly conceding the imbecilic Mr. Brown may have had a valid point.

I didn't know high school teachers used seating plans. I would have thought that was juvenile, telling teenagers where to sit, but actually, I like the idea. Considering I'm all stressed about where I'd sit and this isn't even a real class with real kids, I like that a teacher could take the pressure off.

I breathe out, feeling some tension ease, like I've dodged a bullet.

"Number two," Jaz says, going back to her imaginary destructive to-do list, "is to smash all the goddamn equipment in the room." She jumps across a desk and flings open the cabinet with the glass chemistry beakers. With a quick swipe,

Jaz's arm sweeps all the vials to the floor and the glass shatters musically to the ground. She bounces to another cupboard, flings it open and smashes boxes of lenses and batteries and circuit boards. The equipment, no surprise, looks ancient—no money from the government for new supplies—and it's no match for Jaz's wrath. She pounds them, and throws them and stomps on them.

"Come on, Lyra, help me," she encourages.

I hesitate, not because I care about the equipment, but because I've never seen most of it before. In a classroom of one, with an unqualified set of teachers, there were rarely experiments. All my learning is theoretical. I bend down, on the pretense of shattering a box with red and black dials—I have no idea what it is—but instead I end up studying it.

"Just smash it, Lyra," Jaz cries, and her energy, her enthusiasm is infectious and I lift the gray box over my head and throw it, with all the strength in my arm, toward the window. The glass cracks into a spider web; it doesn't break and neither does the box, but Jaz laughs and cheers. "Yeah! That's what I'm talking about!"

And I feel good. I pick up circular tubes—who knows what they are—and launch them against the cracked glass windows. I feel my anger, and I recognize the lava beast rising, but for the first time, *I'm* in control. *I* will order it to destroy the boxes and the windows and the desks. *I* will decide when and where and how I unleash my fury.

The control is exhilarating.

Jaz whoops and hollers when she sees me launching objects across the room. "Go, Lyra!" she cries.

I do, and she does, and for half an hour, we're two thundering elephants on a rampage. We shred every book and carve up every desk and tear down every bulletin board and then Jaz drags me down the hall and we do the same thing in another class and another class and another, and I'm having so much fun and I don't want it to end. I don't care about the destruction, not the way Jaz seems to—her face is aglow with sweet revenge—but I love that I'm hanging out with another girl my age, doing something *we* choose to do, not something my parents told me I have to do.

Then abruptly I stop. We're in an English classroom, where there's much less to destroy. A set of dictionaries bit the dust, as did a few laminated posters of famous writers, and I'm about to scratch obscene words into a wooden desk with the corner of a metal ruler, but my hand hovers mid-air.

What the hell am I doing?

I can't be tromping doing meaningless, trivial, insignificant shit. My parents are *dying*. I should be planning my escape tonight so I'm ready the moment the sun sets, not skipping around the school like a . . . a . . .

Like an irresponsible teenager.

"You okay, Lyra?" Jaz asks. She, too has a ruler suspended over a desk.

I let mine clang to the floor. "Yeah," I mumble, my face flushed, embarrassed. I'm so stupid to have let myself loose like this.

"What is it?" Jaz presses.

"Nothing."

"Lyra, you were a mad woman on a rampage," Jaz says, and smiles. She shimmies onto a desk and absently swings her legs underneath it. "One minute you're a crazed lion and now you're as meek as a little lamb. What gives?"

I almost tell her. I almost tell her how stupid I was to agree to this, how dumb I was to take part, but I don't. I can't. Instead, I shrug.

"Unh-unh," Jaz protests. "You do not get to do that."

"Do what?"

"Shut me out," Jaz says, with a gleam in her eye. "Maybe your imaginary friends from your overcrowded classrooms back at your home school would have let you get away with such appalling, anti-social behavior, but not around here, no way. Not on my turf." She grins widely to show me she's joking, even as I consider taking offence, and then she laughs and I can't help but crack a small smile.

Imaginary friends in overcrowded classrooms . . . Wouldn't that have been an entertaining notion to mess around with on all those boring, lonely days.

I hoist myself onto a desk facing her, and cross my legs under me. "I guess," I say, unsure where to start, "I feel like I shouldn't be having fun like this."

Jaz looks genuinely puzzled. "Why not?" Then her eyes widened, "Oh, Lyra, honestly, we're not going to get in trouble, I swear."

"No," I say, realizing how she misunderstood me. "I mean, I shouldn't be having *any* fun."

Again, Jaz looks perplexed. "Why not?"

Now it's my turn to stare at her, confused. "Maybe because we're in the middle of a pandemic that's wiping out half the country and the other half is being killed in a relentless war overseas."

"All the more reason," Jaz says. "If the world is going to hell in a hand basket, why not enjoy the ride?"

"Are you serious?"

"Yes!" she says. "Look, I've got only a few days left to live. You got immunity, so you might not know what that's like."

How right she is.

"Think about it, Lyra. The world has always been fucked up, right? It was a mess before the plague, and probably before the war. If we waited for the world to straighten itself out before we had fun, we'd never do anything."

I don't know what Jaz sees on my face, how she interprets my expression, but it's like a brilliant realization washes over her.

"You haven't, have you?" she asks.

"I haven't what?"

"Had fun!" Jaz cries. "You've never had fun."

I'm about to bluster through my protests, to tell her how wrong she is, and how dare she presume that she knows the first goddamn thing about me, that I know fun, like when Jonah and I were jumping off cliffs and dirt-biking on tracks, or when I hung out with little five-year-old Holly, but the words fade on my lips.

Jaz doesn't wait for me to respond. Instead, she hops off the desk, grabs my arm and pulls me down, too. She rushes us out of the room with an energy, a zest, that makes me forget she's sick. We run through the halls—another rule we're breaking, Jaz gleefully points out—and fly down the stairs. She leads me down a darkened hallway where, at the end, she yanks open a heavy set of double doors. Jaz ushers me into the auditorium. It's cold in here, part of the abandoned wing, and the room is dark, thick as velvet, with only a tinge of red coming from a few battery-powered exit signs. But my eyes quickly adjust to the inky light, and I can make out silhouettes of seats running down toward the stage.

"Come on," she urges.

She leads me up on stage and into its center. It's weird, standing here in the vast, dark space. I know the seats are empty, but still I feel like invisible eyes stare up at me. I take a step back, but Jaz pushes me forward.

"What are you doing?" I ask, resisting.

"Having fun," she replies, "without wrecking anything."

She steps up beside me, spreads her arms wide, and starts to sing. It's a pop song I've heard on the radio, but I don't really know it. I wonder why anyone knows it. Pop songs—any songs or music or movies or TV shows—seem incredibly indulgent these days. I've never understood how the entertainment industry can keep chugging along when there are more important issues, like, oh, I don't know, a *war*, a *plague*, going on.

But looking at Jaz's face light up in the dim red glow of the exit signs makes me wonder. I watch her sing, an imaginary microphone held up to her mouth as she dances and spins and twirls around the stage, her movements sluggish from her fever, but nonetheless, she looks like she's alive. She skips to the front of the stage and spreads her arms, like she's embracing the love from her phantom audience then turns to me, smiling widely. I look on, amazed that she can have so much fun singing a pop song that's lighter and fluffier than cotton candy.

"Come on, Lyra," Jaz calls to me in a sing-song voice. "Join me."

"I don't know the song," I say.

"Who cares?" she shrugs her shoulders. "Just sing something!"

I don't, of course, because I'd feel silly and I don't *do* silly. Dangerous and adventurous, sure, but not silly.

Not fun.

Then I think why *not*? Why not do fun? Or silly? Who's going to see me? Jaz? She doesn't care. And that's her point, right? That the world is fucked up anyway so we might as well enjoy what we can. I'm starting to think she's right. I know the world is fucked up—I know that better than anyone. And I hate it. I hate the goddamn war and the plague. I hate that Jaz may die, that Norma will die, that my parents could die. I hate that I'll be alone and isolated and lonely.

I'm not alone right now, or isolated or lonely. I have a friend, someone my own age who is dancing and singing and doing all those silly things teenagers are supposed to do.

So maybe I should be doing it, too. Enjoying what I can. It's what I always wanted. To hang out with friends and do what friends do when they hang out. I can't say dancing around a darkened auditorium singing frothy pop songs was what I initially imagined, but it's the only option available to me, so why not do it? Mom and Dad won't mind, I'm sure. At least not for a day. They'd understand I'm just passing time until dark, until I can slip out of this death camp unseen. They'd know I'm not abandoning them. They'd be okay with me singing one song . . .

I step toward Jaz who spins in a fluid circle, her eyes closed, her arms spread wide. My voice floats over to her. "Teach me the chorus?"

Jaz's eyes fly open. She stops twirling and grins at me in the dim light. "Now *that's* what I'm talking about."

# CHAPTER 8

Back in the vault later that afternoon, I watch Jaz care for Mo. With his head in her lap, she covers his feverish brow with a damp cloth, then lets her hand linger on his flaming cheek. She talks to him, too softly for me to hear, but her tone is light even as her face sags with fatigue and I see Mo try to smile. I wonder what she's saying. Is she telling him about our destructive adventure this morning? Or our performance center stage? I hope so; I like the idea that Jaz would want to talk about me, that I'm conversation worthy.

But that's stupid. Jaz and her dying brother have a million other things to talk about, like their shared years together, their shared family, their shared memories. They're probably talking about their last vacation, or a prank their big brother Joseph played on them, or something their dad said to make them laugh. They wouldn't be talking about me.

A melancholy gloom seeps into my body. No one will be talking about me as they are dying—there's no one *to* talk about me. Even when my parents recover, I know they won't talk about me to anyone. In fact, they'll be more paranoid once we get away from Moto and Hendricks; if we were caught once, they'll be petrified it will happen again, and will double down on where we hide.

It makes me jealous of Jaz and Mo, of their relationship, of their connection. I wish I still had that, the way Ivy and I did as kids. I wish she were still here so I'd have somebody to talk to about old times. *Remember when we went swimming in the ocean for the first time, Ivy? Remember when a big wave washed you under and when you popped up, spitting out a mouthful of salt water, you exclaimed that the ocean tasted like one big potato chip? Remember?*

I wonder if there's enough memory storage in my head for all the years ahead of me. Will my memory grow bigger than everybody else's? Will future scientists discover that my brain grew six sizes during my never-ending years? Or will they find that my memory has overridden all other portions of my mind, so I'll be able to name everybody in my Grade 3 class, but no longer be able to read? Or maybe I have the same memory capacity as everyone else—I'll just end up forgetting stuff from my past to make room for new memories that crop up. The thought scares me. Will I end up forgetting my childhood? My home? Will I forget Ivy? My parents?

I shiver, even though it's hot in the vault. I wish I could stop thinking. I wish I could press pause in my head and stop worrying about what's to come—not just what's to come next week or next year, but what's to come next century.

I hear Jaz tell Mo to close his eyes, to rest. I hear her reassure him that she'll be there when he wakes up. I catch her eye in time to see the unspoken fear reflected on her face. *If* he wakes up.

I feel for her. I wish I could do something for her. I think about telling her that I've been there, that I've lost a sibling to the plague, too, and I know she must be crumbling inside knowing that Mo's death is near. But that won't comfort her because all I can tell her is that it gets worse—the waiting, I mean. I remember what it was like to be trapped in that god-awful hospital room hoping, wishing Mom and Dad would come in to tell me Ivy had died because I couldn't handle the anguish of the anticipation. That's not exactly reassuring, so I say nothing to Jaz.

When Mo falls asleep, Jaz gently places his head on a pillow and comes to sit next to me. I'm alarmed, suddenly, to realize she looks worse. Sweat beads on her forehead, her skin is waxy, her eyes are glazed.

*Oh my God,* I think, *she's going to die before I can save her.* A wave of nausea rolls through me. I lean my head back, my throat tight.

"You okay?" Jaz scoots closer to me.

I lift my head off the wall and feel a sudden bout of dizziness. My eyes take a moment to focus on Jaz. I blink and blink again. "Yeah," I say. "It's just hot in here."

Jaz frowns. "It's as fucking cold as the North Pole," she counters, shivering as if to prove her point. She leans over and puts her hand on my forehead. Her fingers are ice. Immediately I pull away.

"Lyra," she says, "you're burning up."

I shake my head, but that makes me feel like there's a hammer pounding in my skull and the pain is intense. I know pain, I'm used to pain. I close my eyes and try to concentrate the pain away. I focus on it because that's the only way I know how to cope with it. I suck it up, I live with it, and then it's done. I know it will be done. It's always done. The pain never lasts. But, God, this feels worse. I feel like the pain is eating me up from the inside. I feel like my bones are on fire under my skin. I feel like someone is sticking hot knives down my throat. I squeeze my eyes shut and hold my breath. *This will pass, this will pass.*

But it's not passing. The pain, the ache, the dizziness, it's all worsening, and I don't understand. Usually when I get hurt, I scream at the initial agony, but then the pain recedes. Little by little, it always eases up. That's what I count on—my injury being a little less painful with every passing minute.

But not now. Now it's increasing. Every minute I feel worse and worse. Why?

My stomach heaves, and abruptly I jump up and run to the bathroom. I stumble and trip going out the door, but I don't make it past the main office before I bend over, my stomach convulsing, and I hurl. Puke pools on the worn carpet as I double over, still retching. The smell, the stench, reaches my nose and I clench my stomach, heaving. I feel like I'm being turned inside out.

A hand presses into my shoulder and I recoil. I see it's Jaz but still I shrink away from her, embarrassed. I can't remember the last time I threw up. Besides the plague all those years ago, I can't remember the last time I was sick. I've had sniffles every now and then—I'm not a robot—but those viruses are no match for my phoenix cells. Usually my body fights off the illness before I even realize I'm sick.

I lean against a desk and bury my head in my knees. I still feel woozy and I feel like I'm going to puke again, but I clench my arms around my stomach, trying to stop myself.

"Lyra," Jaz says with a note of alarm. She comes over to me, again touches my shoulder, and again I flinch, humiliated by my weakness. I can't let her see me like this. My head swirls and I see a kaleidoscope of colors exploding behind my eyes. Jaz's voice sounds like it's a million miles away. "I thought you said you were immune," she says.

Weak as she is, she tries to hoist me up, and this time I don't resist. When I stand, the world spins and my knees buckle, but Jaz catches me. She circles her arms around my waist and makes me lean against her. I collapse into her and I hate myself for it. I'm supposed to be the strong one, the invincible one, the one who is saving everyone, but I can't even walk on my own.

Jaz leads me toward the staff bathroom where she helps me clean up, which must be doubly awful for her, since she's sick, too. She wipes the puke from my chin, and washes my face and rinses out the ends of my hair and the whole time I can't look at her, I'm so mortified. She disappears, then returns a moment later with a small tube of toothpaste, a toothbrush and a chipped coffee mug. The mint toothpaste in my mouth makes me gag but I do feel better after I'm done.

Jaz helps me back to the vault. Wincing, she eases me onto her thin mattress and spreads a blanket over me. She pauses for a minute, catching her breath, then slowly she pulls herself to her feet and mumbles that she's going to clean up the carpet.

I lie still—my muscles burn when I move—trying to make sense of what's happening. The plague, obviously. Hecate got me. I am in her clutches, burning alive. But how? I'm not supposed to get sick. It's why Hendricks sent me, because I'm the only one who could survive the plague. So why am I sick? Why aren't my phoenix cells protecting me? I feel a well of panic rise up. They've got to protect me; they've got to start healing me *now*. I have to get better before dark; I have to get Jaz's blood back to Hendricks. I have to get back to my parents.

When Jaz returns to the vault, she checks on Mo, who's still sleeping, then kneels beside me. She looks wan and pale, but more than that, she looks defeated.

"I'm sorry you're sick, Lyra," she says heavily.

I try to sit up, but my head is a rock; I can't lift it from the pillow. "I'm not supposed to get sick," I mumble.

"Guess someone forgot to tell your body that." Jaz tries to smile, but there's despair behind her words. I see her eyes travel to my leather jacket, where her vial of blood is stored. I see hurt reflected in her eyes.

"I didn't lie to you," I snap at her. She nods, but I know she doesn't believe me.

"It's just hard when you have hope," Jaz laments. She closes her eyes, looking drained. "And then you don't."

"No," I say. It hurts to speak; the words burn like acid in my throat. "I'll get better. Before dark. You'll see."

Jaz looks at me with such profound pity that I want to spring up from the mattress and shake her until she gets it. I can still save her. I can still do this.

"Your cheeks are burning with Hecate's fire," she says softly. "I know the rash."

Weakly, I shake my head, but the effort to speak becomes too great.

"I'm sorry you came," she says.

Her words stab me through the heart. I thought she liked me; I thought we were friends. But now I see I was stupid to think so. How could she be friends with me? I bought her attention with promises of cures and vaccines and false hope. It wasn't me she was interested in; it was what I said I could do for her and her brother.

"You're brave, though," she continues. "Sacrificing yourself like this."

Brave? I'm not brave, I try to tell her, but I can't force out the words.

"I'm here because I was stupid enough to go to a park," Jaz says ruefully. "But you, you're here because you tried to do something to help. A real hero."

No, I want to retort, I'm not a hero or selfless or noble. I'm not laying down my life for a principled cause. I didn't even *choose* to come here. I was forced into it because my parents are sick. I'm doing it for them, don't you see? I didn't come here to save the world, I came here only to save them.

But all I can do is shake my head. Even that gesture is meek and pitiful—I swear to God my head will explode if I move it more than a millimeter.

*Enough!* I scream to my phoenix cells. Fix yourselves already. Fix me. Because I can't live with this unendurable pain, with the fire that's burning inside, the fog that's clouding my mind. It's worse than last time, worse than when I was eight. It has to end. It should have ended. Why hasn't it ended?

Then a thought worms its way into my fevered brain. What if it won't end? What if my cells can't heal me? What if they've met their match with this strain of Hecate's Plague?

My skin crawls.

What if I *can* die?

What if I *will* die?

I feel walloped, suddenly, like my life has been thrown off course, like I'm careening off a track, heading for a spectacular collision. Could it be true? Is there something stronger than my phoenix cells? Have we been on the run for nine years because of a *lie*? Am I really not invincible? Immortal? I'm shaken to my core.

*I can die.*

My whole perception of life suddenly changes. Suddenly I see it as fragile and delicate, like a rose that can easily be crushed by a closed fist, and I'm scared. Drenched in sweat and fear, I tremble all over.

*I'm dying.*

Abruptly, I reach out and grip Jaz's hand like I'm drowning. I need her to pull me up, pull me back to life, but I feel her fingers slip from my palm. I try to twist my head to see her, but I can't move. I'm paralyzed and I'm sinking. The light around me fades. The vault disappears. Jaz disappears. I see my parents in my mind, but soon they disappear, too. Darkness descends.

I am dying.

# CHAPTER 9

A dim, diffuse light seeps across my closed eyes. I sense it beyond my eyelids, as it grows stronger, brighter. The light hurts, so I shift my head to avoid it, but it seems to be all around me. I can't seem to escape it, so I decide to slowly open my eyes.

I'm looking at a gunmetal gray ceiling, sharp with reflected light. I wince, and turn my head. I see a thick, open door. I frown, because it all seems familiar. If this is heaven, it's not terribly original. Or beautiful. But then I recognize where I am, and it's not the afterlife.

I'm in the vault in the school-turned-quarantine camp. And I remember the rest. The plague. Jaz. Mo.

Me dying.

But I'm not dead.

Gingerly, I sit up. My head aches, but it's a dampened, muffled discomfort, nothing like the pounding I felt earlier. I stretch my limbs—stiff, but well. My stomach has settled and the fire in my bones has gone out.

I am alive.

I survived Hecate's Plague again.

My phoenix cells came through for me again.

I'm relieved, obviously, but I'm far from elated. I'm actually worried—really worried. I've never come that close to death before. I've never before thought that I actually *would* die. Through all my broken bones and cracked skulls and even the gunshot wound, I've never doubted the power of my phoenix cells to keep me alive.

So why did I doubt them when I got sick? Is there something wrong with my cells? Is their ability to heal waning? Or was the virus just so strong that it took all my cells' strength to fight it? It makes me realize how little I know about my body. It heals, yes, but how? And why? I wonder, for the first time, if there's a limit. Maybe my cells have a breaking point, like an elastic band, and I've stretched them too far. Maybe they have only a certain number of "repairs" in them and after that, they shut down. The thought terrifies me. What if, one day, I pull a dumb stunt like train dodging, and I do get hurt and my cells don't heal? I wish, suddenly that I could talk to Hendricks, that he could answer all my questions, but then I think maybe he wouldn't *know* the answers because he hasn't tested my cells inside me because he hasn't had me to test.

I feel a wave of irritation at my parents—have their efforts to keep me out of the government's hands ensured I will never know about my own body, my own fate? It's not like I can saunter into any old doctor's office, so was it fair of them to keep me from the only people who could tell me about *me*? Did they have that right? It's *my* body, after all.

But they didn't care about my cells, not like that. They didn't care to know about what my phoenix cells were and how they work. In fact, we never talked about my "condition." Ironic, I think, considering that's what upended our lives. But Mom and Dad showed no curiosity; they just pretended I was a normal kid.

Well, I'm not and now I want to know why.

But if I want answers, I'm not going to get them hanging around here. I spring to my feet—already my headache has disappeared and my stiffness has dissipated—and I look around, wondering how long I'd been unconscious. Without windows, I can't tell if it's dark yet. Can I safely leave? Maybe I'll have to risk it even if it's not. I notice Mo still in the corner, still sleeping, and I'm curious where Jaz is.

"Lyra?" someone says.

I turn around. Jaz is standing in the doorway, her eyes wide with shock.

I rush over to her—she looks like death warmed over. Her cheeks are sunken; her skin is gray. The rash, which had seemed mild, has exploded across her face. She smells of vomit and peppermint and her hands that clutch her toothbrush are ghost-white. She leans against me as I guide her to the cot and she sits down heavily. I frown, worried.

"You're . . ." she pauses, then swallows, and I see it's hard for her to talk. Like it was for me. I remember the burning in my throat, the lack of air in my lungs and I think how strange it is that I can actually appreciate her suffering. I never thought I'd ever understand how someone feels when they're dying.

"You're alive," Jaz manages to say.

"Yeah," I say and even though it's proof that I was right, I feel embarrassed, exposed. I grab a blanket and drape it over her shivering body. I feel awkward. Like the agents watching my gunshot wound heal, I feel like Jaz has just seen me naked.

"How?" Jaz squeaks.

"I told you I have a sort-of immunity."

Jaz closes her eyes and takes a shallow breath. "You were basically dead, Lyra." The sentence, spoken in a whisper, leaves her winded.

I don't look at her. What am I supposed to say? *Oh by the way, didn't I tell you that I'm immortal?*

I try to ignore her comment, so I busy myself with a water bottle. I unscrew the cap and help Jaz take a sip. She coughs, then swallows, but she doesn't let me off the hook.

"Explain," she rasps.

And I know I have to. I owe her that much, at least. I think of my parents' number one command: Never tell anyone about your phoenix cells. They were afraid word would leak out to the agents and we'd be caught. But we already are caught, so what does it matter now?

"I have a special kind of cells," I say for the first time in my life. "They heal from every injury or illness." The words sound strange—not just their meaning, which is odd enough, but hearing them pour from my mouth. It's like I'm pulling out my insides and I immediately want to snatch the words back and bury them deep. I'm scared, suddenly, of what Jaz will do with them. She can laugh at them or ignore them or mock them, and I have absolutely no control over it.

What Jaz does, though, to my surprise, is accept them.

"You're . . ." she tries to speak. "You're serious."

I shrug. I'm sitting beside her, healthy and whole. The evidence is obvious.

"How—" Jaz can't finish.

"How is it possible?" My very own question. I shrug again. "I was born this way. I don't know why. I don't even know if anyone else knows why. Doctors discovered my . . . condition . . . when I was eight. When I survived Hecate's Plague the first time."

Jaz's mouth drops open. "So *you* must have antibodies," she says, almost hopefully, as if she's the first to have this revelation.

I shake my head. "My body didn't create antibodies to fight the virus," I explain. "It used my phoenix cells. That's what the doctors call them—because the cells always rise from the ashes." I smile wryly.

Jaz looks like she's about to speak again, but I cut her off. "I don't really know anything else," I say, "like how they work or why. Just that they do."

Jaz nods. "It's why you're here."

"Yeah," I say and I'm happy for the change of topic. I'm also happy to regain my focus because I've got to get out of here. I've got to get Jaz's blood to Hendricks so I can save my parents. And save Jaz, too. "Is it dark yet? I really need to leave."

I see a shadow cross Jaz's eyes. She hesitates before she answers.

"Jaz . . ." I'm suddenly anxious.

"It's not dark," Jaz shakes her head, "because it's Sunday afternoon."

"It's *Sunday?*" I choke. "Not Saturday?" I don't understand. I arrived Saturday and since my cells never take long to heal, it should still be Saturday.

"It's Sunday," Jaz repeats. "Afternoon."

*Oh my god, oh my god, oh my god.* I've lost a full day. Twenty-four hours—gone, vanished, disappeared. I stand and start pacing across the vault, two steps in each direction. This is bad, very bad. My parents got sick on Friday. Nobody lasts longer than three days . . . They could be dead already.

No. There's still a chance. Sunday isn't over. They may still have time. I may still have time.

"I can't wait for dark," I say, my mind whirling. I've got to chance it, risk being seen and shot at by the guards. Goddamn it, why didn't I do this yesterday? Why did I let Jaz convince me to wait? Now I've wasted a whole day, and I had to suffer through Hecate's Plague in the process, *and* I'm still bolting in broad daylight. I snatch up my leather jacket and check for the vial, which is still there, still intact. Goddamn Jaz, wanting to play it safe. The lava beast of my anger stirs in the pit of my stomach. What the hell was she thinking? Does she *want* to die? I mean, every minute she made me squander here was one less minute Hendricks had to extract her antibodies—if she has antibodies—and create a cure that could help her, too. I storm toward the vault door, my chest tight. I feel like I'm breathing fire. Jaz and her fucking suggestion to wait could cost my parents their *lives*, and I swear, if that happens, there'll be holy hell to pay.

"Lyra, wait," Jaz calls and there's more power in her voice than I thought possible.

I spin around, seething. "Wait? *Wait?* Waiting is what got me into this mess." I'm yelling loud enough that Mo stirs on his mattress. Jaz shoots a look of daggers at me, and crawls over to her brother, cradling him. He looks bad. His skin is the color of ash, his lips the color of bruises. When he looks at me and I see that the light, the life in his eyes is dim, my anger evaporates. Such a waste, I think, that Mo's life will be cut so short.

"I have to leave now," I soften my tone. "It's our only shot." I let Jaz believe that the "our" refers to her but really I mean it's the only shot left for my parents and me.

Jaz nods like she understands. She breathes in as deeply as she can, then, with effort, she speaks. "You're right. But so am I. If you leave in daylight, you'll be shot."

I'm about to protest when Jaz raises her hand. "You need a diversion," she says.

"Diversion?"

"Something to draw the guards' attention so you can slip away unseen."

"Like what?"

Jaz doubles over with a bone-rattling cough, pain etched across her face. When she finally catches her breath, she answers. "Me."

"*What?* No," I say. That's stupid. How can she think that would work? She'll be the one shot and killed, so how can we come back to save her if her blood holds the key to a cure?

I'm not the only one who thinks it's a terrible idea. I see Mo's face flash with fear. Weakly, he shakes his head, grasping for Jaz's hand.

She turns to her brother, pleading for understanding. "It's the only way," she says. Tears well up in her eyes and I can see the offer of her sacrifice scares her.

"It's not," Mo croaks. "I can do it."

Jaz looks dumbfounded at the idea. "No," she says, shaking her head vehemently. "I won't let you."

Mo tries to rise, and I see the effort tires him. "I'm dead already, Jaz. Lyra can still save you."

I press my lips together. *He's right,* I want to say. We all know he'll be dead in a day or two at most, so let him help me. But I bite my tongue, since I know Jaz won't appreciate me ushering her twelve-year-old brother to his death.

Mo, like Jaz, struggles to speak, but he perseveres. "You gave the blood," he whispers to his sister, "and I'll help get it out so we'll both save the world." He tries to smile, but his lips barely move. "Lyra will call it the Smith Cure and we'll be famous."

A faint laugh, the echo of a chuckle, slips out of Mo's mouth and I want to slap him on the back and say, *Yeah, absolutely, buddy, I'll make sure everyone knows how you saved the world.*

Jaz sees my smile and rounds on me, fire in her eyes. "You *want* my brother to walk into a firing line?"

I sigh, which was maybe the wrong thing to do, but I'm getting exasperated. Yes, I could use their help and no, I don't want to see either one of them die by gunshot, but I'm running out of time. Either one of them decides to sacrifice himself or herself to help me, or I'm on my own. I'm not afraid of getting shot; I've obviously survived worse, but I *am* afraid of getting caught and being dragged back in here. If that happens, if I can't get Jaz's blood to Hendricks, then the whole mission was for shit and my parents die.

"Jaz," Mo is saying, "let me be a hero, okay?"

Tears sting the back of my eyes thinking about a twelve-year-old boy going out in a blaze of superhero glory to help save the world. I don't remind him there's a chance Jaz's blood won't have the antibodies or that Hendricks may not be able to create the cure even if it did. In his last hours on this Earth, I will leave him with his gallant idea. And who knows? Maybe how he imagines it will be exactly how it plays out.

"You can barely walk," Jaz says to Mo and all three of us know that means Jaz has conceded. Mo's lips curl slightly, his best effort at a smile.

"I'll help him," I say, but then I realize Jaz is right; he has to be mobile or the whole diversion is useless. "You really think you can walk?"

"Yeah," he says weakly. "I got super-human strength."

Does he? I mean, can he truly muster enough energy to help? It's one thing to want to and another thing to be capable of it. I remember the agony I felt before I passed out; could I have forced myself to stand, to move, to walk into the line of fire? Can Mo?

Jaz's face is strained with emotion—pride, fear, sadness, longing—but she nods. It takes her a minute to gather her strength. I'm impatient to leave, but now that Mo and Jaz are going to help, I have to wait.

"I'll take you to the music room," Jaz says, breathing heavily. "There's a side door to the parking lot." She pauses to catch her breath. "It's closer to the fence than the front or back doors. I don't think many people know about it, so maybe there will be fewer guards over there."

I feel a flutter of excitement—is that appropriate, when I'm condemning Mo to his death? But it's true. Hearing Jaz's plan, I feel hopeful, suddenly. I'm glad I met someone who knows the school.

Jaz pushes herself to her feet and I get Mo to lean against

me to save his strength. I wrap my arm around his waist. He's tall, gangly, but wow, he's light. Did Hecate take all his weight or was he always a skinny kid? I wish I knew. I wish I'd seen him before, the kid he was in life, not the kid he is now, on the verge of death.

Jaz is weak, too; she uses the furniture in the main office as support, then drags her hands along the wall in the halls and pushes on. We pass a bunch of people, but I can't tell whether they are the same as the ones I saw yesterday or not. It's like the make-up of the school, the quarantine camp has changed, shifted, evolved in just one day.

Jaz leads us down a long narrow hall, away from the library, the cafeteria and the gym, which means it's almost empty. Good. The fewer people who see us, the better.

Jaz turns into a doorway not too far from the auditorium. It's a big room, with chairs and risers and a drum kit at the top. A row of black cases—school instruments, I'm guessing—sit undisturbed against the wall. Jaz sinks into an old, battered rec room couch in the corner and Mo sits down heavily beside her.

"No vandalizing this room?" I ask.

"No," Jaz says, and smiles. "This room was fun."

"You played?" I ask.

"Sax," she answers, and I smile because now I'm picturing Jaz standing in the middle of this music room honking into her shiny gold saxophone. Jaz, jazzin' out.

She points to a narrow door next to a long line of windows that overlooks the school's side parking lot. Across the asphalt is a lawn. It's wide, but nowhere near the size of the playing fields out back or the long drive out front. What's more, the fence on the far side is lined with trees I can climb up and over. And Jaz was right; I see only one guard patrolling this whole area.

A jolt of hope rushes through me. "I think I can do this without you guys," I say and instantly I'm relieved. What was I thinking, marching a twelve-year-old kid to his painful death?

I've *been* shot. It hurt like fucking hell—and I was only shot in the arm. So no, I can't let Mo be mowed down by excruciating gunfire. Forget about playing heroics—it only sounds noble in the movies. In reality, Mo's death would be brutal and agonizing and possibly slow, so how can I let him suffer for my sake? No, Mo deserves to die quietly in his sister's arms.

I study the guard sauntering back and forth, his rifle carelessly slung over his slouched shoulders. He's obviously relaxed, bored most likely, as Hendricks predicted, and doesn't seem to expect action.

"I'll wait till he's at the far corner," I say, "then I'll make a run for it."

Jaz frowns. "He'll see you before you get to the fence. By the time you're over, you'll be caught, or shot."

"Then I'll just have to outrun him," I say.

Jaz looks at me skeptically.

"I'm a runner," I reassure her. "Been running my whole life."

"You'll still name the cure after us?" Mo asks.

"You've both saved the day," I smile. "The Smith Cure it is."

Jaz pulls herself to her feet and throws her arms around me. Her hug is surprisingly strong for such a sick person and I return her embrace. It's the first time I've hugged a girlfriend before and I'm really going to miss her.

"Hang in there, Jaz," I whisper. "I'll come back for you."

"I know," she replies. "But it's okay if you don't. I'm good."

We both know she isn't but we both pretend she is.

I crouch in front of Mo. I don't try to hug him—that doesn't seem right—but he holds up a weak hand and gives me a fist bump.

Jaz walks with me to the door. I pat the pocket of my jacket, feeling for the vial. We watch the guard, waiting for the right moment. My pulse races. My stomach fills with butterflies and my skin tingles. The guard nears the far corner. Jaz inches open the door. I take a deep breath.

"*Go!*" Jaz hisses.

I run.

I sprint. I bolt. The cold April wind wallops me, but I ignore it. I pump my arms, I pound my feet and I keep my eye on the fence and the tree I can easily climb. I'm almost there.

"Hey!" I hear a roar from my right. The guard.

My heart hammers in my chest—it's going to burst—but I have to get up and over. Up and over. Up and over.

I'm ten feet from the tree, maybe less, when I hear the crack of the rifle. A bullet whizzes by, but it's way off the mark. The guard is still too far away, his angle too narrow.

Almost . . . almost . . . I think of the tree as safety, even though I know the guard will be on me when I jump to the other side of the fence. My hand scrapes along rough bark. I pull one leg up. God, I wish it were late spring, I wish there were leaves in the tree to hide me. I reach for another branch; I miss and almost topple backwards, but I regain my balance and grip the bough.

That's when I hear it: the shout of a boy. No, the war cry of a hero. I can't help myself. I stop and turn. To my horror, I see Mo straggle across the parking lot, whooping and yelling with the energy of a crazed man. At the same time, I hear Jaz's agonized cry and then I see her bolt after her brother.

And for a moment, I forget that Mo and Jaz are helping me. I forget that they're providing the diversion I desperately need. Time slows down as I watch the guard swing his rifle toward Mo, aim, and fire. I watch as he shoots over and over and over. I watch as Mo is flung back by the force of the bullets and knocked to the ground. I watch as his body trembles and shakes from new bullets ripping into him. I watch as blood spurts from his wounds. I watch as Jaz scrambles to her brother and cradles his head, the way she did in the vault, and I watch as she screams in rage and grief. Only then do I realize the bullets have stopped and I have to flee.

I pull myself up high enough to clamber the fence. I hear a rumble of troops coming from my left, from the front of the school, and a lone set of boots pounding toward me from my right.

I jump. I land hard, rolling on my ankle, and a shot of pain streaks through my foot, but I ignore it as I pick myself up. I have to run. Mo died so I could escape; I can't get caught now. I can't have him die in vain.

I look for Hendricks's black van, but I don't see it. Is he still here, a day later? He should be, I think, since he said this blood and this cure means everything to him, but I can't exactly hang around at the front of the school waiting for my ride. Instead, I head for the houses across the street. I need to slip into one of their backyards to lose the soldiers. Then I can double-back and look for Hendricks. I run and run hard, but then I stumble—my ankle gives way. I hop, I hobble, I limp, but I keep moving. *Faster!* I'm at the side of a house when I hear the soldiers behind me. I hear another crack of their guns, but I duck behind a bush and they miss. I can't stay, though, I can't let them trap me. I crawl my way through the bush to the back and burst into the neighbor's yard. There's a kid's playhouse, and I think about hiding out there, but that's dumb; they'd find me in an instant. I scan my surroundings—peeling fences and bare trees and unswept patios. I keep running. I don't glance behind me; I can't afford to waste a millisecond. Besides, it doesn't matter where they are as long as they're not yet on top of me.

I veer through another yard and then another that backs onto the first. I pick my way forward and—there! I see pavement. I fight my way to the edge of the backyard jungle and look out—and my stomach drops. The school's entrance is almost directly in front of me. I've gone in a near-circle, coming out on a crescent that bends around near the guard post. On top of that, I don't see Hendricks's van. Two soldiers remain, their rifles raised, on high alert. If I burst onto the road now, they'll see me. But I hear other guards trampling through the lawns behind me. If I stay, they'll catch me. My mind whirls in panic. *What do I do?*

I slide to the front of the house I've been hiding behind, and while I'm now facing the street, my back is pressed tight against the wall in the late afternoon shadows. I scan my surroundings. There. I notice the house two doors down has a crawl space under its porch. If I can sneak in there without being seen, I can hide out, at least until I can come up with a better plan.

I move torturously slowly. I want to race to the porch and dive under, but I'm afraid any sudden movement will attract attention. My heart pounds—I swear, they'll hear it—but I try to breathe. My ankle aches, but it's nothing really. I see the soldiers from the backyard rush onto the road, but they haven't spotted me yet. I creep along one house, dash across the side lawn to the next, then scamper under the porch. Did they see me? I'm afraid to peek out. I hold my breath, waiting for disembodied hands to reach in and grab me.

I listen hard. I hear the shouts of the soldiers, gruff orders, but I can't make out their words. I wait in terror, not just because I may be caught, but every minute I'm stuck in here is a minute less my parents have to live.

"*Come on, come on, leave, dammit,*" I wish I could shout. "*Let me go, I'm not contagious.*"

Suddenly I freeze. I hear footsteps in the yard. I hold my breath; I don't move a muscle.

"Lyra!" My name is a hiss.

I shiver.

"Lyra, please, I'm a friend. Come out and I'll help you disappear."

I tremble to my core. I don't recognize the voice. It's male, deep and resonant and desperate, and a part of me wants to believe him, to reach out my hand and have this strange savior whisk me off to safety. But it's a trick, I realize. No one except Hendricks knows I was in the quarantine camp and no one except Jaz and Mo know I got out, so who the *hell* is this guy? I scramble away from the entrance of the crawl space, terrified.

"*Please*, Lyra," the man says again, sounding frantic. "I know George Hendricks."

It's as if Hendricks's name is a magic word. I stop scuttling backwards, my mind reeling. I want to believe that Hendricks sent this guy to protect me, that he told someone to wait for me if he couldn't be here himself, and I convince myself it could make sense since Hendricks would want to protect the vial of blood, but I know better. I know it's over. I've been caught again. Moto mostly likely found out that it was Hendricks who let me escape and Hendricks must have told him where I'd gone. The bastard.

Still, it doesn't take me long to weigh my options: scream bloody murder to alert the soldiers and let them throw me back into the quarantine camp or surrender to this guy and have him drag me back to the lab. At least with option number two, there's an outside chance I could still find a way to get the blood to Hendricks.

I scoot forward and extend my hand. My captor grasps it and yanks me out. He pulls me up beside him and I'm surprised that he's my age, maybe a bit older, a teen with a coffee cream complexion. His eyes are black pearls, deep and intense, and he looks scared. I'm puzzled. He's definitely not like the agents who took me down in Jamestown.

The guy pulls me up to the porch under which I was hiding, then shoves me toward the front door of the house.

"What are you *doing?*" I hiss. If the homeowners see me, see us, if they heard the gunshots, they'll know I'm the quarantine camp escapee and I'll be back where I started.

"Trust me," he says as he glances furtively around.

For the moment, we're sheltered from the road under the deep roof of the verandah, but I know that won't last long. I can hear the clomp of the soldiers boots charging down the street.

The guy rattles the door. Locked. But he doesn't give up. He readies his elbow and crashes it through the window panel to the left of the door. He winces at the impact, glass cracks and he punches again. Finally, the glass cascades to our feet and he reaches through, unlocks the door, and hurries me inside.

"What the *hell*?" I start, but the guy doesn't listen. He slams the door, locks it, and hurries me up the narrow oak staircase. We reach the landing. His eyes dart left and right—it's obvious he doesn't know this house—but finally he makes a decision, and shoves me into a bedroom. It's small, with a narrow bed in the corner and an antique roll desk against the wall. There's a closet, sloped with the roof of the house, and the guy shoves me in.

"Stay here," he whispers.

He races out of the room and down the stairs. Despite his insistence, I creep out of the closet, toward the door of the bedroom. I hear the tinkle of glass—is he sweeping up the broken window?—and the scrape of furniture.

What is going on? Who *is* this guy? I'm sure he's not an agent, but then why is he here? Is he a junior researcher at the lab? Is that how he knows my name? But why would Hendricks send him?

My heart starts to race when I hear the guy open the front door. I hear voices. Soldiers. I can't make out their words, but they're angry.

"No sir," I hear my new savior say. "Nobody here but me. Heard the gunshots—but no fucking plague victim gonna drive me outta my house."

The soldiers grunt, but I can't make out what they say.

"The window? Fucking vandals. Happened the other day when I was out findin' food." A pause. "Check the house?" the boy continues. "Sure. Ain't nothin' here."

Terrified, I scuttle back into the closet. It's filled with fur coats and I feel like I'm drowning in animal pelts. I hold my breath against the repugnant odor of mothballs and slink to the back.

A minute later, the bedroom door creeks open. I turn into a lifeless statue, I don't even dare breathe, as the soldiers clomp through the bedroom. One pushes his way into the closet, and starts to push aside the coats. I feel the air trapped in my lungs as the hangers squeak on the rod. The soldier grunts and I hear him step back. I hear the closet door close but it's only when I hear their footsteps recede from the room, do I finally draw a breath.

A few minutes later, the closet door swings open again.

"They're gone," he says unnecessarily.

I emerge slowly. I decide to play it cocky. I step into the bedroom, my arms folded, and I glare at him. But I can't make sense of him. He's wearing jeans, a black wool coat, grey fingerless gloves and black Doc Marten shoes. He's breathing heavily, as if he's just run a marathon, and his eyes are still glazed with fear. Something about him seems familiar.

"Who the hell *are* you?" I demand.

He blinks in surprise, as if he expected me to know.

"I'm David," he says. "I'm Mama Jua's grandson."

# CHAPTER 10

The guy from the funeral.

The one who lowered his grandmother's casket into the ground.

"What are you *doing* here?" I ask. My head spins. I can't make sense of how one part of my life—my friendship with Mama Jua—has ended up entangled in the other, fucked-up part. Mama Jua knew we were on the run, but I never told her why. She didn't know about my phoenix cells or the agents, or any of it. So how does her grandson end up in the middle of this mess? How does he know me? And how did he know where I'd be? *I* didn't even know where I'd be.

"I had to find you," he says. "I had to warn you not to go back to George Hendricks."

Shit. Now I understand that this is what I feared when I first heard David speak my name: "Moto sent you," I say, dismayed. Moto must have found out that Hendricks helped me escape. He must have learned where I was going. But did he think luring me back with the grandson of my friend as opposed to hunting me down with agents, would actually work? Does he think I'm that gullible?

"Who's Moto?" David asks.

I shake my head and brush past him out the door. I have no time for his games.

"Lyra, wait," he says, scrambling after me, but I run down the stairs, ignoring him.

When I reach the front door, David jumps in front of it. "*Wait.*"

I try to get around him, but he doesn't move. Frustrated, I take a deep breath. "Let me out."

"No."

No? Who the hell does he think he is? "Move," I say, and try to reach for the door handle. My parents' lives are at stake and no one, least of all some mysterious guy, is going to stop me.

But David doesn't move and I'm nervous. He's tall and muscular, and obviously stronger than me. How am I going to get past him? We face off, my heart hammering, but I won't back down. Finally, David blinks. He steps away and I grab for the handle.

"Your parents are dead, Lyra," David says, his voice thick and heavy.

I stop moving, my hand stuck to the door handle. I think for a petrified moment it's true, that my worst fear has been realized, that I'm orphaned, that I'm alone, but then I shake my head and refocus. He's lying. My parents aren't dead yet; they still have a few hours. I know their situation is perilous, but they're not dead. I'd know it if they had died. I'd have felt it if the only people I have left in the world, the only people who care about me, who love me, had died. No, David is playing me. He's using some sort of sick manipulation to get me to do what he wants—I don't even know *what* he wants—but it won't work. I'm not going to fall for his tasteless stunt.

I glare at him hard. "You sick bastard," I say, then I turn my back on him and yank open the door.

"They died of the plague this morning," David says quickly. "Your mom died about 9 a.m. and your dad died an hour later.

They were at the Fort Potomac military research facility in an isolation chamber near George's lab. They arrived two days ago, on Friday morning, after federal agents caught you and your parents in Jamestown. After my grandma's funeral."

I shiver, unnerved. He has so many facts right, but no, he must be wrong. I feel for him about losing his grandmother, I do, but that's a fucking sadistic thing for him to do, to take his grief out on me.

"Why are you doing this to me?" I say, turning around slowly.

"I'm not doing anything *to* you," he snaps. "I'm trying to save you."

I huff at his arrogance. "I don't need saving, thank you very much." What I need is to get back to Hendricks so he can cure my parents before it really is too late.

He arches an eyebrow sardonically. "Really? That's not what it looked like to me when I found you cowering under the front porch."

Bastard.

"Look, I don't know what you want and frankly, I don't care. Whatever you say, my parents are alive." I take a deep breath, trying to calm myself. I have to say in control. "I have the blood Hendricks needs to make a cure." I tap the vial in my jacket pocket. "I just have to get it to him, and then my parents will be okay. They're at risk of dying, yes," I concede. Dad taught me that tactic. When you're debating an opponent, always acknowledge the facts. That way they can't accuse you of using rhetoric and lies to win your argument. "And it's true that Hendricks won't have a lot of time," I continue, "We're up against the clock, but it hasn't yet run out. Sunday isn't over."

David sinks heavily onto the stairs. He wipes his hand across his face, rubbing his eyes. "You didn't know . . ." David says, as if that explains everything. "I thought my grandmother would have told you . . ."

"Told me what?" I demand. I'm impatient and irritated with him.

"That George is family."

I stare at him as if he's speaking Greek.

"Mama Jua's family," David clarifies. "George Hendricks is married to my mother's cousin," David explains. "My grandmother is his wife's aunt."

I feel disoriented, like David is telling me the sky is green and the grass is blue. Hendricks knew Mama Jua? The doctor from my childhood, the one who sent us on the run, knew the one person in my life who wanted us to stop running?

This is crazy. I shake my head, clinging to reality. The grass is *green* and the sky is blue. Mama Jua lived in Jamestown and Hendricks lives in Washington and that's that. My former life and my current life are separate.

*Right*?

Because someone would have told me. Mama Jua would have told me, because we didn't keep secrets from each other. That's why I trusted her, because she was honest with me. She wasn't just a benevolent old lady, she was a *person,* a woman with a past, one filled with mistakes. She told me so. She told me all about how she'd screwed up raising her three children, how she'd told them—and everyone—that their dad died when, in fact, he'd abandoned them. She thought it wasn't fair to burden the kids so she kept it secret until her oldest daughter found out when she was twelve.

"She's barely spoken to me, since," Mama Jua lamented.

*That's* why I know Mama Jua didn't lie to me, because she said she learned her lesson. She wasn't going to keep secrets.

So it has to be just a coincidence that Hendricks knew Mama Jua. It doesn't mean anything.

"George was at the funeral on Friday," David says. "He saw you."

My brain catches up to David's comment. Hendricks was

at the funeral. *Hendricks* was in the same cemetery as me. The man in the rich black suit. The man helping David wriggle away the planks under the casket.

"George turned you in," David says.

Dr. Hendricks? No, David has it all wrong. Dr. Hendricks helped me *escape* the lab; he wouldn't have turned me in only to get me out.

I shake my head. "Hendricks got me out," I say.

"Did he?" David challenges me. "Did he get you out? And why—to escape? To run away again? To live your own life? Or to be his errand girl?"

I jerk back like I've been slapped. "What are you saying?"

"George orchestrated all of this. What happened to you, your family, the blood . . ."

"No, that's not possible . . ." I say. "Dr. Hendricks was helping me . . ."

"Was he, Lyra? Or has he been manipulating you this whole time?"

I recoil as if his words are fire, as if they've scorched my skin. "No," I insist. "I'm not stupid."

David looks at me with sympathy and it grates on my nerves.

"I'm *not*," I insist.

*Or am I?* The thought sends shivers down my spine. Hendricks's midnight visit, his escape route, his plan to get Jaz's blood . . .

"You're the only one who can get in and out of the quarantine camp alive," he says. "He knew that."

Could it be true? Could Hendricks have engineered my capture so he could use me to retrieve the antibodies?

"George heard about the girl in the quarantine camp the day before Mama Jua's funeral," David says, "From a security guard at the lab, I think. The girl's his niece, or something. George was desperate to test her blood, but there was no way he'd get into the quarantine camp—or at least get in and get out. But then he saw you in the cemetery, and, well, he thought his prayers had been answered."

I shake my head.

*No . . . It can't be.*

I feel like I've been dragged into a vortex, like everything I knew or thought I knew has been sucked up and swirled around in a twister. All this time *Hendricks* is the bad guy?

"How do you know all this?" I whisper. Maybe David is wrong, maybe he's missing some facts. Or he's invented it. Maybe he's just a kid who wants to cause trouble. I mean, Hendricks being at the same funeral as me is hardly proof of his villainy.

"He told me," David explains.

I raise an eyebrow. "He *told* you? Just like that? He said, 'Hey David, let me tell you about a girl I know you've never met?'"

David presses his lips together, thinking before he speaks. "I have . . . leverage," he finally answers. "When I asked, he had no choice but to answer."

Leverage? No choice? What the hell is David talking about?

"*Why* did you ask?" I demand. "Did Mama Jua say something to you about me or Hendricks before she died?"

David looks surprised. "No, of course not."

"Then why are you here?"

David suddenly looks sheepish. He drops his gaze, and mutters, "I feel like I owe you."

"You *owe* me?" I cry, exasperated. "You don't even *know* me!"

"I saw you," David mumbles, his eyes still downcast. "On your street." A pause. "When you got shot."

I suck in a deep breath.

How does he know I was shot? Not even Hendricks knows I was shot; my arm had healed long before I met the man.

"I was in Mama Jua's house after the funeral," David admits. "I heard the commotion. I saw you running." His voice fades.

I close my eyes. I'm back on the street, reliving the terror of the agents closing in on me. I see Mama Jua's house, my sanctuary but now I see David peering at me through the window.

Hiding.

"No one helped me," I whisper.

The closed curtains in all the neighbors' houses, the ominous absence of the neighbors themselves, all of them peeking out their windows, watching me run for my life as if I were their entertainment . . .

And David was one of them.

"I'm sorry, Lyra," David pleads. "I should have done something to try to help. As soon as I realized what was happening, I confronted my mom and I made her tell me everything, but it was too late."

"Your mom?" I asked. What does David's mom have to do with it?

David sees my surprise. "Oh," he says quietly. "You don't know that, either."

"Know *what?*"

"That my mom was helping your family."

Is he out of his fucking *mind*? My parents didn't even *know* Mama Jua, let alone her daughter, David's mother.

"Ahimsa?" David prompts, but I don't understand. What does Mama Jua's resistance group have to do with my family and me? Ahimsa fights the government's draconian plague policies by hiding plague victims and their families so they won't end up in quarantine camps, and they arrange secret funerals, like Mama Jua's, to make sure people die with dignity. Ahimsa has nothing to do with me.

"Wow," David says under his breath, "I thought you knew everything." I glare at him as he continues. "My mother Emmanuelle founded Ahimsa almost a decade ago as a nonviolent, anti-war protest organization. George and his wife

Margaret, my mother's cousin, joined soon after their only daughter was killed in battle overseas."

David recounts his story like a newsreader, objective and emotionless, but my mind is a mass of swirling confusion. Why is he telling me this? Why is this relevant?

"George used his position in the military lab to feed Ahimsa as much inside intel as he could," David continues. "When he learned that his colleagues wanted to permanently remove a girl from her parents so they could use her cells—that's you, I assume—he arranged for my mom and her contacts to hide your family."

I gape at David. *Hendricks* arranged for us to escape? My parents always said they whisked me out of the hospital after Hendricks's warning and then we just ran. They didn't get help from anyone then or any time since. My parents made sure of that. They made it crystal clear we could trust no one. When we did pick up and leave, it was without planning, without forethought. We'd drift around the country like a tumbleweed, heading in whatever direction the wind blew, and land wherever we wanted. There was no *help*, no outside person, no one masterminding anything.

But David persists. "Every time you needed to move," he says, "my mom would set you guys up in a place where she knew people who could help. Jobs for your parents, a place to stay, old textbooks for you, that kind of thing. In return, your parents would keep their ears to the ground and pass on any names of people they thought might be sympathetic to Ahimsa. My mom says they were a big help in recruiting new members."

No. This is not true. None of it is true. My parents did *not* keep their ears to the ground or pass on names or recruit people for an anti-government protest organization. They didn't know anybody in the towns we landed in and they certainly didn't get help from anyone. There's no *way* they would do that. It would have been too risky. *And*, they would have told me. They wouldn't have kept a whole *network* of secret helpers from me all these years.

"I'm not lying," David says defensively.

I shoot daggers from my eyes at him, but he meets my gaze, challenging me. "How else would I know that before Jamestown you were in Nevada and before that California?"

I shudder, unsettled at how much he got right.

"How else would I know that Mom sent your family to Jamestown because my grandma offered to keep an eye on you guys? How else would I know that Mama Jua arranged for your parents to rent the empty house down the road from hers?"

I back up against the door.

No, no, no, no. Mom and Dad did *not* know Mama Jua, and Mama Jua did *not* know them. She was *my* friend. *Mine*. Not my parents' friend. They'd never even *met* her.

She wouldn't have lied to me, and neither would my parents.

No.

This stupid, fucking boy is just wrong.

"Lyra, there's more," David says. He stands and takes an ominous step toward me.

*Stop!* I want to shout. *Haven't you fucked with me enough?*

"Your parents didn't just contract the plague," he says. "George purposely infected them so he'd guarantee you'd return to the lab instead of going back on the run."

I gape at him, wide-eyed.

"Did you hear me, Lyra?" David presses. "George is dangerous. He killed your parents."

# CHAPTER 11

I laugh.

What else can I do? Because what David is suggesting is preposterous. Hendricks purposely infecting my parents? David must be insane. Doctors, scientists, don't go around infecting perfectly healthy people, that's just crazy. My parents must have been infected in the stupid jail cell or wherever they're being held.

Except . . . how did my parents get so sick so soon? If they caught the plague in custody, they wouldn't have gotten sick for up to a week. But they showed symptoms right away, on Friday. That must mean they picked up the virus *before* we were captured.

Holy shit. Did *I* infect them? I was in contact with that little boy at the park. Did *I* pass on the plague to them without knowing? But no, that makes no sense. If I'd picked up the virus from Mama Jua, I would have gotten sick like I did in the quarantine camp. So, it wasn't me. It must have been somebody at Mom's work. The truck stop is full of transient people—there's no way of telling who might have been contagious.

Well thank God we did end up getting caught, then, because at least now my parents have a shot of getting better. Feeling reassured, I decide not to bother responding to David.

I don't need him to mess with my mind; I've had enough problems for one weekend. I stride to the door and fling it open, ready to walk.

"There are still soldiers out there," David calls to me.

I hesitate on the doorstep. *Damn, he's right.* If I go out now, they might recognize me and haul me back into the school.

"I can help you," David says.

I step back and let the door swing shut. I take a deep breath. "I don't need your help."

"Yeah, you do."

I turn around, irritated. "No, I really don't."

"Fine." David settles himself on the couch. "How are you going to get out of here?"

I grit my teeth, frustrated. "I don't have to answer to you."

"Okay." And he sits there, staring at me.

"Leave me alone," I snap at him.

David holds up his hands. "I'm not doing anything."

I walk away from him into the kitchen. I have to think. How do I find Hendricks? He wasn't waiting for me, so does that mean he gave up on me? Or did he never have much hope that I'd succeed in the first place?

The thought scares me. If that's the case, does that mean he's given up on a cure? On my parents?

I start to feel panicky, my mind whirling, but it's like a spinning tire stuck in the snow. I can't get any traction; I can't think what I should do. I can't go back to the lab to look for Hendricks—too many bad guys—and I can't wander around the city looking for his black van. Where can I find him? At home? It's Sunday afternoon, so maybe he'll be there.

I make up my mind. I'll track him down at his house—once I figure out where he lives. I search the house for a computer, a tablet, a phone—something I can use to find Hendricks's address online, but there's nothing. The place is empty of all electronics.

I go back into the living room; David is still sitting there, watching me closely.

"Do you have a phone?" I clench my teeth when I ask because I don't want to owe this crackpot anything.

"Why?" Even as he asks, he pulls it from his pocket, but he doesn't give it to me.

"Can I borrow it?" What, is he going to make me grovel next?

"You're calling George?"

"No."

David exhales. "Lyra, talk to me."

"No."

He sighs again, but this time he holds out his phone.

I snatch it and start searching for Hendricks's address, but it doesn't take me long to discover he's unlisted.

"Shit," I hiss.

"Can't find George's address?" David asks and I look up at him, surprised. "I can see the screen from here," he explains.

*Stupid, Lyra, stupid.* I fling the phone back at him, frustrated and annoyed.

"I know where he lives," David says.

I glare at him. He's playing with me, but David just shrugs. "I told you, he's family. Look," he stands up, "let me drive you there."

"Why? You want me to stay away from him."

"Obviously I'm not very convincing, am I?"

"So you're just going to drop me off?"

"Sure, if that's what you want."

"I don't trust you."

"You don't have a choice."

*Fucking hell.* He's right again. If I want to get out of here unseen, I need help. If I want to find Hendricks as soon as possible, I need David.

"Fine," I grumble. "Let's go."

David smiles, like he knew I'd see reason, and it infuriates me. "Are you going to screw with me?"

He shakes his head. "Just trying to help."

Reluctantly, I follow him back through the house to the kitchen.

"I have a car on the next street over," David explains. "If we sneak out the back and through the neighbor's yards, I think we'll evade the soldiers."

"Let's go," I say, unbolting the door. I step carefully outside, listening for the sound of soldiers tromping through the streets, but all is quiet. David slides past me, motioning me to follow. We slip through a few backyards, then sprint across the street, climb over a fence and end up next to a battered blue station wagon.

"It's Mama Jua's car," I exclaim. I know it well. Mama Jua would often let me drive it when we went to the orphanage. "Driving is for people in a hurry," she'd say. "I'd rather sit back, relax and be chauffeured."

"I don't think she minds that I borrowed it," David replies wryly. "Get in the backseat and hide under the blanket until we're out of the area."

I scramble in and do what he suggests. I pick up an old wool blanket. It's gray and black, with large geometric patterns and I recognize it, too. Mama Jua told me it was hand-woven by her sister.

"It's as ugly as hell," Mama Jua said. "But it's full of love so how could I throw it out?"

I curl up on the floor of the backseat and drape the ugly wool blanket over my head. It smells of Mama Jua, of her lilac talcum powder, and I decide I'm going to take it with me when David and I get to Hendricks's house because it reminds me that Mama Jua was full of love, too, and I have nothing else to remember her by. I don't really care whether David agrees or not—I was with Mama Jua almost every day these last few months and he wasn't, so I deserve to have something of hers.

David crawls through the neighborhood, driving carefully to avoid attention, and then, when we speed up on the highway, he tells me it's safe to come out. I scramble over the front seats and sit beside him.

I stare outside as we hurtle across the city, my own mind going a mile a minute. Ahimsa. My parents getting help. Is David right? Did my parents lie to me all this time? I think back on all of our moves, trying to remember if there were hints or clues I missed that would indicate our plans weren't random. But I can't. There weren't any. We went where we wanted, when we wanted, and there were many times when *I* chose our next route. Dad would spread out a map on the hood of the car, tell me to close my eyes and point. Wherever my finger landed is where we went. So how could Ahimsa arrange all of that? Unless my parents talked to David's mom *after* we chose where we were going? Did that make sense? No, none of this makes sense.

Which is why none of it is true. My parents weren't extraordinary secret-keepers; they couldn't have hidden a whole Ahimsa network from me.

Which means David is lying.

But a small voice burrows through my thoughts: *why*? Why would David lie? What's in it for him? To mess with me? Why do that if he says he came to protect me?

I'm so wrapped up in my turmoil, that it takes me a while to realize we're still on the highway—driving *out* of Washington. I sit up straighter, then twist back to see the city fading in the distance.

"Wait, where the hell are you going?" I ask.

"To George's house," David replies, but he seems to be concentrating a little too firmly on the road.

"Where does he live?" I demand.

"On the outskirts," David answers vaguely.

He's lying. Goddamn it, now I know he's lying. He tricked me, the bastard. He never had any intention of driving me to Hendricks. "Pull over," I say.

Now David looks at me. "No."

"Pull *over*," I insist. "I'm getting out."

"No."

My blood pressure rises; I feel my cheeks flush with anger. "*No?* Now *you're* kidnapping me?"

David brushes off my accusation. "Not kidnapping you. Protecting you."

"By keeping me against my will?"

David says nothing.

"I'll jump out of the car," I say, putting my hand on the door handle.

"We're going more than seventy miles an hour," David answers calmly, like he thinks I'm bluffing. "That's insanity."

*No, it fucking isn't,* I think. I've never jumped from a speeding car before, but it can't be worse than my fall down the canyon wall in Utah. I actually lift the tip of the door handle. But then I think it through: I may survive, but the glass vial of Jaz's blood, the only thing that can save my parents, may not.

*Shit.*

I ease my hand off the handle and cross my arms, angry and frustrated. Goddamn it, what am I supposed to do now? How am I going to get back to my parents? Every mile David chews up is a minute of my parents' lives he's shaving off.

"Please," I beg. "I need to get back to my parents."

"I told you—" David takes a deep breath as if *he's* irritated, but then he softens his tone. "Lyra, I'm really sorry your parents already died."

"They didn't," I insist. "They're not dead."

David's expression is grim, but he says nothing.

And it's his sad silence, his bleak resignation that suddenly jolts me with fear, hijacking my anger. What if he is telling the truth? What if he's right?

"David, please," I beg, starting to feel jittery. "You're being cruel. Please tell me you're joking."

David's jaw tightens. "I wish to God I were."

"No, you don't understand," I say quietly. I hear my voice quiver, but I can't make it stop. "They can't be dead. They're all I have." I try to imagine for an excruciating second what my life would be like without my parents, being on my own, all alone, but I can't do it.

David glances over at me, his eyes full of sympathy.

"We've been on the run since I was eight," I tell him. "It's just been the three of us all these years."

"That must have been tough," David says, and he sounds genuine.

"Yeah, but it was good, too," I say defensively, as if David had been dissing my parents. But my reaction surprises me. *Good?* For years, I've been fighting my parents to stop running, and now I say it's good? But then I realize I'm not lying. It actually was good. Parts of our lives really *were* good.

"I had my parents to myself," I say, but I don't know why I'm explaining this to David. What business is it of his? Why would he care? Yet still I find myself talking. I find that I like talking about my parents. I like thinking about them.

"I never had to share them with the rest of the world," I continue, and it's true. Because I didn't have anyone else, they always made sure they were there for me. When we took off from California, when I had to leave Jonah, I remember being a wretched mess. I cried quietly in my new bed every night for a week, I missed him so much, and I'm sure Mom heard me. She might even have guessed why, although we never talked about it. Instead, every morning, she'd bring me a cup of chamomile tea, settle on my bed beside me, and flip through a magazine.

"You'll be late for work," I remember telling her.

"You're more important," she replied, without looking up from her article.

David looks over at me. "Not sharing your parents . . . that sounds nice," he says wistfully.

"It was," I agree. "Whenever I wanted, Dad would stop what he was doing and come for a run with me, even though he hated running," I smile at the memory, at Dad groaning good-naturedly as he tied his shoes. When I complained about his whining, he defended himself.

"It's how I psych myself up," he'd say, grinning, and then we'd take off down the road or over the trails or wherever.

"I'm with your dad," David tells me. "Why run when you can be a couch potato? It's much more comfortable."

"What? And miss out on the endorphin rush? The runner's high? To push yourself so hard you're rewarded with this incredible euphoria? You'd give all that up to sit on your ass?"

"Yes," David laughs. "Because your runner's high or euphoria or whatever the hell you want to call it doesn't exist. I know. In all my life, I've never once experienced it."

"You're not serious," I say. "Everyone feels it. The biological effects of exercise have long been proven."

"Guess my body didn't read the textbooks," he jokes.

I laugh. "Mine either," I say.

We're quiet for a minute, my mind still on running and on my dad, when I notice the car slows down, and then David pulls off at the next exit.

"What are you doing?" I ask. Is he turning around? Are we going back? Should I get my hopes up? Or is he just taking another route to his demonic lair?

He doesn't answer until he's crossed over the highway, gotten back on in the opposite direction and is headed toward Washington.

"Taking you to George's house," he says.

My heart flips a little with excitement, but still I'm wary. "Why'd you change your mind?"

"Because I see now that it's the only way you'll accept the truth," he answers heavily.

No, it's the only way *he'll* accept the truth, I think. The truth that he doesn't know what the hell is going on, no matter how much he thinks he does. Still, I try to be gracious. "Thank you."

"But there's a catch," he says.

I knew it, the bastard.

"I come with you. When you talk to George."

"Why?" I ask. I don't care, actually, if that's his only condition. As long as I can get the blood to Hendricks and he can start working on the serum, David can go wherever the hell he likes.

David shrugs in response, but doesn't elaborate. "Do we have a deal?"

"Deal."

We drive in silence the rest of the way. When David pulls up in front of a beautiful colonial house, my pulse starts to race. This is it. I'm so close now. When I was trapped in the quarantine camp, when I got sick, when I woke up and realized I'd lost a day, I truly feared I'd never succeed. But I am succeeding. I'm here, mere steps away from Hendricks and mere hours away from a cure. Soon, I'll be disappearing with my parents into the wild blue yonder and all of this crazy, stupid weekend will be forgotten. No, not forgotten. I'll remember how close I was to losing them, and I won't complain to them again about where we go or when. I'll keep my mouth shut and be the good obedient daughter they deserve.

I follow David up the richly landscaped path, but instead of going to the front door, he walks around back.

"What are you doing?" I hiss as I jog after him.

"I told you, I don't trust George."

"He's not going to kill me."

"I'm not going to give him the chance to get you," David says. "If we're out here, we won't be trapped. We can easily escape through the forest behind the house."

I shake my head, but in the end, what does it matter? Hendricks's front hall, his backyard, who cares?

The lawn, still a winter brown, is lined with elaborate garden beds. A few butter-yellow daffodils sprout up among the moist dirt, and I recognize the budding, dark ruby amaranth flower, like Mama Jua's gift to me. The plants remind me of the small little plots Mom used to plant in whatever house we were in during the spring. "You're wasting your time," I'd tell her. "We'll be gone from here by the time the flowers are in full bloom."

"It's not about seeing them, Lyra," Mom would say. "It's about knowing they're here, knowing that someone else will enjoy them. I like to think of it as my mark on the world."

I understand now, because *my* mark is going to be helping make the cure for Hecate's Plague, even if no one but Hendricks will know about it.

David suggests I wait at the back of the lawn near an elaborate goldfish pond ringed with stone while he gets Hendricks. I think his precautions are useless, but I humor him.

I watch as David knocks at the back door. A moment later, Hendricks swings it open.

Thank God he's here.

He looks surprised to see David, but then his eyes fly up to where I'm standing and he smiles. He scurries after David down the flagstone path, and I'm surprised by how much older he seems, as if he's aged a decade in only a day.

"Lyra!" he cries, relieved. He grasps both of my hands in his. "You made it."

I twitch at his comment, annoyed that he makes it sound like I'm merely late to a dinner party, instead of *him* being the one who deserted me at the quarantine camp.

"You left me," I say, dropping my hands from his. I feel the full weight of the task I had to do, the burden I had to bear, the risks I had to take. All Hendricks had to do was sit in a goddamn van, and he couldn't even do that.

Hendricks startles at my tone. He glances fleetingly at David before turning back to me. "I had to leave," he says as if it were obvious. "The soldiers were getting suspicious. They'd already stopped to talk to me twice on Saturday. It was all I could do to keep them off our scent."

All he could do? *All* he could do? All he had to do was *sit* there and spin a few lies, while I did the death-defying work.

"Besides," he adds petulantly, "you weren't supposed to be in there so long. Get in, find Yasmine and get out."

"I *couldn't* get out, not until dark," I snap.

"I waited until long after dark," Hendricks retorts. "You didn't come."

"I got *sick*," I say.

Hendricks shakes his head, then rubs his wrinkled eyes, like he's disappointed in me. "You were in there too long," he chastises. "If you'd been in and out the way we planned, if you hadn't waited for dark, then you wouldn't have picked up the virus."

"Wait," I say, my skin prickling with dread. "You *knew* I'd get sick? And you didn't warn me?"

"You didn't need to know," Hendricks replies. "And if you had listened to me, if you'd just gone in and come out quickly—like we *planned*—you wouldn't have gotten sick."

My eyes widen. He's blaming *me*?

"But it's no matter," Hendricks's face brightens, and his eyes gleam with a childlike hope. "You're here now, very much alive. You have the blood?" he asks eagerly.

I pull the vial from my jacket pocket and I reach out my hand.

Excitedly, Hendricks grabs for it, but at the last second, I snatch it back.

*You didn't need to know*. That's what Hendricks said. I didn't need to know that I could get sick again from Hecate's Plague, that I could almost have died. Then I hear David's voice in my head. *Your parents are dead, Lyra*. Is that something else Hendricks feels I don't need to know?

"Are my parents still alive?" I ask, holding the vial back from Hendricks. I watch his face carefully. He blinks in surprise—but was that a shadow of guilt? Or am I imagining things?

"Why, yes, of course," Hendricks exclaims. "They're very sick, though," he says gravely. "We have no time to lose."

He reaches again for the vial, but again I withhold it.

Why? Why am I doing this? I went to a world of trouble to bring this blood back here; why am I not giving it to him? Because of what David said? A stranger? Someone who doesn't know me or know what's going on?

Someone who didn't have to get involved. Someone who has nothing to gain by coming after me.

"Prove it," I say.

Hendricks blusters. "Prove what?"

"That my parents are alive. Bring them here, then I'll give you the vial."

*What am I doing?* I can't afford to waste another minute of my parents' precious lives by playing games.

"Lyra," Hendricks says soothingly, as if to a child. "You know they're too sick to travel. You can come to the lab with me, if you like. I'll sneak you back in and you can see for yourself."

"No!" I cry. I'm not going back there. I'm not risking getting caught.

"Then what do you propose, Lyra?" Hendricks asks innocently.

I think fast, I think furiously. Should I even go through this charade? Hendricks is right—how can he prove to me my parents are still alive if they can't come here and I can't go there?

"Let me talk to them," I say.

"They're too weak for a phone call," Hendricks says, then his tone stiffens, like an impatient father. "We don't have time for this. We're wasting precious seconds. Hand me the vial."

David jumps in quickly. He glares at Hendricks. "Have Lyra choose a question only her parents would know the answer to. Then get your assistant in the isolation chamber to ask them. If your assistant relays the correct answer, Lyra will know her parents are alive and she'll hand you the blood."

David and Hendricks stare at each other, hatred burning in each other's eyes.

"I told you to stay out of this, David," Hendricks growls. His face darkens and his body tenses, coiled and ready to spring, like a cornered animal.

I look from one to the other and my pulse starts to race. David still thinks my parents are dead. He thinks his idea about the secret question will call Hendricks out.

"And I told you I won't stay out of it," David snarls. "Lyra deserves the truth."

I see Hendricks's gaze falter, anxious and frightened.

No . . . it can't be . . .

Wildly, I try to catch his eye. "Dr. Hendricks?"

But he won't look at me. His shoulders droop.

"She'll find out, George. The truth always gets out."

Hendricks straightens, as if he's regrouping. With a great effort, he rearranges his expression and offers me a thin smile. "Lyra, could you please give me the vial? It's all that's standing in our way of finding the cure, and we desperately need a cure. You saw the quarantine camps yourself, you know better than anyone how devastating and cruel this plague has been. We have to stop it, and now you have the power to do it. Just hand me the vial."

I grip the thin glass in my hands, the blood that may save my parents. I start to tremble. "I did what you asked because my parents are sick. I did it to save them, not save the world."

Hendricks whirls toward David, with a look of unfathomable exasperation. "See? I told you that's all that would motivate her."

David's voice again echoes in my head. *George purposely infected them so he'd guarantee you'd return to the lab instead of going back on the run.*

With rising anger, dread and foreboding, I turn to Hendricks and I ask very, very slowly, with what's left of my control, "Are my parents alive?"

Hendricks's face falls. He slumps into himself, the posture of a defeated man.

"No . . ." I whisper. I double over like I've been punched in the gut. It's true. David was right. My parents are dead.

The world tilts on its axis.

I try to breathe.

If David was right about my parents, was he also right about Hendricks killing them?

With a strength of will, I raise my eyes to meet his. "Did you infect my parents?"

"I'm sorry," Hendricks says heavily. His eyes remain downcast; he refuses to look at me. "I had no choice."

My mind is exploding. Behind my eyes I see a whirl of angry red flames, of fire, of hell itself erupting "You *killed* my parents?"

"I didn't *want* to!" Hendricks says. "I tried to lie about them being sick, but you insisted on seeing them. I had to infect them, then, and I had to do it with a concentrated dose so they'd be visibly ill when you saw them. You had to believe they were sick, otherwise I knew you wouldn't have agreed to return. The only way I could ensure you'd come back was if you knew your parents' lives were at stake. I told you, it's all about psychology." Then, defiantly childishly, petulantly, he adds, "But it was *always* about more than your parents. It was for the greater good. I knew you'd never see that, so I had to do what was necessary. And honestly, I thought you'd get back sooner. If you'd gotten here yesterday, then there would have been a chance . . ."

David roars at him. "You're blaming *Lyra?* You sick bastard."

Hendricks ignores him. "Lyra, please, you have to understand, it was for the greater good," he repeats. "I had to sacrifice your parents' lives to save millions more."

My body is convulsing in violent tremors, like I'm being pummeled with a dozen sledgehammers. He had to sacrifice my parents. For the greater good. I look at the vial of Jaz's blood in my hands, the vial that was supposed to have saved my parents. The vial that shouldn't have been necessary because they shouldn't have needed saving.

"Lyra, give me the blood, okay?" Hendricks speaks like he's trying to calm a wild animal.

I *feel* wild. I am wild. Rage overwhelms me and I can't control it.

"*This*?" I shout, holding up the vial. "This is what you want?" And before I think of the ramifications of what I'm doing, I smash the vial into the rocks at the edge of the goldfish pond with the strength of a thousand warriors. The glass shatters and Jaz's blood, the answer to my hope, my future, my life, spills, ruined, into the muddy water.

# CHAPTER 12

"You *bastard!*" I shriek, lunging at Hendricks, at his sniveling, pathetic little form. I dig my nails into his cheeks—I want to tear him apart—but David grabs me by the shoulders and pulls me back. "Get *off* me," I screech, flailing my arms to shake him off.

Hendricks uses the moment to scuttle off the garden path, but he doesn't get far. I shove David back and leap again at Hendricks. I catch the collar of his coat before David again holds me off. He wraps his arms around my waist and twists me away.

"Let me *at* him!" I cry, struggling against David, but he tightens his grip to the point where I'm lifted off my feet.

"Calm *down*, Lyra," David hisses, wrapping me in a bear hug. His arms pin me like a straitjacket and I wrestle against him. "We have to go," he says into my ear.

I don't listen. I can't listen. I won't listen. I'm not going anywhere, not until I rip apart the man who murdered my parents.

Hendricks crumples to the ground in front of the goldfish pond, frantically swirling at the bloody water in the pond as if he could scoop out the antibodies with his bare hands.

"What have you *done*?" he moans.

"What have *I* done?" I shriek, bitterly aware of the echoes of my mother's dismay when I told her about Holly, right before she and my dad were captured. "When *you* were the one who purposely infected my parents with a disease that has no cure?"

"I told you— " Hendricks starts, but David cuts him off.

"No. You don't get to speak," David says, his voice low and menacing. "We're going now and I swear, if you try to find us, if you look for Lyra, I will *ruin* you."

David still has his arms around me. He starts to pull me backwards, but still I resist. "No!" I cry. "He can't get away with it!"

"We don't have a choice, Lyra," David says. "It's either him getting caught or us. I came to save you, not him. Let him stew in his own self-destruction."

"No . . ." I say, thinking I will protest, but my energy wanes. Suddenly I feel like a ragdoll, limp and sagging, in David's arms. It's not that the fight goes out of me, it's that I have no more strength with which to fight. David bundles me against his chest protectively, like a knight rescuing a damsel in distress.

Am I? Is that what I am? Am I so helpless, so pathetic that I need a man to save me?

Obviously, since I couldn't even save my own parents.

The thought twists a dagger through my heart, a blade with a serrated edge ripping it to shreds. I failed them. I failed my parents. I look at the smear of red water in the pond, the remnants of the blood that was supposed to save them. But it's too late. *I* was too late. If I'd made it here earlier—yesterday, the way I was supposed to—then they'd still be alive.

No.

Hendricks wouldn't have saved them; he killed them. *He* killed them, not me. The lava beast rises within me and I'm relieved. This is better, feeling this rage. I can deal with it. I can cope with anger. I've dealt with it my whole life. I know it. What I don't know is the guilt and the grief and the despair that feels like it's eating me from the inside out, so I just simply won't let those things get to me. I won't acknowledge them. I won't accept them.

David pulls me away, out of reach of Hendricks, out of his garden and into the forest, and I turn my wrath on him.

"You're in on it," I spit. "You *knew.* You knew my parents were dying and you did *nothing*."

I see a wounded look flash across David's face.

Good. He *should* be hurting, the asshole. Telling me this, dragging me here . . .

David suddenly lets go of me. He steps back, his hands raised in surrender.

"Go," he snaps. "Go back, finish him off."

I pause and look at him, confused.

"Go," he hisses, waving me away. "You want to get yourself caught? Be my guest. I was trying to help, but if you're so hell-bent on revenge, then I'm not going to stop you. But *I'm* not taking the risk."

"Risk?" I snarl. "What risk for you? You turn Hendricks in and then you go back to your cozy little family." I am thinking of the tight circle I saw at the funeral. Bitterness seeps into my veins. It's not fair. I've had everything taken away. My sister, my home, my childhood and now my parents. And what has David lost? He still has a home, he still has a family.

David glares at me, then shakes his head. "I'm *eighteen*, Lyra."

It takes me a moment to understand.

"You're dodging the draft," I say.

"Yeah," he says heavily. "Since my birthday last month. The Conscription Service is relentless. You know they won't let any eighteen-year-old slip through their fingers. Gotta have more bodies to send home from the war, I guess."

I'm pulled up short by David's comment. I didn't know. I didn't know the Conscription Service tracked down every eighteen-year-old. I know it's mandatory for every teen, male and female, to enlist on his or her eighteenth birthday, but I never thought anything else about it. Obviously *I* wasn't about to saunter into an enlistment center on my eighteenth birthday; I never thought there were other people who might not, either.

"So, no, Lyra, I don't have a cozy little family to go back to—not that I ever did," he adds cryptically. "But I do have a life that I'm not about to throw away on a goddamn useless war, so I'm leaving. Oh, and you're welcome, by the way."

I blink at him.

"For saving your ass," he says. "I fucked up at my grandmother's house when you got shot, but now I've made up for it. I *did* something. If you want to get yourself killed in your hot-headed revenge, then that's your problem, not mine. I'm out of here."

I open my mouth, ready to bluster at him that he has *some* nerve, that I never *asked* for his help, that I didn't *need* his help, that I don't need his help now to take down Hendricks, when suddenly I realize he's right. I won't get myself killed, obviously, but I could very well get myself caught. Then where would I be? Back in that basement bedroom in the lab, a slab of meat to be tested? Is that how I should honor my parents? By risking everything they fought for—my freedom—to avenge their deaths? Is that what they'd want?

Then another thought, another fear slams into me.

I'm on my own. I'm truly alone.

And I have nowhere to go.

I can't go home—it's the first place the agents will look for me—but I don't know where else I could go. Or how I'd get there, or how I'd survive once I did. I have no money, no contacts, no skills. I don't know how to evade the authorities or how to get a job.

Wow. How is that possible? How is it that I've been on the run for more than half my life, but I don't know *how* to run? Was I so busy fighting my parents to stop running that I never learned how? Did they try to teach me, but I would never listen? It never occurred to me that I'd be on my own. Oh, someday, for sure, when I was an adult, and my parents died peacefully of old age, but not now, not at seventeen.

"Good luck, Lyra," David says sarcastically. He turns around and walks away.

I look back at Hendricks's yard, then I twist to see David's retreating form. Avenge my parents or save myself? My anger coils, a snake ready to strike, and I want—oh, how I want—tear after Hendricks and knock him to the ground and pound him until he's—

*Dead? You want to kill him, Lyra? You want to* become *him?*

I shiver, unnerved by my rage.

"David?" I call out. Without a second's hesitation, he turns back to me. "I'm coming with you."

He looks relieved. "I was hoping you'd say that."

I hurry after him, still shaking.

We get back to the car, climb in and David starts driving.

"If you can't go home and I can't go home, where are we going?" I ask.

"To an Ahimsa cabin," he answers. "One of the hideouts my mom's group uses."

"Back in Jamestown?" I ask nervously. That'll be dangerous, with agents lurking around.

David shakes his head. "We'll go to Pennsylvania for now."

"Ahimsa has hideouts in Pennsylvania?" I'm surprised. I always assumed Mama Jua's Ahimsa group was local.

"We have hideouts all over the country," David replies.

I never thought about how many people might be resisting the government like that. "That's impressive," I say.

David snorts. "No, it's not."

I look over at him, surprised.

"What's impressive about scurrying for cover?" he says, and I notice he grips the steering wheel tighter. "Hiding sick people and their families, giving them funerals? What will that accomplish?"

"Dignity," I answer hotly, thinking of Mama Jua, of her life, of her death, of her funeral. She was the one who taught me how important dignity is, how essential it is for people to feel in control of their lives or even their deaths. She made me see the value of caring for others to give them that dignity. That's why I started volunteering at the orphanage, because I could see the difference I made when I helped out.

Because I could *feel* the difference it made in me when I helped out.

"Dignity is not going to bring down the government," David retorts. "Dignity is not going to end this plague or this war. *Action* is going to end this plague and this war. *Doing* something, not sitting on our asses hiding out in cabins."

"I believe you just informed me that we're going to sit on our ass in a cabin."

David grimaces. "There you have it, the crux of my dilemma. I want to fight the government, but I don't want to fight their war."

I try to follow his logic. "If you fight the government, you'll be caught and sent off to war."

He nods. "So I hide out, like I've done all my life."

I feel a prickle on my skin. "All your life?"

"Most of it," David says bitterly. "Mom's poured her heart and soul into Ahimsa. We're on the move all the time, setting up new safe houses and new networks."

"What about your dad?"

"He died before I was born," David says, pressing his lips together. "I never knew him."

"Oh." I don't know what else to say. I can't even imagine

not knowing my dad. I love my dad. He was the greatest, except for the whole dragging-me-across-the-country-against-my-will thing, but otherwise, he was always there for me. It hurts—God, it hurts—to realize that I'll never again hike with him through the mountains or watch another screwball comedy with him or gaze up at the stars together, but is that worse than never having had those memories in the first place?

"My mom and dad met in Washington," David starts talking. "Dad worked as an Arabic–English translator at the Arab Union League and Mom was finishing her nursing degree. They met in a bar and, so the story goes, they fell madly in love at first sight."

Something about the picture he paints reminds me of when I was little, when Mom would come home from work on the base and Dad would be in the kitchen cooking dinner and he'd stop chopping vegetables to pull her into a big hug and then he'd kiss her full on the lips and Ivy and I would groan in disgust and then we'd wrestle our way in between them and they would laugh and Dad would always say, "Someday, when you're older, you'll do the same thing, girls."

I never thought about it until now, how happy my parents were together. They fought, of course—and it was always about me—but they always made up. Whenever I complained to Dad about Mom, he'd gently remind me I was talking about the love of his life. "You know I can't live without her, honey."

Now I guess he doesn't have to.

I wonder if that's a slim, miniscule, microscopic blessing in disguise. That because my parents died together, neither one had to suffer the loss of the other. After everything my parents had to go through in their lives—losing Ivy, deserting the army, giving up their home, their friends, their family, living with me—maybe it's better that it's only me who has to suffer.

"My dad's parents were diplomats from Jordan," David continues, "and they went crazy when Dad told them he wanted to marry a divorced Black girl from New York who already had a kid in tow—that's my half-brother Matteo—instead of marrying a rich, upper-crust Arab girl." David smiles as if he's picturing the scene. "When his parents learned Mom was pregnant with me, they disowned him. They never talked to my mom or dad ever again."

"Really?" I say, surprised. "People do that?" I mean, my parents had to cut off contact with their parents, well, my mom's mom, anyway, who may be still alive for all I know, but that's because they had no choice. It's not because they wanted to. How could anyone just stop talking to their family?

"They never even met me," David says bitterly. "They wanted nothing to do with me."

"You're not serious," I say.

David nods. "At least I had Mama Jua," he says, and smiles. "She more than made up for my missing grandparents."

I smile, too. How right he is.

"Anyway," David finishes his story, "my dad died of a heart attack three months before I was born, so I never knew him."

"That sucks," I say.

"Yeah," David agrees.

And then there's nothing more to say. I look out the window, watching the world pass by, the houses and roads and trees. The world I don't belong to, the one I can never be a part of. I feel overwhelmed, suddenly. My escape from the quarantine camp, the news of my parents' death, Hendricks's betrayal, David's history—which sounds almost as fucked up as mine—all prove to me how impossible my goal was. All I wanted was a nice, normal life with a nice, normal family. Was that too much to ask? Obviously . . .

A great weight settles over me, a thick blanket that suffocates me. I draw my arms around my chest and pull my knees up, as if I can shrink to escape the heaviness, but it doesn't work. Instead, it closes in on me, crushing me. I start to shake, my insides convulsing. The pain is so intense. I squeeze myself harder, trying to hold together, but I crumble. Big, wet tears drip down my cheeks and I start to sob.

*It hurts, it hurts so much.* I ball my fists, my nails digging into my palms. I forget to breath.

David stretches out his hand, but I'm curled against the door, so he doesn't reach me.

"I'm sorry," he whispers.

I cry and cry and then I fall asleep. We don't talk again until hours later when we reach the Ahimsa cabin.

David leads me up a steep rocky path to a little cabin on the edge of a cliff overlooking a beautiful line of hills.

"It's the Blue Ridge Mountains," David says.

He shows me inside the cabin. It's a small, one-room cottage with a king-sized bed covered in a tattered quilt in one corner and a small kitchenette, its sink and counter stained with rust, in another. Scattered about are men's clothes and a backpack, a sleeping bag and boots.

"It's your bachelor pad?" I ask.

David smiles. "I didn't exactly think I'd have a guest. It was only supposed to be my sanctuary until I could make my arrangements."

David offers me a mismatched chair at his small, round kitchen table. I sink into it, exhausted. Was it only this afternoon that I said goodbye to Jaz? That I watched Mo die? My God, how does time fuck with us like this?

I try to refocus on David. "What arrangements?" I ask.

"My escape plan," David explains. "I'm going to slip across the border into Canada. My brother Matteo is there—he evaded the draft a few years ago."

"He'll help you?" I ask, and I can't help but feel jealous that David has a brother, that he has family to help him.

"His dad, Christian, went with him," David says. "He was my mom's first husband. They were high school sweethearts—obviously it didn't work out, but they remained friends. After my dad died, we moved to New York City, where Christian lived, and he often included me in his father–son visits with Matteo."

"Like a stepdad kind of thing?" I ask.

"I guess," David shrugs. "He felt sorry for me, not having my own dad," David says and I can't tell if he sounds bitter or pleased. "I guess he kind of adopted me informally—he's the closest thing I have to a father." David shakes his head, like he doesn't want to parse through his emotions for Christian, the dad who isn't his dad. "Anyway, Christian helped Matteo escape the draft and he's agreed to help me."

"But if you go to Canada, that means you can never come back."

David flicks his eyes away from me. "It's the price I have to pay."

"Is that what you want?"

He's silent for a moment and then says, "I don't have a choice."

I guess neither one of us has a choice. Neither one of us has ever had a choice.

"Come with me," David says suddenly.

I look up at him. "What?"

"To Canada. I'll get in touch with Christian and Matteo; we'll make sure you're safe."

I stare at David. I don't know what to say. Leave the United States? Leave my home? But where is my home? In a country whose government wants to abuse me? The answer seems obvious—David is handing me the golden ticket—yet still I hesitate because no matter how many times we had to move, no matter how many towns I lived in, my parents never gave up on our country. When they spread out the map to choose where to go, it never included Canada or Mexico or anywhere else.

*But our country killed them*, I remind myself.

Our country wants to imprison me, to use me, to exploit me.

Then I get angry, the emotion I crave, the feeling I understand. *This* is the country to which I'm swearing allegiance? A country hell bent on a decade-old war in the Middle East that cannot possibly be won? A country that kills its citizens to stop the spread of the plague instead of investing in research to prevent it?

Maybe I *should* go to Canada with David.

Maybe I should run away.

"Think on it," David says hopefully, and I wonder why he asked. Why does he want me to come? He said it himself: He's paid back whatever debt he felt he owed me. Why would he want to burden himself with an angry, bitter girl?

He quickly changes the subject. "You must be wiped. The bathroom's right there if you want to take a shower, and then why don't you crash on the bed?" He pauses, and adds, as an afterthought, "Unless you're hungry?" He looks panicked for a moment, like he's about to search for food, but I stop him.

"I'm not hungry."

I do wash up—I thought I'd feel like a new person after a hot shower, but I don't; I feel just as miserable and unsure and lost as I did before—and then I fall onto the hard, lumpy mattress.

"Sorry, it's not much," David apologizes.

I think about where I've been the last few nights: passed out on a thin cot in a vault in a school-turned-quarantine-camp and before that on a single bed in a cell underneath a top-secret military lab. Even the night before that, Thursday, when I was home, in my own bed, I didn't sleep well, knowing I'd be waking early for Mama Jua's funeral.

"No, it's great," I say, collapsing under the covers. "And . . . thanks."

❖

When I wake, the soft dawn light shines through the huge windows facing east, and I remember that my parents were murdered yesterday. I'm tormented by my last image of them, lying scared and helpless, dying from Hecate's Plague in Hendricks's isolation chamber. *You're totally alone*, I think. The grief strangles me, a noose tightening around my immortal neck, the pain as real, as intense as if I could actually die, and the knowledge that the pain will never disappear terrifies me.

David is sitting at the table, reading a crumpled newspaper. He offers me breakfast—a protein bar—and we take our weak coffee in chipped enamel mugs out onto the deck. I can see for miles in every direction, the peak of mountains and the tops of ridges and for a moment, I feel I am the overlord of the world, looking down on my domain from my throne above, and not an orphan, not an outcast, not freak of nature destined to live out my endless days isolated and alone.

"Matteo can't meet us for at least another week," David says, and I don't bother to ask how he learned this information. I don't have the energy to process how a secret underground network that spans the whole country works.

I nod, as if I've already accepted David's offer to join him, but I can't think about it now. I can't think about anything. Any kind of thought, any kind of memory hurts too much, so every day when David slips off to do whatever he does and I simply sit on the deck, staring at the unmoving mountain, trying to empty my mind. It works for a few days, where I am a blank slate, but after a while, I notice wisps of thoughts seeping into my head. I'm grateful for what David has done for me, but still I feel a third wheel, a hanger-on, an add-on. David has his brother and his sort-of father, and I have nobody. I am not the center of anyone's life, and they are not the center of mine, but then, in a rush of clarity, I think of Holly.

I miss her. I miss her little twig-like arms that slapped around my neck every time she saw me, and her wide blue eyes that danced with excitement at whatever adventure I proposed: a trip to the frog pond in the forest where I showed her how to catch the green-speckled creatures by their legs, pet them and let them go, or a spy mission to investigate the secret recipes of the ice cream parlor down the road, or a challenge to slay the dragons that had begun to invade the sparse little playground near the orphanage. It was the most fun I ever had and I can't stand that she probably thinks I abandoned her. I told her I'd drop by Friday afternoon and now that it's been almost a week, she must realize I'm not coming. I suddenly realize I could go back.

I've relied on David this whole time, falling into his plans. Maybe I need to carve my own path, figure out my own life. And maybe I should start where I wanted my life to be: Jamestown. I know it's dangerous to go back for good—but maybe it's not dangerous to return to the orphanage and see Holly. The agents may not know about my volunteer work there and they can't possibly blanket the whole town, so maybe I could sneak back, and see Holly. I'll set myself up someplace nearby, then settle down. I'll be more cautious about where I go and what I do. In fact, the more I think about it, the more I think how brilliant it is. The agents will expect me to go underground. They won't expect me to *settle* back in the same place I was captured from. If I make sure they don't catch sight of me, then they'll eventually realize I'm not returning, and then they'll move on. They won't bother coming back because they'll think Jamestown has been checked off their list.

I jump up from my wooden chair on the deck, stoked that I have a plan. A way forward. A future.

I tell David when he comes back from his errands.

"You're serious?" he asks.

I nod. "It's a risk, obviously, but so is crossing into Canada. And if I go with you, I'll never see Holly again. She's all I've got left, David."

He frowns, and suddenly I'm irritated. "What, you don't think I can take care of myself?"

"It's a lot harder to hide than you think," he says.

My eyes flash with fire. "You think I don't *know* that? I've been hiding half my life."

"No, your *parents* were hiding you half your life. *My* mom was hiding you for half your life. Not you."

My mouth drops open. He has the *nerve* to question my life? Then I decide it's not worth the fight, so I clamp my mouth shut. I'm done with this conversation. I stomp into the cabin and grab a new backpack David found for me. I stuff in some of the clothes he got.

David follows me inside. "Lyra . . ."

"I'll pay you back for this stuff," I say. I don't know how; I still have no money nor any way of getting money and if David disappears into Canada, I can't exactly drop it off when I do get it, but I'll figure something out.

"I don't want you to pay me back. I want you to come with me." He comes up behind me, puts his hands on my shoulders and gently spins me around. His hands feel warm, firm, and against my better judgment, I let him turn me. He leans his face toward mine, slowly, hesitantly, as if he's giving me time to pull away, but I don't. I let him bring his lips to mine. I let him kiss me. And I kiss him back. My lips tingle and my stomach swoops and I press into him. He circles his arms around me, and pulls me close and I don't ever want him to stop.

When he does pull away, he keeps me locked in his embrace.

"Come with me," David repeats.

His body feels so warm, so strong, that I imagine for a moment what it would be like to stay with him, to be close to him all the time. I imagine him kissing me like that every day, and I imagine how good it would feel. But isn't that stupid? Thinking we could be happy like that all the time? Relationships don't work like that. Besides, we hardly know each other, so what would happen if he stopped liking me? I'd be stuck with him in Canada, dependent on him, on his family. Didn't my parents want me to be independent?

"Why did you come after me?" I ask. I've asked before; he said he owed me. I think there's more to it.

"I had to meet you," David says and a faint blush rises to his cheeks. "We talked about you all the time, Mama Jua and me. She told me everything about you. Your quiet life in Jamestown and your connection to Holly. And she told me—" here David pauses, his cheeks flushing "—that you were my soul mate."

My eyes fly up to his face as my own face reddens. She told me the same thing and I had just laughed. Was there even such a thing as a soul mate? I always hoped that someday I'd find a boyfriend, someone to love me, but I never actually expected it, not with my parents' strict no-talking-to-*anybody*-policy. It's kind of hard to a) meet somebody and b) form a relationship when you can't see them. I know. I tried with Jonah. And the result was that my parents dragged me off in the middle of the night without giving me the chance to say goodbye.

But my parents aren't here anymore. They can't make those decisions for me.

Only I can.

There's a glint in his eye, a sparkle. "Want to find out?" he asks.

Do I want to find out if this man is my soul mate? If I'm his? Is this for real? I want to say yes—I want to take a crazy risk and know that I won't ever be alone—but I can't drag him into my fucked up life. I haven't told him about my phoenix cells—Mama Jua obviously couldn't have told him *everything* about me—so he may not realize I'll always be hunted.

"I can't . . ." I pull away from David. I turn away.

"Because of Holly? Let's take her with us."

"What?" I face him again, almost laughing.

"Sure," he says, warming to his idea. "She's an orphan, right? The foster system broke down a long time ago, so she'll be stuck in that shelter for the rest of her childhood. Why put her through that when she can come with us? We'd be her family." He blushes—he has, after all, just proposed we become family to each other—then he pauses, as if struck by a scary thought. "You think she'd like me?"

I laugh. "Yes, yes, she'd love you."

"Great," he says. "Then it's all set. We go to Jamestown, spring Holly from the orphanage, and sneak across the border. Christian and Matteo will help us get settled."

"We can't just take a kid . . ." I object, but my tone sounds half-hearted. David . . . Holly . . . a family . . .

"Who's going to miss her? The government? The people who would kill her if they thought for even one moment she'd been in contact with a Hecate Plague victim?"

I think about the little boy in the park, the one Mama Jua sacrificed herself for. David is right. If Ahimsa hadn't covered up the sick kid as well as Mama Jua's illness and death, then all those kids in the shelter would have been sent to a quarantine camp. So really, we'd be saving Holly, because we could ensure she's never at risk like that again.

"Okay," I say, even though I know it's ridiculous. "Let's do it."

"Done!" David exclaims, grinning. He comes over, cups my cheeks in his hands and kisses me.

I'm terrified at what I have just agreed do, crushed by grief, but alongside those truths is this other one: I like when he kisses me.

## CHAPTER 13

Four days later, it's done. We slipped into Jamestown, spirited Holly away, and made our way to a farm not far from Jamestown where we're hunkered down in an old trailer on the back field. Now I'm waiting anxiously, nervously, uneasily for David to get back from seeing his mom.

To Holly, though, it's all a great adventure. She was apprehensive when we got her, afraid she'd get in trouble with Alexis, and I have to admit I hesitated, too. Alexis would be livid, but I knew David could smooth it over with her later, after Holly was safely in our hands. He'd tell Alexis that Holly was integral to a secret Ahimsa plan and he'd convince her that Mama Jua would have approved. So when I helped Holly pack her few meager possessions, I reassured her it would be all right. I promised her that everything would be okay. I knew she didn't believe me, not right away, but when she saw the trailer, she squealed. "It's like we're living in a dollhouse," she said.

"Don't get too used to it," I laughed, "because we've got much bigger places coming up."

"Palaces?" Holly asked, giggling.

"And castles," I replied.

Actually, I have no idea what accommodations we'll have in Canada. David doesn't know either. His brother has been scant on details, including when and where we should cross the border to meet him, but I guess it doesn't matter. Not when I'm defecting to another country with a child I am not related to accompanied by a guy I just met.

I step on the lower bunk to reach Holly and kiss her goodnight. She grabs the sides of my head, brings my face close to hers and wiggles her nose against mine. She giggles, and I try to laugh, too, but her nose is like ice. The nights are cold and the trailer has no heat.

"*Tisbah ala khayr*, Lyra," Holly says.

"Tisbah what? Is that a new secret code?" I ask. Holly loves them. She makes up strange phrases and ciphers all the time. She says she's going to be a spy when she grows up and I don't doubt she has the imagination for it.

"No, silly," she laughs. "It means 'good night.'"

"Oh! A secret code for good night!"

"No, it's a real language," she says, "It's called Arabic."

"How do you know Arabic?"

"David taught me. He says we're gonna mix up English and Arabic to make our own code."

Holly's eyes dance in the flickering candlelight, but I'm confused. David knows Arabic? Why didn't I know that? How much more don't I know about him? God, that's a stupid question. Of course, I don't know anything about him. We've only known each other for a week and it's not like I'm one to talk. I still haven't told him about my phoenix cells. I know I should—they kind of define my life—but I don't want to. I don't want them to define my life anymore. I don't want to be the phoenix-cell freak and I don't want David to see me that way. I just want to be Lyra.

"When's David coming back?" Holly asks. "I wanna tell him I got you," she says smiling.

"Yeah, you got me," I admit, and I'm happy she and David are getting along. I knew they'd like each other and it's nice I was right. "David will be back soon."

I hope I'm right. He's been gone a long time, and I don't like it. I didn't want him to go see his mother; it's too dangerous. The Conscription Service always watches the families of draft dodgers—if Mama Jua's funeral hadn't been secret, he wouldn't have been able to go—so it's not safe for him to risk a visit with his mom.

"I don't know when I'll see her again," David told me. "I have to say goodbye."

"But you said you weren't close to your mom, that she always ignored you for her Ahimsa work, so why would you risk everything to see her?"

"I can't leave things with her the way they are," he said.

I hear the last words I said to my parents echo in my head: *I'm done*. "Okay," I say, "Go."

But it's late and I'm worried now. David should have been back hours ago.

I crawl onto my bunk and I pull a sleeping bag up around my shoulders like a blanket. What should I do if he doesn't return? I don't know how to contact his mom, or his brother for that matter. And even if I could, why would his brother help Holly and me? He doesn't know us; he doesn't owe us anything.

*You are such an idiot, Lyra*. How did I let myself get so dependent on David? How did I think it was okay to let him make all the arrangements? To let him take charge? That's got to change, I vow. I've got to learn to be more self-sufficient.

The door creaks open and David slips inside, clicking off his flashlight.

I exhale, relieved.

"David!" Holly calls out and he crosses to her in a single step. He's like a giant in the trailer, hitting his head on the low ceiling. "I got Lyra! She didn't know 'tisbah ala khayr'."

David laughs. "Good for you, Kiddo."

"Teach me more," she begs.

"In the morning," David promises, still chuckling. "Good night, Holly." He blows out the candle and motions for me to follow him outside.

I do, but I keep my distance. I don't know why. I still feel jumpy about him being gone for so long. He shouldn't have made me worried, but I won't let him know how much I need him.

So instead, I pick another fight.

"How come you didn't tell me you speak Arabic?"

It's dark outside. The night air is cold and damp and holds the threat of rain. It's bleak and cloudy; there are no stars tonight, but in the murky shadows, I can see he's surprised.

"I don't know," he answers lightly. "It just never came up."

"You should have told me."

David's tone darkens. "Why?"

"Because—" But I don't have a "because." In fact, I can probably guess why he didn't. I assume he learned because of his Arabic father, the one he never knew. He probably wanted to feel connected to him somehow, and maybe admitting that to me would be too personal. Maybe he didn't feel like he could open up to me, confide in me. And maybe he couldn't do that because he doesn't trust me.

I cross my arms defiantly. So that's it. He doesn't trust me. Well then, I don't trust him, either.

"Maybe this isn't a good idea," I say, but I don't know what I mean. He and I aren't a good idea? Running away together isn't a good idea? Staying in the trailer isn't a good idea?

"*What* isn't a good idea?" David asks, slightly bewildered.

And before I know what I'm doing, I blurt out, "Why do you want to be with me if you don't even trust me?"

"Lyra, for God's sake, what are you talking about? The Arabic thing? You think I didn't tell you because I don't trust you?"

I know I'm being stupid, but I can't help it now. I double down on my anger. "Yes."

"You want to talk about trust, Lyra?" his voice is low and cold. Very cold. "You want to explain why you haven't yet told me about your phoenix cells?"

A long shiver snakes its way down my spine.

"Hendricks told me," David says.

I slouch onto the doorstep, defeated. There it is. The end of the line of my illusions about living a normal life. David now knows what a freak I am.

"Nothing made sense without that piece of the puzzle," David says. "I saw you get *shot*, Lyra," David reminds me. "I saw your arm was a mangled mess, yet the agents did nothing for you. *You* did nothing for you. You didn't even seem to notice. If it had been me, I would have been screaming that they take me to the hospital or at least give me first aid. It wasn't natural, Lyra, so I made George tell me why."

It wasn't natural.

It's not natural.

*I'm* not natural.

"So, you know everything, then?" I say, my voice deadened. "Why the agents are after me? What the scientists plan to do with me?"

"Yes."

My insides burn with betrayal, with shame, and with utter, profound dismay. All this time he didn't tell me he knew . . . All this time I thought I was just Lyra when all along I was the phoenix-cell freak. Is that why he's with me? Because I'm an anomaly? A circus-sideshow character who fascinates him?

"You didn't tell me," I say. My chest feels heavy, as if rocks are crushing the air out of my lungs.

"*I* didn't tell *you*?" David exclaims. "*You* didn't tell *me*!"

I leap up from the steps, angry at his anger. "I *couldn't*," I hiss. I walk away from the trailer, afraid of waking Holly.

David comes after me, but his demeanor softens. "Why, Lyra?" he asks quietly.

I whip around to face him. "Because I'm a *freak*, David! A freak who will live forever. If I told you, then you'd only see a freak." I drop my head, my voice shaking. "You wouldn't see me."

David gently lifts my chin, makes me meet his eyes. "Why do you think I'm here with you? Because you're immortal? Because you'll have a life long after I'm gone?"

I pull away from his hand, but I don't say anything.

"From the second Mama Jua told me about you, I wanted to meet you. *You*. Not your cells."

"Mama Jua didn't know about my cells."

"Exactly," he says. "And from the moment George told me about your cells, I *still* wanted to meet you. I came after you, didn't I?"

"Only to see action," I snap at him. "You told me you hate your mom's duck-and-cover resistance. You told me you wanted to *do* something. Well, I was that something, wasn't I? I was your damsel in distress, your excuse to take action, to rise up and fight."

David shifts uncomfortably, and I know I'm right. He didn't even know me when he barreled down to Washington. He just wanted to be an action hero.

"Does it matter?" David asks, coolly. "I still came."

"Because you felt sorry for me," I say, rounding on him.

"*No*, you idiot, because I love you!"

My eyes widen, my mouth drops open in shock.

"I've loved you from the first moment I saw you hiding behind the tree at Mama Jua's funeral. Love at first sight. My parents were right. It does exist."

David comes over to me and wraps me in a bear hug, just like he did in the cabin. And I let him, just like I did in the cabin. He feels so good, he feels so right, but I'm scared.

I'm scared it's too good to be true. I'm an angry, isolated girl, a freak of nature, a mutant, an aberration with no friends and no family.

I pull away from him and sit on the trailer steps. "I don't get to love," I say.

"Why not?" he asks.

I don't answer. I don't know how to answer.

"Please, Lyra, talk to me."

I have nothing more to lose, I realize, so I do talk. Slowly, hesitantly, softly, I talk about my life, family, my childhood before the plague. How much I missed my mom when she was deployed and how much we fought when she was home. I talk about getting sick, about being in the hospital, about getting better. About the medical tests, about Ivy dying. I talk about our life on the run, about all the towns we lived in and all the jobs my parents had and all the midnight moves we made. I talk about Jonah, about how we met on the trails in the forest, how we met secretly every day after that, and then how I just disappeared from his life. I talk about moving to Jamestown and meeting Mama Jua and volunteering at the orphanage and meeting Holly. I almost stop there, because I'm drained. Exhausted. Flayed. I don't think I can tell David any more, about my decision to defy my parents, which led to our capture, which led to Moto and the military lab.

But David urges me to continue, so I do, and to my surprise, with every sentence, every story, I feel lighter, freer, calmer. Is this what having a boyfriend is all about? Someone real, who knows the real me? It's scary, opening up to him. I'm pulling out my soul, laying it bare, and he can crush me with just one little laugh. But, like Jaz, he doesn't. All he does is listen intently as I tell him what they did to me in the lab that first day, how Hendricks came to get me out, our plans to retrieve Jaz's blood. He listens as I tell him about going into the quarantine camp and my fear about never coming out. He listens as I tell him about Norma, the friendly greeter who is most likely dead now, and Jaz and our destruction of the classrooms and dancing in the auditorium. I tell him how Jaz helped me escape and how Mo threw himself into a hail of bullets to give me a chance to escape.

"But I blew it," I conclude. "When I smashed the vial with Jaz's blood, I blew our whole mission and Mo's sacrifice."

David squeezes my hand. "She died, Lyra. Jaz died the day after you left."

I whip my head toward him, a rock in my heart. Why does everyone I love die? "How do you know?" I ask softly.

"My mom passed me the message from George."

I look at him, startled, but David senses my concern. "She doesn't know anything about you. She thinks I left you back on the run in Washington. She deals with a million secrets a day. She knows when she's not supposed to ask."

"So that's it, then. Our only shot at saving the world from the plague and I smashed it to smithereens."

"You know it's not on you. It's on Hendricks. *All* of it. There's nothing more you could have done."

I lean against his chest and let him hold me. We stay like that for a long while, even as the temperature drops. I'm cold, but I don't want to move. My eyes are heavy and they drift closed, but then I hear a rustle of grass off in the distance, and I snap them back open.

David hears it too. Awake, alert, we both bound to our feet, peering in the darkness. The rustling doesn't stop, and it sounds too heavy to be an animal. I scuttle to the end of the trailer, and peek around, toward the farmhouse far off by the road.

My heart lurches.

I see flashlights, four of them bobbing their way here. They're still a fair ways off, but they are distinctly moving closer.

"Agents," I whisper to David, and as soon as I say it, I know I'm right. Had it been the Ahimsa farmer coming to check on us—something that should never happen—there would have been only one beam of light.

As quietly as possible, we hurry inside the trailer. David wakes Holly and puts a finger to his lips. "We can't make a sound," he breathes into her ear. The trailer is dark, but in the ambient shadows, I can see the fear etched onto Holly's face. I want to sit her down and reassure her everything will be fine, but I can't. Because I don't know if that's true. Instead, I quickly gather up our packs and our sleeping bags. I feel around for anything else we might have left out—a stray sweatshirt or a can of soup—because they can't discover *any* evidence we were here or they'll scour every inch of ground for a one-hundred-mile radius. David helps Holly into her coat, then scoops her up and whisks her outside. Loaded down, I follow them, shutting the door behind me very carefully.

The trailer is between us and the agents. If we hurry, we can sprint across the field and jump down the steep embankment to the riverbank before they make it around to the door. I can hear them now. Their voices are still indistinct and I can't make out what they're saying, but they sound professional, determined. We run, crouching as low as we can. The inky, murky sky gives us some cover; I can barely see David and Holly a little ways ahead of me, so hopefully the agents won't spot us either. I clutch the packs and bags awkwardly, moving as quickly as I'm able, which isn't very fast at all. My steps are small and slow.

Behind me comes a shout. Instinctively, I turn and I catch the arc of a flashlight spread across the field. I dive to the ground. My pulse races and I hear the blood pounding in my ears. I don't dare stand up. I can't risk the light catching me, so I shimmy, snake-like on my elbows. I make slow progress, but I'm afraid to go faster. I have to stay flat.

I'm convinced that any second I'm going to get a bullet in the back, but I don't. Instead, I finally make it to the ridge of the embankment. I ease myself over and slide down the side. David rushes to me, and hurries me behind a copse of trees at the water's edge. Holly is there, shivering. I pull her to me, holding her close.

"It's okay, sweetie, we'll be okay," I tell her, but my breath comes out ragged and words come out wrong. How will we be okay? The agents almost found me—if they search carefully around here, they *will* find me. But how did they know where to look? No one knew I was here, not even David's mom. Then I realize it must have been the goddamn farmer whose land we're on.

But does it matter? The point is the agents are here. The agents will always be here. Even if I flee to Canada, the agents will be wherever I am. Eventually, they'll find me.

I will always be hunted. No matter what I do or where I go, there is no way out.

I am, and always will be, the prey.

# CHAPTER 14

"We're almost there," David says over his shoulder.

I reposition Holly on my back. She's too tired to keep her legs crossed around my waist, so I hook my arms under her knees. I feel her little hands slipping from around my throat, as her head bobs with sleep. "Hold on, sweetie," I say, but I don't know if she hears me. It's so late, past midnight for sure, and long past when a five-year-old should be tucked and snuggled in bed. I think of Holly's narrow cot in the shelter where she was sleeping last week when we snuck in and spirited her away in the dead of night, and I think of sleeping in the woods last night after we escaped the agents, and I think again about whether we did the right thing.

*Yes, of course we did*. I chastise myself. We saved Holly. We saved her from the plague.

"She's getting heavy, David," I whisper. "I don't know how much longer I can carry her." I wonder if I should have traded Holly for our three packs when David offered to take her but I couldn't let her go. I love the feel of her warm breath on my neck, her soft cheek next to mine.

"We're close," David tries to reassure me. He stops and peers into the darkness, his back to the road. We're standing on the gravel shoulder, ready to scramble into the ditch if we see headlights, but so far our luck has held and we haven't seen any cars. I guess nobody has much need to drive toward a boat launch on Lake Erie in the middle of a frigid April night.

I smell the lake air, the damp mist rising from the water just beyond the trees and I feel a surge of hope. We *are* almost there. David's plan is coming together. I was so relieved when he was able to contact his brother and move up our plans—I have to get out of this country *tonight*. So once David steals a boat from the marina around the corner, once we're on the water, we'll be home free. Almost. We still have to sneak into Canada on the other side of the lake, but David assures me it won't be hard.

"Matteo told me this was the best place to cross," David told me. "And at night there will be no patrols on the water."

But a prickle of fear ripples through me. What if there are border patrols on the lake? Or Canadian guards scouring the opposite shore? We're only an hour's drive from Buffalo—it's not like we're in the middle of nowhere.

"But how does he know for sure there won't be patrols?" I pressed him on Matteo's plan.

"He just does. He understands our predicament. He knows all about laying low."

Laying low. *I* know about laying low, and David and Matteo are nowhere near my league, despite David's Ahimsa experiences with his mom. That's because once David crosses into Canada, he's safe from the Conscription Service. Matteo told him that Canadian police don't really go after American draft dodgers. But my pursuers, on the other hand, will not let a pesky invisible line on a map stop them.

Yet then I just feel resigned. What choice do we have? Turn around and hand myself over to the murderous Hendricks and his mad scientists? Return Holly to the orphanage where she'll eke out a threadbare existence? Have David answer his call-up so he can go off to die in a war he despises?

My stomach churns with mixed feelings, and I wish they made dream catchers for emotions. If the Indigenous webs can catch evil spirits from entering a person's dream, why can't they stop bad feelings from seeping into your mind?

"This way," David says. He swings the thin beam of his flashlight onto an overgrown path and trudges onto the near-frozen ground. The wind picks up the closer we get to the lake; it's cold and bitter and I worry that Holly may not be warm enough. She's wearing her winter jacket, but it's thin and worn. It's probably third- or fourth-hand, donated by some do-gooder who felt it still had some life left in it. But is it enough to protect Holly? I'll have to get her a new coat when we get to Canada. David said his sort-of-dad will help us with money. But still I worry. What if he won't? David isn't Christian's biological son, after all—he's not even his stepson. Why would he pay for David, let alone Holly and me who are strangers to him?

I shake my head and try to refocus on the drop of hope I felt a few minutes ago. I've got David and I've got Holly and it doesn't matter what else happens. I wrap Holly's little legs tighter around my waist. I'm not alone anymore and we've got a plan. We can get our lives back.

*What lives?*

I almost let out a scream at the nagging voice in my head. *Go away!* I'm talking about our lives. David's and Holly's and mine.

*Your lives? On the run forever?*

If that's what it takes to stay safe.

I stop suddenly and shiver, as if I've been drenched in ice water. I recall my mom's words which she threw at me in answer to my asking that exact question the move before last, when I thought then about refusing to go: "If that's what it takes to keep you safe, Lyra, then that's what we have to do!" Mom screamed at me. I'd just come in from a secret date with

Jonah, my skin still flushed from kissing him, and I couldn't imagine never seeing him again. But I had capitulated, like I always did, and we skittered away in the night—this time, dragging my broken heart.

"We always have to keep moving, Lyra," Dad said. "You understand, right?"

Now David turns around. "Lyra, you ok?" he asks. I can barely see his dark skin in the thick, clouded night, but the whites of his eyes shine with worry.

"Yeah." I take in a sharp, deep breath and I try to smile. "Just getting tired."

He nods, no doubt uncertain whether to believe me, but he carries on nonetheless. In a few minutes, we emerge onto the edge of a tiny beach. We're in small cove, surrounded by winter-worn trees, bleak and leafless, but still secluded. David lifts Holly off my back and I sit heavily on the coarse sand, shivering again. It's as cold as snow. David cradles Holly, then eases her gently into my lap. She doesn't even stir.

"Can you grab Mama Jua's blanket?" I ask David. He obliges and I drape it over Holly. "You think she'll be warm enough on the water? We'll be in this wind for hours."

David presses his lips together, hesitating. "We'll be fine," he says.

I'm not convinced as I imagine being out on the lake in the glacial air and lashing wind and waves that could sink a schooner. "Maybe we should wait for a calmer night," I say.

David lets slip an exasperated huff, but he tries to hide it. "And go where in the meantime?" He kneels down behind me and pulls me into him. I lean back against his chest, soaking in his warmth. "We don't have a choice, Lyra," he reminds me softly.

"We never have a choice, do we?" I answer bitterly. It's all I ever wanted. I remember telling Mama Jua, "It's my life, it should be my choice!"

"Life is always about choice, isn't it?" she'd say. And

somehow I always felt like she was agreeing with me, even when her words contradicted mine.

"We will have a choice," David says, "when we get to Ontario."

*What choice*? My inner voice sneers, but I'm in no mood to listen. Instead, I stare out at the wall of black in front of me, sea and sky stitched together. The night, the lake, seem impenetrable. "You sure you can get us a good boat?" I ask.

David pecks my cheek then jumps to his feet. "You doubt me, I see," he says jovially. "Well, I will return with the finest vessel for m'lady and then you can call me Captain Jua!" he cries into the night as if we were alone in the world, and I laugh. It's why I need him. He understands me, and can still cheer me up. I wish Mama Jua had pressed harder to introduce us months ago when she first told me about her grandson. I wish *I* had pressed harder to make her. What would have happened to us if we had met last fall? Would I have still defied my parents to stay in Jamestown? Would David have defied his mom about dodging the draft so he could fight the government instead of hiding from it like Ahimsa does?

Funny how both David and I wanted to stop running—me from my parents' suffocating isolation, David from his mom's neglectful remoteness—and yet here we both are. Running, running, running . . .

*It's for the best,* I remind myself. It's what my parents wanted. A sharp stab of pain cleaves my head—the knife that splinters my mind every time I think of them, of what I did to them, but I force myself to remember them anyway. It's my penance. It's the least I can do. Suffer as they suffered. And how they suffered, all these years, to give me my freedom. How can I repay them by throwing it away?

And David, too, owes it to his mom. She's dedicated her life to helping others escape the government's clutches; he can't let her own son fall into its maw.

*And Holly? What does Holly owe?*

Shut up!

David leans down and kisses me, his lips soft and warm. "I won't be long," he says. "Then everything will be all right." He jogs down the beach and disappears into the night.

I put my fingers to my lips, feeling the lingering shadow of his kiss. I wish I could believe that everything will be all right, the way I believed it when David first suggested we run to Canada. But now I'm afraid. Last night was too close. The agents shouldn't have found us in the trailer, but they did. We were careful, and still they came. We can be careful for the rest of our lives and still they'll come. The border won't stop them, no matter what David says. It may stop David's pursuers, the military Conscription Service, which has thousands of other eighteen-year-olds to go after, but it won't stop the agents going after their one quarry. How long do I really think I can last on my own? A week? A month? A year? I don't have the skill or resources of my parents. And as much as I wish it were true, David doesn't either—and neither does his brother and sort-of father. Sooner or later, Holly and I will have to run again. Mom was right. It's my fate.

Holly stirs in my lap, stretches and opens her eyes. For a second, in the dim night, I see fear streak across her face and then she sees me. She wiggles into a sitting position, still on my lap. I wrap my arms around her, keeping her warm.

Keeping her safe.

"Where are we?" she asks. "Still on our adventure?"

"Yep."

"How much longer, Lyra?" She tilts her head back to see my face.

"How much longer, what, sweetie?"

"Till we go home."

Holly's question is like a punch in the gut. I feel winded, unable to breathe. It's my own little voice, exactly the same.

I don't know how to answer.

"Don't you like our adventure?" I squeak. I squeeze her tightly, as if to remind her I'm here, I'm all she needs.

I feel her head nod against my arm. I want to leave it at that because we're well on our way and David will return with the boat soon, so there's no turning back.

"What are you missing about home?" I find myself asking.

"Janna told me I could play with her doll," she says, then, almost apologetically, adds, "I wanna play with her doll." Holly drops her chin, like she's embarrassed about her secret desire.

My heart pinches with guilt, but then I quickly shake it off. I have an idea. I lift her off my lap and set her on her feet. She sways, still sleepy, and the wind buffets her, but she regains her balance. She's strong. She's a survivor. Even after losing both her parents, living in the orphanage, Mama Jua's death, she keeps standing and smiling. I remember what she said to me last week when I told her my mom and dad had also died. This little girl, this small, five-year-old child threw her thin arms around my neck, and whispered in my ear: "You don't have to be sad, Lyra. Heaven's a really nice place." I laughed and smiled because the certainty with which she said it, made me believe it.

"Come with me," I say, wrapping her mittened hand in mine. We leave our packs by the trees and walk across the cold, dark sand. The waves, unseen, lap at the shore with a strong, beating rhythm. It's a drumbeat, a heartbeat, that crescendos as we near the water.

I mean to tell Holly our plans, to play up our voyage across the lake, to tell her we'll be pirates, that we'll cry "arrghhh!" into the wind and hoist our skull and crossbones flag and pretend there's a parrot on board, who always squawks for crackers. I'll say the sea is ours to rule, that no one will stop us on our quest for buried treasure and I'll even draw her a treasure map, x marks the spot, and she'll love our game and our journey so much she'll forget about Janna's sad little rag doll.

Instead, Holly pulls up short. My momentum carries me another step before I feel the tug on my arm. "We're almost at the edge of the water," I say. "Come and see it. But we can't dig out our bathing suits just yet. It's a little too cold to swim." I smile, even though I know she can't see my face in the dark, but I think she'll laugh at my joke.

She doesn't. She grips my hand tighter and pulls me back, a little whimper escaping her lips. I kneel beside her, and wrap her in my arms. The poor girl is trembling. "It's okay, Holly. I know it's dark, but it's just a lake. David is getting us a boat and then we can become pirates and—"

"No," she says, shaking her head. The motion starts out slow, but builds to a violent shudder. She yanks herself out of my embrace and tears back toward the trees.

"Holly!" I shout after her, confused. What just happened? Holly's never acted like this before. She's always been up for fun and adventure. She's daring and bold and courageous—but this?

I find her huddled by the backpacks, her arms tucked in, her knees up to her chest. She's quivering and shaking and crying.

"Holly," I say gently. I put my hand on her shoulder but she jerks away. A flare of frustration fires up inside me. "What is it, sweetie?"

Holly says nothing; she just buries her face in her lap. I can hear her muffled gasps for breath, her squeaking sobs.

"Is it the water?" It's all I can think of—she's been so gung-ho on every part of our trip so far, even the long walks and cold nights in the trailer.

I see a little nod of her head and I feel immediately relieved. The water. Of course. Her dad was in the navy.

Maybe she got scared for him when he was away, just like I was terrified Mom would never come back. But now that I know that, I can explain it to Holly.

I scoot beside her, but not too close; I don't want to overwhelm her.

"I know it looks scary at night, but it's just a big lake. You've seen lakes before, right? It's just a bunch of water and we'll drive across it and we'll be safe in our boat. And you know what the good news is? If you don't like the boat ride, you don't have to go on another one ever again. Once we get to the other side, we're going to stay there."

Holly chokes out a sound, but I can't make out what she says.

"I didn't hear you, Holly."

A whimper: "Sea monsters."

Is that all? I laugh with relief. Her fear isn't about capsizing boats or sinking ships, like I thought. "Sea monsters aren't real, sweetie, so it's okay. "Come on, I'll show you. We'll go down and wait for David by the water. I'll prove to you that you'll be safe. I'll hold your hand the whole time."

Another violent shake.

"Holly . . ." I'm trying to be reasonable, trying to be understanding, but I feel a prick of irritation. I do my best to subdue it. "When David comes, we have to get on the boat. We can't stay on the beach."

Suddenly she flails herself off my lap and onto her feet. Her tear-streaked face, level with mine, is full of a fury I've never seen in her.

"*NOOOO!*" She screams at the top of her lungs. She punches me with her small fists then sprints up the path toward the road.

Shocked at her outburst, I spring up and run after her. "Holly!" I cry, but the path bends and I can't see her. David has the flashlight, so I'm stumbling in the dark. My heart pumps faster, my chest tightens. Where *is* she? Fear seeps through me, a fear so dark and profound I can barely breathe. *I can't lose her, I can't lose her, I can't lose her.*

I hear a yelp, a squeal, then a thud. I round the bend and there is Holly, splayed on the ground, her foot caught on a tree root. My chest fills with air, my body tingles with relief. Holly lets me pick her up, lets me cradle her. She's not hurt. No twisted ankles or broken bones, no cuts or bruises I can make out in this darkness. It was just a little tumble.

"Please no water," she whimpers. "Please no water."

I start to say, "We have to, we have no choice," but I stop, hearing the protest I made a thousand times: "It's my life, it should be my choice!"

And hearing Mama Jua saying, "Life is always about choice.

Do I have a choice? Does Holly? She didn't ask to be dragged into this mess. But then, neither did I. I didn't ask to be born with a genetic mutation. I didn't ask to be hunted down like a wild animal.

I can't escape it.

*But Holly can.*

Oh my God, that's true. Holly *can* escape this fate. She doesn't have to go on the run. She doesn't have to live with the fear of the enemy stalking her, the dread of the predators closing in on her. She doesn't have to live the paranoid, nomadic existence I grew up with.

Unless I make her.

Unless I make her live the life I hated.

The realization wallops me with the force of dynamite. My mind is blown apart. What am I *doing*? How can I do this to Holly? For my own selfish needs? So I don't have to be alone? What kind of surrogate sister am I, then? I imagine Ivy, if she'd lived, having to be dragged around from town to town with us, leaving friends and schools behind, all because of me.

She would have had the same isolated existence as me, not for her own sake, but for mine. We would have been together, we would have been each other's only friends, but at what cost to Ivy?

At what cost to Holly? Ivy may not have had a choice because of our parents, but I'm *not* Holly's parent. I'm not her family. I have no right to steal her away from the life she could have, the stability she needs—the risk of plague or not. The orphanage sucks, yes. She'll never have much, unless she's adopted—and who wouldn't want to adopt a cute, precocious kid like her?—but she will have three meals a day and clothes on her back and a chance to go to school if schools ever reopen. She'll have Alexis, who might be a stern director about running the orphanage, but is a caring matron about the orphans themselves. She'll have a chance.

She'll have a choice.

I shift Holly so she's holding onto my front, her arms around my neck. I stand and walk back toward our packs. Holly's grip tightens in fear as we move toward the water, but I squeeze her into a hug.

"No water, Holly," I say. "We won't go on the boat."

Instantly, her fingers relax. She huffs out a little puff of air, as if expelling a demon from her body.

We return to the trees, and I sit down, Holly still leaning against my chest. I smooth her damp hair off her face, and stroke her cheek the way Mama Jua used to with me.

*Life is always about choice.*

"How about we go home tomorrow?" I ask Holly. "Maybe Janna will let you play with her doll then."

## CHAPTER 15

I pace back and forth in front of the cluster of trees close to where Holly sleeps in the secluded cove, wrapped in Mama Jua's blanket, her head resting on my backpack. The night wind has died, but the cold air still prickles and I feel like it's February instead of April. I wrap my arms around myself trying to keep warm. Again I worry about David. Again he's been gone a long time. I hope he hasn't capsized; I hope he can manage the stolen boat on the waves.

But then I worry about what's going to happen when he does get here. I have to tell him I'm taking Holly back, but how? *Hey David, just wait here while I drop off Holly at the orphanage, which is a two hours' drive away—oh, except we don't have Mama Jua's car anymore—and then I'll skip back to the boat launch and we'll continue on our merry getaway?*

That's not going to work. And the more I think about it, the more I realize, with my heart cracking, there's only one thing that will work: I have to leave David. In my head, I run circles around every possible scenario. David comes with me back to Jamestown, then we start our escape over, as if Holly had never come. We return here, re-steal a boat and make it across the border. We'll contact Matteo and tell him we got delayed, and he'll reschedule our rendezvous, so no harm, no foul. Except the agents found us in the trailer last night. They're close. If we don't slip away now, they'll likely find us. It's a risk *I* have to take, because Holly is *my* responsibility, she's here because I insisted, but David doesn't have to take that risk. David can get in his newly-acquired boat, slip across the water and disappear, safe forever from the tentacles of the American military. I can't let him give up his life, his freedom because I made a colossally selfish mistake by bringing Holly.

The thought of leaving David crushes me. How is it possible to hurt so much over someone I met only a week ago? It doesn't feel like a week, though. It feels like a lifetime, like we've always been together, like we'll always be together. He's in my head all the time. I can't stop thinking about him when we're apart and I can't stop staring at him when we're together. Mama Jua said I'd know love in my lifetime. I never believed her, not with my freaky phoenix cells and the isolation that comes with them, but did she know? When she was joking (was she joking?) about setting me up with her grandson, did she *know* David would be the one?

It's bullshit what they say, I decide. That it's better to have loved and lost than to never have loved at all. It's killing me to know what I have to give up, to know what I'll be missing: David's strong embrace, his deep laugh, his cheerful optimism.

But I have to let him go.

I have to stop thinking of me, me, me. I thought of me and I got my parents killed. I thought of me and I kidnapped Holly. If I think of me now, I'll get David shipped off to war and get him killed. I can't live with myself if that happens.

I stop pacing and stare out into the dark night. The clouds have thinned, revealing a gossamer moon. I see no stars; I wish there were stars. *I wish I may, I wish I might, have the wish I wish tonight.*

But the world is not made up of wishes.

The world—my world—is made up of agents and plagues and phoenix cells and hard choices. I cannot escape it. I can't escape my fate.

How did I get this fate? Why did I get this bizarre genetic mutation? What was it about the combination of my parents' cells that created my own? And why didn't it happen to Ivy?

"*You were just born this way*," was Mom's usual, unhelpful reply.

But *why*?

Then I think about all those cells of mine in Moto's lab and all the years of research his scientists have done on them. Have they figured out why I am the way I am? Do they have the answers I want?

The answers my parents never had, the answers my parents never wanted. "What does it matter, honey?" Dad asked every time I asked. "It's who you are now that matters."

Is it? Who am I? A physicist? A singer? Am I a leader? A follower? A loner? What do I like? Running? But am I a runner because that's who I am or because I've never had another option? I liked volleyball when I was twelve and still allowed to go to school. I liked playing with the other girls and chatting with them on the bench. I remember cheering each other on at tryouts and shouting and clapping when one of us spiked the ball over the net. Would I have been good? Or would I have given up sports for drama? Would I have auditioned for my high school musical and taken to the stage like Jaz and I did in the quarantine camp?

I feel overwhelmed, suddenly, with all the might-have-beens, and I'm reminded of a boy, Eric, who was in my class the year I got sick. He has autism spectrum disorder (had? Did he die of the plague?), although I didn't really know what that meant at the time. I remember what he'd told me after he'd gotten my friend Chloe and me in trouble one day for saying that we'd rifled through the teacher's desk to retrieve Chloe's confiscated pack of gum.

"Why'd you rat us out?" I screamed at him in the play yard after school. "You said you wouldn't tell!"

"But Miss Bunston asked me if I knew who did it," he answered, and only now, in my memory, can I see his quizzical expression. He truly had no idea why I was angry.

"That's when you *lie*!" I shouted back.

"I can't lie," he responded evenly.

"Everyone can lie," I snapped, heatedly, still seething over a week's worth of recess detentions.

"No," he said. "I can't."

"That's stupid," I sneered and I turned to walk away. But his next words struck me, stuck with me.

"It hurts my brain too much to lie. I can't keep track of everything that could have happened if I lied."

I didn't say anything, but Eric continued. "What if Miss Bunston had asked if I knew where you and Chloe were? I could have said you were on the play structure or in the sand pit or on the swings or on the hill or maybe you were playing tag or chasing Andrew and— "

He stopped, and though I didn't understand what he meant when I was eight, I feel like I get it now. The possibilities of "what-ifs" are too overwhelming. What if I'd had the talent to become an architect, or an accountant like my dad? What if I'd had the skill to become a doctor? *What if? What if? What if?* Like Eric said, it hurts too much to think about. The truth—reality—on the other hand, is simple. For Eric, only one true thing happened: Chloe and me breaking into the teacher's desk. That's all Eric had to keep in his head. For me, only one reality exists: my phoenix cells. That's all I have to focus on.

And then it hits me like a bolt out of the blue.

What if my choice in life isn't whether I live a normal life or not, but *how* I live my phoenix-cell life?

The revelation staggers me and I stumble to sit on a fallen log, my head swirling. *What am I saying?* I choose a life on the run and learn to like it or I choose a life in the lab and learn to live with it? How is *that* a choice?

But then a vague notion starts to form in my head, and I feel like an answer, a solution drifts at the edge of my consciousness, a wisp of an idea, but real, its contours slowly forming.

I try to force it into focus—and surprisingly, I think back to something David told me about Hendricks, about how he'd been kicked out of Ahimsa because, desperate for a cure for the plague, he started hounding my parents to let him use me and my cells. He became so obsessed with the idea that my body might be the key to the cure that David says he tried to bring us in a few times—until Emmanuelle, David's mom, shut him out the group as a way to protect us. "Making a deal with Hendricks is making a deal with the devil," my parents would have said. The potential reward of a cure was not worth the risk of Dr. Moto or some other psychopath getting his hands on me. My parents feared that if they gave me up for the greater good of a cure, they'd lose me to the base evils of greed and power. They feared if I went in, I'd never come out—cure or no cure.

But what if it wasn't their choice to make?

What if it's *mine*?

What if—am I actually thinking this?—after I return Holly, I turn myself over to Hendricks and he can use my body to find a cure for Hecate's Plague? What if that's my purpose? I won't become a neurosurgeon—or a concert pianist or cab driver or plumber—but maybe I can become . . . what? What would I be, other than a vessel?

*Valuable.*

I would be valuable.

I *am* valuable. The military has been telling me that for the nine years they've chased me across the country.

So maybe now *I* choose how I'm valuable. Maybe I choose how my cells are used.

I'm not stupid, though. I know I can't just waltz into the lab and dictate to Moto or Hendricks how they'll use my cells. I saw how heartless they are; once they have me, they'll use me anyway they want, super soldiers and all.

Unless I can work out a deal: they can have me for their nefarious tests—*if* they use my cells to find a cure for the plague first. They would most likely promise and then renege, but maybe a cure for the plague that could save hundreds of thousands of lives is worth the risk.

I feel a jolt of excitement, adrenaline, and sheer terror course through me. I think of my two possible life paths, the one I was leading and the one my parents were keeping me from. Path A: I stay on the run, hopping from town to town, isolated, alone, an ephemeral ghost on the fringes of society, unable to pursue an education, a career, a *purpose*. I would be free, but at what price? A drifting, meaningless existence. Or Path B, where I hand myself over on the condition that Dr. Hendricks uses my cells first. Moto said the scientists can go only so far working with cells in a petri dish—that's why they need me there—and maybe that's why Hendricks hasn't yet succeeded. But if he studies my cells *in* my body, maybe he'll find a solution. It's a long shot, I know; it's why he had me retrieve Jaz's blood with the potential antibodies rather than waste time experimenting on me.

But what if?

These new, heady possibilities make me dizzy.

Am I *actually* thinking about turning myself over the Hendricks, the man who *killed* my parents?

My hands start to shake and I press them together, trying to stop the tremors.

What do I have to lose? Not Ivy, Mama Jua or my parents, anymore. Not Holly or David because whether I run or surrender, I'll never see them again.

So what do I have to gain?

When the answer comes to me, suddenly my decision seems easy.

Hope.

For the first time in my life, I feel a tiny flicker of hope for my future. Hope that maybe I can help cure the plague. Hope that maybe there's a reason I am the way I am. Hope that maybe I'm not a freak of nature, but a force of nature.

Hope.

I sit with the strange new feeling, anxiously guarding it like a candle in the wind, terrified that a stray thought or a rogue emotion will snuff it out. I'm scared, I'm petrified about what I'm choosing because there's no coming back from this.

But then I laugh, a cackle, really, because I think of how badly I wanted to make my own choices, and now that I can, I'm beyond frightened.

I hear the ripple of water, the soft growl of an engine.

David.

My stomach churns; I want to throw up, I'm so nervous. I walk to the water's edge and I see the silhouette of a small powerboat veer toward the boat launch. Expertly, David docks the boat and cuts the engine. In swift, fluid movements, he ties it up, hops out and jogs over to me. The moon is brighter now so I see his warm eyes, his triumphant smile.

"The sucker left his keys in the glove box," David says, his voice low but cheerful. "Obviously didn't think someone would steal a boat in the middle of April, the fool."

I open my mouth to say the words I've planned. "I'm not going. Holly's not going. You have to go on alone. I'll miss you. I lo—"

But I can't do it. I can't say it. Any of it. I'm paralyzed.

I see his face, his forehead creased with worry. "Lyra, what is it?" he asks. "Is Holly okay?" He swivels toward the copse of trees, but I put up my hand. It seems I can move.

"She's fine—well, no, not really, I mean, yes, she's okay, but she's afraid of water and—" I cringe. It's all coming out a garbled mess. How do I do this?

David cups his palm to my cheek and I lean into his warm hand. I'm shaking now, because as soon as I say it—"I'm leaving"—it'll be real, and now I'm not sure if it's a good idea. It sounded so reasonable in my head, the hope and greater good and finding my purpose, my answers, and all, but the reality is that I'll be locked up in that windowless basement room, imprisoned as a lab rat forever, hundreds of miles from Holly, a whole continent away from David. What was I *thinking*? No, the better option is to scoop up Holly, pray she stays asleep, climb onto the boat with David and sail off into the sunrise. It'll be that easy. A few steps to get Holly, a few steps to the water and we're home free. And Holly will be okay. She's a kid; she'll adjust. I'll buy her a rag doll like Janna's and then she'll be fine. She'll love our adventure.

*Like you did?*

My heart sinks because I know I'm fooling myself. I can't take Holly to Canada with David and me, and I can't risk David returning to Jamestown with Holly and me.

I pull away from David. I can't look at him. Instead I stare at the water, into the black void that will soon mirror my life.

"I can't go," I tell him.

"Go?" David asks, and I wish suddenly that he could read my mind. I wish he were in my head right now so I wouldn't have to explain.

I take a deep breath.

"I can't ruin Holly's life," I finally say. "I can't do to her what my parents did to me."

David puts his hands on my shoulder and I wince at his touch because I'm melting, melting, melting. I want to go with him, I want him to stay, I want him . . .

He gently spins me around and lifts my chin so I have to look into his dark chocolate eyes. I see worry, confusion, concern.

"Your parents kept you *safe*," he says. "That's what you're doing for Holly."

"No, David, you know I'm not. Holly was safe at the orphanage. She didn't need to be dragged into my fucked-up life."

"It's *not* fucked up," David replies vehemently. He squeezes my shoulders, as if he can press common sense into me.

"Fine, *I* am, then," I say, suddenly weary. I haven't even gotten to my message, my trifecta of conclusions—Holly goes back to the orphanage, David sails on to Canada and I become a human guinea pig—and I'm already weak.

"*You* are not fucked up." David is insistent, defiant. "What everyone *did* to you was fucked up, but that's not you."

"David, I'm a *freak*! A mutant, an aberration! You think it's normal to heal instantly from gunshot wounds and deadly plagues? You think it's natural to live forever?"

"You're not your phoenix cells, Lyra," David challenges.

"The government thinks so," I retort. "It's why they've been after me for more than half my life. And my parents thought so, too. It's why they kept me isolated and on the run all those years. It's all because I have phoenix cells. It's all because I *am* a collection of phoenix cells."

"No, you're more than that," David insists. "You don't have to let your phoenix cells define you."

I shake my head sadly. "Yes I do," I say. "That's what I realized when you were getting the boat. Don't you see? I can't keep pretending I'm normal. I am who I am. I can't outrun my fate."

"You *think* you're who they say you are, but they don't get to choose," David counters. "*You* get to choose who you are."

"Exactly. It's *my* choice."

I take a breath. I hold it in. I exhale. I look David in the eyes. "And I choose to turn myself over to Hendricks."

"*What?*" David's screech echoes across the water, and I try to shush him, afraid somebody might hear. "After everything we've been through? You're going to, what, just throw in the towel?"

"I'm not giving up," I say, but I sound meek even to my ears. "It's just . . ." How to explain?

"Tell me," David says, his tone dripping with sarcasm, "how is you turning yourself over to those monsters *not* giving up?" Before I can answer, before I can defend myself, he continues. "God, Lyra, your parents hid you for nine years, they *died* for you, and now you're going to throw away their sacrifice?"

His accusation slices through my soul. I want to slap him, punch him, kick him, *hurt* him, like he's hurting me.

*Is he right?*

"Goddamn you, David," I seethe. "Are you purposely trying to make it easier for me to leave you?"

"That's what it's about, then, isn't it?" he growls. "You want to leave me. You don't want a quiet, anonymous life."

"*You* don't want to live a quiet, anonymous life!" I yell, forgetting to be quiet, going on the attack. "*You* don't want to hide for the rest of your life. You want to go and fight!"

"I want to fight the government, not their bloody war, Lyra," David snaps.

"Exactly," I say, crowing. "You want to fight. You're a man of action. It's why you came after me in the first place. Ahimsa didn't have to warn me about Hendricks; there was nothing in it for the group, yet you went out of your way, you risked your life outside the quarantine camp to find me. You told me yourself you're sick of your mom's conceal-don't-feel philosophy when it comes to resisting the government."

"Don't you dare bring my mother into this," David says through gritted teeth.

"No? Why not?" I'm on a roll now. A dangerous, spiteful roll, but I can't stop myself. "Why can't I talk about your mother who all but abandoned you for her cause? Who suppressed your every desire to *fight* the injustice, not just run from it."

My poisoned arrow hits its mark and I see the wound, the hurt in David's eyes, but still I continue. All my anger, all my hatred, my frustrations, my pain, my agony spill out. "Is this what you've become, David? A shadow in the night? A coward?"

The word isn't even out of my mouth before I want to suck it back in. I've gone too far. *I'm sorry,* I want to cry. *I didn't mean it. You're the bravest man I know.* But I can't. My lips are glued shut, my vocal chords stripped away. The accusation hangs in the air between us, the guillotine that will, any moment, cleave us, our relationship, in two.

I sink to the ground, burying my head in my knees. How could I have twisted David's innermost fear, the one he confided in me as a sign of his trust, as a blade against him? My insides shrink into a knot of pain; I am frozen.

I hear David stomp away and I know I deserve it, I asked for it, but I can't bear to think this is how it will end—how we will end. Hot tempers, bitter recriminations and hurt.

"I love you, Lyra," he murmurs. "I thought you loved me."

My head flies up and I see that David hasn't gone far; he hasn't stormed off. Instead, he's settled himself on the cold sand, his elbows propped onto his knees, his back to me, staring at the black water.

Love. My heart constricts in pain. It hurts to think he's gotten me all wrong, that he thinks I don't love him. When I speak, my voice is soft, quiet, broken. "I love you more than you can understand." And I realize it's the first time I've told him that.

David suddenly scrambles to me and wraps his arms around me and I collapse against his chest, thinking, *This is what I want.*

"Then stay with me," David insists. "It's what Mama Jua would want."

I think of Mama Jua and her funeral, of watching David lower his grandmother's casket into the ground and I think of how she did, in the end, bring us together. We sit like that for a long while, his arms wrapped tightly around me, my hands entwined in his. We don't talk, and our silence is magic, like we've suspended time. There is no future, there is no past. There is only us, the two of us, alone together.

Even still, even as I'm cocooned where I want to be, worry seeps in. It's like Christmas morning, I think, the ones I remember as a child, when Ivy and I would rush to our stockings, squealing with delight. Yet even before I tore into the first present, I remember feeling sad, knowing that a few rips of the wrapping paper and it would be all over. This moment was what I'd been desperately, impatiently, excitedly waiting for—it was finally here!—yet I couldn't enjoy it because I knew the moment would, *poof!*, disappear too soon. And I was always right. And the disappointment always hurt.

David finally speaks and when he does, he breaks the spell. Time restarts; the real world intrudes. "You're right about Holly," he concedes. "We shouldn't have brought her with us. So let's take her back and then we'll decide what to do, okay?"

I press my eyes closed as a wave of dismay washes over me. He doesn't understand.

"I can't risk you getting caught," I tell him.

"Well, it's a good thing it's not up to you, then, is it?"

I hear the smile in his voice, and a wave of irritation washes over me. Stiffening, I detangle myself from his arms and turn to face him. His eyes dance in the moonlight like we're playing a game and I huff in frustration. This is so not a game. "David, one of two things will happen if you come back to Jamestown with Holly and me," I say. I hear the distance in my own voice. It's crisp and cold and I wonder how I could change gears so quickly. A moment ago I was murmuring soft, heartfelt declarations of love. Now, to the very same person, I'm icily chastising him.

"Number one: the agents catch us before we reach the orphanage, they return Holly, send you off to boot camp and hand me over to the mad scientists. Number two: we evade the agents, return Holly, I turn myself in, you miss your chance to slip across the border and wind up in boot camp."

"We don't have to go to Canada," David says.

God, he just won't give up.

"We'll disappear in America," he says. "My mom will help."

"Your mom *can't* help, anymore," I want to shake him, hard, to shake sense into him. "The military will be watching her, waiting for her to contact you. You were lucky you didn't get caught yesterday when you saw her. We can't risk that again, so we can't use her connections the way my parents did, and we can't survive on our own." I grip his hand, squeezing it hard. "Don't you see, David? We can't run. *I* can't run anymore, and you won't have to. Once you get to Canada, you'll be fine."

David flings off my hand, his own anger rising up to meet mine, as he jumps to his feet. "I won't be fine!" he says. "I won't be fine knowing you'll be chopped up and reassembled. I won't be fine knowing I could have protected you and I didn't."

"Protect me?" I snap at him, my heart racing, my anger, the lava beast, reawakening, roiling inside. I stand up to confront him. "You can't protect me. My parents tried for nine years and look what happened to them. You think you can do better? Cut me off from the world, leave me languishing? For how long, David? How long do I live in suspended animation while you protect me? And what happens when you die and I'm left all alone? You get to become the knight in shining armor, but what about *me*? What do *I* get?"

"Me!" David shouts, fighting back. "You get me, for as long as I live. It's all I can give you, Lyra. *My life* is all I have. Isn't that enough?"

His question slams into me with the force of a tank. *Isn't he enough?* Put aside the fact that we've just met, forget that we're still teens and most people don't end up with their first love, assume we *will* be together for the rest of David's life, *isn't that enough?* Isn't his love, his devotion, his commitment enough?

*No.*

The voice in my head.

It won't be enough. I had my parents' love and devotion and commitment and it wasn't enough. I felt trapped and isolated and—

I try to think of the right word.

Useless. I felt useless.

My parents had a purpose. Their life's mission was trying to keep me safe, and David will have a purpose, trying to do the same. But I would still have nothing. I would still *be* nothing. I would still *offer* nothing.

But how do I explain to David that I'm not rejecting *him*?

I can't.

Because I am rejecting David. I can't have David and a purpose and answers to my questions about my phoenix cells.

"Life is always about choice," Mama Jua said.

I have to choose: David or me?

The silence between us widens, deepens, darkens, and the silence tells David what I can't.

"You're choosing Hendricks over me," he says flatly. I can't look at his face, at his pain. My insides scream at what I'm doing to him, what I'm doing to me.

"No," I say, and try to keep my voice steady. "I'm choosing people like your grandmother and my parents and my sister. People like the ones your mom tries to help, people dying of the plague, people being treated no better than livestock by their own government."

"It won't work," David says bitterly. "You said Hendricks tried before and failed."

"Nine years ago," I counter. "Science and technology have come a long way since then—and now he'll have *me*."

"You're risking your life for nothing," he says, and I hear what he means. *You're rejecting me for nothing.*

"Not for nothing," I say, almost pleading now. "For a chance, a shot at making life better. Don't you think it's worth it if I can save even one person?"

David glares at me, his eyes full of fire, of fury. "For every person you 'save'," he snarls, long and low, "you'll kill me ten times over."

His words are an explosion in my chest. The shrapnel tears through my body, lodging in my skin, my muscles, my bones. I feel my heart shatter and splinter, then disintegrate. There is nothing left. Inside, I am hollow.

I turn, my movements robotic, and walk toward Holly, still asleep under the trees. I shake her awake and ease her gently to her feet.

"Let's go home, sweetie."

I pick up her pack and mine, grasp her little hand in mine, and turn toward the road.

Still sleepy, Holly looks up at me. "What about David?"

"David can't come with us," I say. "He has to finish his adventure."

"On the pirate ship?"

I picture David wearing a black eye patch and a peg leg, cruising across the lake in an old wooden boat with black sails, a wicked grin on his face.

"On the pirate ship."

"Will he look for buried treasure?"

"Most definitely."

"Will he show it to me when he comes back?"

The smoldering ruins of my heart flare up in pain. I can't tell her he's never coming back.

"Most definitely."

Satisfied, Holly drops my hand and skips ahead, singing a made-up song about Janna's little rag doll. I think of the distance we have to go and I think of where I'll end up.

*Come after me!* I cry to David inside my head. *Come with me!* I want him to stop me, I want him to support me. I want him to run and be safe, I want him to stay and be strong.

*I want, I want, I want.*

Behind me I hear only the sounds of the waves lapping at the little beach and the chug of a motor.

For the first time in my life, I've made my choice.

I take a deep breath and don't look back.

# CHAPTER 16

I'm riding shotgun in the cab of a transport trailer, hitchhiking to DC, and I've been trying to understand my luck.

What luck? I'll never see David again. No, wait, not true. I will see him again. And again and again and again, over and over and over. I'll see in my mind's eye his final, hurt expression, the one on his face when I turned my back on him by the lake. Long after David has moved on from me, long after he's found another girlfriend, a wife, someone with whom he can have a real future, I will continue to be haunted by the lasting image of his anger and his hurt.

Stupid, fucking love.

And I'll never see Holly again. All I'll see of her forever is the back of her head, her blond hair a halo in the harsh light outside the orphanage's door as I shooed her back inside after our long walk from the lake. I wished I'd stopped her, pulled her to me for one last hug, to feel her warm little arms circle my neck, but I knew I had to let her go back to her real life, the life she's destined for, the one without me. I know she doesn't understand that I'm actually never coming back, that she'll soon feel abandoned—or maybe she won't. She's only five. Maybe she'll think I was part of a dream, or a vague memory, or maybe she won't even think of me at all. If I strain my own memory, I can barely remember anything before I was five, so maybe that will be the same for her. Maybe *that's* my luck: To not have Holly remember me, to not have Holly feel abandoned by me.

But that's not my luck. My luck is not as lucky as that. My luck, I think, as I sit, weary and exhausted, leaning against the door of a rattling truck driving further and further away from everyone I've ever loved, is that I simply haven't been picked up by agents yet.

I expected them to be guarding the orphanage; they'd been swarming around Jamestown for days and they almost caught us last night, so I don't know why they weren't outside the shelter. I don't know how I was able to get Holly back inside without being seen. Or how I was able to sneak away from town, plod along the highway, stick my thumb out at all of the passing vehicles, and finally get a lift from a kindly trucker named Frank, who asked no questions about why a teen girl was hitchhiking to Washington in the dead of night.

That's my kind of luck. Not true-love, fairy-tale, shiny-happy-people kind of endings. My luck is simply being able to turn myself over to the research scientists on my own terms.

Yay for me.

When Frank asked me where I was going, and I said DC, he said he'd take me there. It was hours out of his way, but he said he'd go.

"Why?" I asked.

"No one chooses to be out here hitchhiking alone at three in the morning in the middle of April unless they have good reason," he explained. "I got a daughter, not much older'n you. If she was out here instead of you, I'd want somebody to look out for her." He didn't seem to care that I could be a mass murderer, someone infected with the plague or a runaway with federal agents bearing down on her, and I remember what Norma had told us when she greeted newcomers at the quarantine camp. "People are good and decent."

I wonder if she meant people like Frank.

He tells me to rest. "Close your eyes, honey, get some sleep."

I shouldn't, I know. I've got to stay awake, alert. Frank may seem nice so far, but it could be all part of his plan to catch me off guard and attack me. Or maybe there are agents lurking at a rest stop ahead, ready to pounce.

But then I realize I don't care. I don't care if the agents are following me or if they're about to pull over Frank's truck and nab me and drag me back to the basement lab. I'm going there anyway, so what difference does it make in the end how I get there?

To my surprise, the thought is incredibly liberating. I feel free, suddenly, like a weight is gone, like the heavy millstone that's been around my neck for nine years has been lifted. I don't have to run anymore. I don't have to hide. I know it will be short lived, this freedom, that I'll have it only as long as it takes me to find Hendricks, but for the moment, I savor it. It's like the sweet tang of a lollipop lick. The taste stays on your tongue for only a second, but man, is that second a good one. I wonder if this is what I felt like as a kid, before the first outbreak. Free to go anywhere and do anything, be anyone—including myself... God, I love the feeling. I love the relief and reprieve and respite I feel from my constant blanket of dread. I love that I'm calm, that I'm relaxed. And I love that I drift off to sleep without once worrying about what will happen while I am asleep.

When I wake up, the sky is a pastel of pink and purple and orange, an artist's painting. I look at Frank, still driving, and note that nothing happened while I slept. I look out the windshield and remember a story my mom told me when I was a kid, about how fairies paint the morning sky.

"You can tell what mood they're in by the colors they choose," Mom said.

They must be in a good mood this morning, I think, since the sky is glowing.

"Good morning," Frank says. He's a big, hefty man with a hangdog face, days-old stubble and flyaway gray hair, but his voice is gentle. "We're not too far from Washington, so you let me know soon where you want me to drop you off, okay?"

I frown. I hadn't thought of that. I mean, I thought about where I'll be going, eventually—the basement prison—but I can't exactly have a transport trailer pull up outside the military complex and risk Frank getting embroiled in my troubles. Besides, I need to get to Hendricks first, to make sure he convinces Moto to take my deal, I should have Frank drop me off at Hendricks's house.

Where he admitted to killing my parents.

*No.* I can't think of what Hendricks did—only what he may be able to do. If I'm going to see whether my phoenix cells can help save the world, then I have to put aside the fact that Hendricks destroyed my life.

"You got family in DC?" Frank asks, but then he leaves me no time to answer, "Nah, sorry, shouldn't have asked. Don't mean to pry. I always tell myself not to ask questions when I pick up people—hey don't tell my boss, eh? I'm not s'pposed to offer rides, but how c'n I pass by when I see people like you who need a lift? That damn Hecate took my wife and son an' if I'd been home, it woulda taken me, too. I almost feel like I owe it to the road, to the people on the road, to help 'em out."

I scowl, angry again at this fucking plague. I've had it, hearing about all these people dying. "That sucks about your family," I say, instead of "I'm sorry" because what good does that do anyone?

Frank chuckles. "Ain't that the truth, honey. It sucks big time." He smiles like the two of us are sharing an inside joke. "But my daughter, she was with her grandparents in New York; she's still safe, thank the Lord."

The daughter who's about my age. I feel jealous of her that she still has a dad, and that makes me think about mine, and how much I miss him. I wish it were him sitting next to me, even if it meant we were slinking off to a new town.

"Hecate killed my parents, too," I say softly. I hadn't meant to tell Frank anything about me, but he makes me feel comfortable, at ease, like Mama Jua used to do.

"Ah, shit, I'm— " Frank pauses, then flicks his eyes to me. "That sucks."

I smile. "Yeah."

"Please tell me, honey, that you have family in DC?"

I know he wants me to say yes, to know I'll be looked after, so I tell him what he wants to hear. "Yes, I'm going to see my— " I'm about to lie, to say, I don't know, my cousin or something, when I'm struck with a thought: Family. I do have family in Washington. "I'm going to see my sister," I say.

I'm going to see Ivy.

Before I give myself up, I'm going to see my sister's grave. I can go for real, and not pretend someone else's grave is hers. I can go because I'm finally free for the first time since she died. Mom always said it was better I hadn't gone to Ivy's funeral, but I always felt like she meant *she* wished she hadn't gone. And maybe she was right. Maybe if I'd had to bury a daughter, I wouldn't be able to face it, either, but now is my chance. Before I give up my life on the run, I can say goodbye to the life I had before.

An hour later, the sun fully risen, Frank drops me off near a wooded park close to the Potomac River.

"You sure you can get to your sister's from here?" Frank asks, as I hop out. I feel a little bad, misleading him to believe my sister is a grown-up, responsible adult who can take care of me, but when I see the cemetery in the distance, I simply nod. "You take care, honey," he says. "Be safe."

"Thanks, Frank." I'm about to close the door, but then I stop. "I hope you see your daughter soon."

Frank smiles warmly. I shut the door and watch him rumble away—a good and decent person.

I remember where the cemetery is because we went there a bunch of times when I was little. I remember running around the plush green lawn, laughing and giggling and playing tag with Ivy while Mom and Dad stood mournfully in front of Dad's parents' graves. Since they died before I was born, I never thought of them as grandparents and therefore I never thought of the cemetery as a sad place. If anything, Ivy and I had the best fun, skipping around the tombstones, playing hide-and-seek and follow-the-leader among the angels.

I don't feel sad now, either, when I walk through the unlocked wrought-iron gate. On the contrary, I actually laugh. Here I am, in the bright light of day, not a stone's throw from the enemy's lair and I'm standing, explicitly, defiantly out in the open.

"*Come and get me, you assholes,*" I shout in my head. "*You can't scare me anymore.*"

I assume Ivy's grave is near my grandparents' so I strain my memory, trying to retrace in my mind where they're buried, where Ivy and I played. It takes me longer than I expected to find the tombstones, either because my memory is failing or the cemetery has changed. It does seem fuller—more graves, newer headstones—and I wonder how many of these new occupants arrived courtesy of Hecate's Plague.

*There*, I suddenly think, scanning a grassy knoll near an ancient oak tree. *On the other side, that's where they are.*

I slow my pace, my stomach clenching, my head buzzing, my skin tingling and I feel like I've been electrified. I'm a little surprised I'm so nervous about approaching Ivy's grave. It's not like I brooded over my inability to visit all these years. My parents did, but I never thought staring at a marble slab with my sister's name carved into it would give me peace. Now I wonder if it might. Isn't that why I came? To find closure?

I startle at the caw of a crow, and I'm suddenly reminded of Mama Jua's funeral, the first one I'd ever been to. Did I get closure then? Had I been able to let go, to say goodbye? Hardly, but this time, I feel like something's changed. I try to put my finger on it. Is it because Ivy's been dead for so long, or that my parents are now with her? Is it because I'm here alone? Because of what I'm about to do?

I find myself approaching slowly, reverently, like I'm gliding down the aisle of a church but I have to stop. It feels all wrong, walking solemnly toward Ivy's grave, like she was a priest or a cardinal or a saint. It's *Ivy*, the girl I chased around the tombstones, the kid I toppled off the hill to become the king of the castle, the sister I played with and fought with. How can I act as if she's this untouchable, sacred figure?

Because, I realize with a start, that's what she's been all these years. We—my mom, my dad, me—we beatified her as an angel, a paragon of virtue, a poor innocent soul, unblemished by human frailties. She rose, in my mind, to a stature I could never attain: unchanging perfection.

No wonder I could never compete. How could I, against the memory of a child who could never do anything wrong? Ivy never yelled at Mom and Dad, or stormed out of our house, or defied them when they insisted we had to pack up and leave immediately, or caused their death. Ivy never caused them trouble or frustration or fear of any kind. She remained a perfect, innocent child of six, cruelly taken away by an accident of fate.

But she wasn't perfect and innocent. She was a screamer, a crier, a thrower of temper tantrums beyond compare. I remember how she'd shriek in the middle of the mall, flop down, writhing on the floor when Mom refused to buy her something she desperately wanted. One time it was a little princess crown. Another, a red bouncy ball. It drove Mom nuts because nothing she did or said could calm Ivy. Not even giving in. I remember she conceded, one shopping trip, to buy Ivy a stuffed bunny rabbit and Mom said she couldn't face another meltdown, so Mom marched back into the toy store, bought it and thrust it in Ivy's tear-streaked face. Even cuddling the bunny, her victory, didn't immediately calm her down. Ivy continued to wail and wail and wail and at one point, Mom just looked at me and said, "Thank God I have one kid who will listen."

I wonder now what Ivy would have been like had she lived, had she had a chance to grow up. Would she have been as stubborn and defiant as I seem to be? Worse? Would I have appeared, like I did as a small child, to be the calm, rational one? Would I have shone in comparison to Ivy's misdeeds? Or would she have settled down, matured, and grown into a responsible young adult?

I try to picture what Ivy would look like as a teenager. Taller than me, I think, her hair still blond, her skin alabaster white and smooth. I decide we still would have gotten along, that we still would have been the best of friends. I think she would have been more outgoing than me, more positive, more hopeful. I think, actually, she would have been a lot like Jaz.

I smile, because I like the idea that Ivy would have been like Jaz. Gregarious and friendly and open. I think she would have loved Jaz's idea of vandalizing her school-turned-quarantine-camp, that she would have participated with glee.

Which means that Ivy would not have been perfect. She would not have been a saint or an angel. She would have been a wholly, completely, flawed human.

Like me.

Mom and Dad wouldn't have liked her better, or loved her more. They would have been just as exasperated with her, as frustrated and fearful and angry with her as they were about me.

I almost skip the rest of the way to her grave, as if her ghost, her playful, six-year-old self, was leading me on. And I feel like I'm eight again, running after my beautiful, annoying, fun, irritating sister.

From the top of the knoll, I spot Ivy's grave. It's marked by a small headstone of white marble, tucked beside two larger, weathered slabs of gray. I jog over, feeling inappropriately giddy. *I'm here, Ivy,* I think. *I made it.*

I crouch in front of the headstone. It's a simple oval, nothing ornate or embellished or childlike and I'm pleased my parents had good taste. It makes the marker feel more dignified, more timeless and that's what Ivy deserves. She deserves to be remembered as a person, not as a kid who died young.

"You've missed a hell of a ride," I tell her. "It's over now, of course. But then again, you know that, since Mom and Dad are with *you* now. I guess that's fair, eh? I got them for nine years, now it's your turn."

I see her in my mind as the teen girl I conjured. The tall, lithe, blond girl I imagined, the one who'd be friends with Jaz. I like thinking of Ivy this way, as a teen like me instead of as a kid like Holly. It somehow seems right. And suddenly, it seems like a relief, too, to have separated them. Suddenly I feel like Holly is Holly, her own little person, not a living specter of my dead sister. Isn't that why I was drawn to her in the first place? Because she reminded me of Ivy, right down to the similarities of their names. But how fair was I to Holly, thinking she could stand in for Ivy, thinking she could replace her, thinking she could *be* her? Holly shouldn't have to be Ivy. She should be allowed to be her own feisty, spunky self.

"Do you know why I'm here?" I ask. I picture Ivy perching on her headstone, swinging her legs, tapping her heels against the marble. She'd shake her blond mane.

*Why are you here, Lyra?*

"I'm going to turn myself in," I say. "To Hendricks, the guy who killed our parents."

I expect my ghost-Ivy to protest, the way David did, but she smiles.

*I know.*

"You think Mom and Dad will be mad?" I look up at the sky. "They gave up their lives to protect me and the moment they're gone, I throw it all away."

*Nah*, Ivy says.

"How do you know?" I want her to be right. I want Mom and Dad to understand what I'm doing, to forgive me for what I'm about to do.

*They know it's up to you, now.*

I know this whole conversation is all in my head. I know Ivy isn't real, that I'm probably just telling myself what I want to hear, but it's working. With every imagined dialogue, I feel lighter, freer. It's a different sensation than when I felt the millstone lift from around my neck—that was the agents, the researchers, the government who imposed it on me, weighed me down —but this feeling now is like I'm stripping off layers of . . .

Guilt.

Talking to ghost-Ivy feels like I'm letting go of my guilt. Guilt that I killed her, guilt that I killed my parents. Guilt that I'm disappointing my parents.

*That's* what's different, I realize, from when I was at Mama Jua's funeral, when I felt like I could have saved her, that I should have saved her. Here, today, in this cemetery, I don't feel burdened by everything I could have done or should have done. Maybe I could have saved Ivy by not coming close to her when I was first infected, but how could I have known? I was only eight and not even the medical experts understood how contagious Hecate's Plague was. Maybe I shouldn't have gone to Mama Jua's funeral, which means Hendricks wouldn't have seen me there, wouldn't have sent agents after me, wouldn't have caught us, wouldn't have infected my parents to use them as leverage against me, wouldn't have killed them, but how was I to know that would be the chain reaction? How could I have foreseen a visit to say goodbye to my only friend would have resulted in my parents' death? And maybe I should hold a grudge against Hendricks forever for what he did to my family, maybe I should spurn him and his pathological researchers and say "Screw you," and disappear into the wilds with David. But I'm not turning myself in to become a tortured guinea pig for Hendricks's sake, but for the sake of Jaz's older brother Joseph and Jaz's parents and my new friend Frank and his daughter in New York. They're the ones I want to save.

*You do what you gotta do,* Ivy says.

"Thanks, Ivy," I say out loud. "Take care of Mom and Dad for me, okay?"

I'm ready to leave. I've said my goodbyes. Just before I go, though, I reach out my hand, and trace my fingers across the black words engraved on the white marble.

*Ivy Harmon*
*Our Blessing for Six Years, One Week and Six Days*
*Rest in Peace, Sweet Love*

I like the inscription my parents chose. It's simple, yet specific. Six years, one week, six days. I smile, trying to imagine the same idea used on my own tombstone.

*Lyra Harmon*
*Our never-ending blessing for more than a million years, a gazillion weeks and a bazillion days. Rest in peace if you ever get around to it.*

I turn away from the grave and head back up the little hill, my mind still on the inscription. It just occurs to me that I never knew exactly when Ivy died. I remember she got sick on her birthday; I remember Mom and Dad coming into the hospital where they were keeping me prisoner even though I was no longer sick, to tell me Ivy got sick the night before.

"Like the flu?" I asked, my skin going cold. But I knew I was wrong.

"Like the plague," Dad answered softly.

And I remember that a little while later, Mom and Dad told me she'd died.

One week and six days later, it seems.

I stop dead in my tracks.

Ivy died thirteen days after she got sick.

*Thirteen* days.

Ivy lived ten days *longer* than everyone else who died of the plague.

Except for Jaz, of course. Jaz lived with the plague for ten days before she died.

And Hendricks thought that Jaz had antibodies in her system because she had survived longer than anyone else.

But nine years ago, during the first outbreak, no one knew anything about Hecate's Plague. No one realized that it kills everyone in three days.

Everyone except, it seems, my sister.

Does that mean . . . ? Could she have had . . . ?

I try to take a deep breath, but I feel like I'm hyperventilating. My mind is whirling, spinning, spiraling. The possibilities, the consequences, the impact . . .

What if Ivy's blood had antibodies?

# CHAPTER 17

I walk around and around the cemetery, agitated.

Thirteen days.

Ivy could have had antibodies.

She could have survived if someone had known, if someone had helped her.

Why did no one know? Why did no one help her?

Why did *Hendricks* not help her? He was there; he treated her the way he treated me. He recognized the potential for antibodies in Jaz; why not in Ivy? If he had, he would have found a cure and she would have lived. And the second outbreak would never have happened, and tens of thousands of other people would never have died. My parents would never have died. Hendricks wouldn't have needed to infect them to manipulate me because he already would have *had* a cure.

*Goddamn* that man.

Is he that incompetent, that inept that he missed his shot finding a cure almost a decade ago? If so, that's a huge problem for me because my freedom and my future is riding on his ability to extract a cure for the plague from my phoenix cells.

Or what if he *did* notice Ivy was living longer than the others? What if he tested her blood and she didn't have antibodies and she just died slower? What if there was never any hope of getting antibodies from the blood of someone who dies of the disease? What if my quest to find Jaz had always been a fool's errand? What if Hendricks knew that but risked my parents' lives regardless?

God, I'm so sick of questions. I just want answers.

And Hendricks will damn well give them to me, I decide. I'll make sure of that. I have leverage and I'm no longer afraid to use it.

I leave the cemetery, alert for any signs I'm being followed. I tell myself that I don't have to search for suspicious shadows or listen for unnatural rustles anymore, but old habits die hard. After nine years on the run, I can't seem to let down my guard. Maybe that's for the best, though, because now I'm afraid I'll be picked up before I can have my quiet little chat with the good Dr. Hendricks.

It doesn't take me long to get to Hendricks's house. Given our knotted history, I expected Hendricks's house to be crawling with agents, but I don't see any. Are they hiding or do they think I'd never return to Washington, to Hendricks?

It doesn't matter, I remind myself. If they're here, they're here. If I'm caught, I'm caught. I'm done running.

I take a deep breath and walk up Hendricks's path to the front door. I raise my hand—it trembles—and I ring the doorbell. I hear the chime echo inside and suddenly I'm petrified. What the hell am I doing at the wolf's door?

It's not too late; no one's answered yet. I still have time to sprint down the path and slip away.

I hear footsteps on the other side.

*Go! Run!*

But I don't. My heart hammers, but I steel myself against my fate.

The door creaks open. I hope it's Hendricks and not his wife. I don't know what she knows about me and I don't want to explain.

The door flings open and the person on the other side isn't Hendricks.

It's David.

My eyes widen in shock and before I can understand, he's pulled me into the house, into the front hall, slammed shut the door and smothered me in a tight embrace. I can't make sense of why he's here, but I lean into him like I never left. He holds me like this, like he won't ever let go and for a moment I believe he won't. I believe we'll stay like this forever, the two of us locked together, unmoving and for that moment it's all I want. The realities of my world—the plague and my phoenix cells and the war and David's call up—all disappear as if *they* were the illusion and the only thing that's real is us, together, my arms around him, his arms around me.

He steps back, breaking the spell, and brings my world, my fate and his rushing back to me, scalding me with pain of our reality.

"What are you *doing* here?" I ask, because now that I think about it, I'm afraid. If David is here in his cousin's house, he'll be easily discovered by the Conscription Service. He won't escape the draft, he won't be free from the war, he won't live safely with his brother and sort-of father in Canada.

David doesn't answer right away. Instead, he takes my hand—it feels so good against my own—and leads me into the living room. The house is a museum, proper and formal with important paintings on the walls and china plates on display, and I'm envious of the antique furniture, protected here from the ravages of reality outside these walls.

We sit on the couch, a red-velvet Queen Anne style piece that makes me sit up straight. David doesn't let go of my hand.

"I thought about what you said," David tells me. "That we can't run from our fate."

"*You* can," I challenge him. "Your brother did. Why aren't you with him? You'd be safe there."

"You said yourself I don't want safety. You were right."

"You'd rather be *dead*?" I fire back, because I can't have David die in a miserable, pointless war.

"Yes, goddamn it!" David snaps. He drops my hand and springs up, away from me, and starts pacing and I immediately want to take back my words, my tone, to rewind the clock even two minutes. "Why is it okay for you to be so noble and sacrifice yourself for the greater good of humanity, but not *me*?"

"You?" I shoot back, angry. "What are you offering?" My words sound harsher than I mean, but I can't help it. "*How* is you being killed overseas going to help society?"

David's eyes bore into mine. They bubble with bitterness. "So *you're* the only one who has something to offer the world? You alone are its savior, are you?"

His sneer slices me deep in my soul. Doesn't he get it? My phoenix cells are *all* I have to offer. There's nothing else I can do to give my life purpose. But David can do so much more. As long as he rides out the war, he has his whole future and then he can make anything of himself that he wants. He just has to be patient.

David abruptly changes tack. He drops back beside me on the couch and rests his hand on my knee. His touch stills me as I feel my anger, my fear, receding slightly.

"You were right about me," he says, with a half-smile. "I don't want to hide. I never have. I want to fight."

"You want to fight the government, you said, not their war," I repeat his words from last night by the lake.

"Exactly," he responds. "But there are more ways than one to resist."

"How?"

"Arabic," David responds.

"Your knowledge of Arabic is going to save the world?" I ask, instinctively pulling away from him. "How? By understanding the cries of the people you're about to kill?"

Immediately I regret my words. What's *wrong* with me? David is here right in front of me, we're together and all I'm doing is alienating him?

David's eyes flash with fire, but he shows more restraint than I seem to be capable of. "*You* were the one who said that if you can try to save even one life it's worth it."

"How are you going to do that?" I insist again, because I honestly don't understand how being the government's mouthpiece will save a life.

"There are Interpreter Battalions in the army," David says. "If I'm posted to one of those units then maybe I can help . . . I don't know . . . negotiate a local ceasefire or warn a neighborhood before they're bombed or listen to what they need . . ." He turns to me, defiant, aggressive. "You don't know how your phoenix cells will translate into a cure for Hecate's Plague, but you're willing to take that risk. This is no different."

I let out a breath, deflating, as if his logic has pricked my self-righteous bubble. He's right. It's an incredible long shot that my cells will help end the disease. But it's all I have, all I can do, so how can I fault David for wanting to do the same? Come to think of it, his knowledge of Arabic may end up saving more lives than my phoenix cells.

His efforts may end up being more important than mine.

His victories may end up being greater than mine.

I feel a sharp, unexpected stab of jealousy, but then my next thought is shame. Is that all I care about? The credit, the glory? Is that who I am?

"Lyra," David is talking to me, and I drag my attention back to him. He shifts closer to me. "You were right yesterday when you told me we have choices. I understand now why you're doing what you're doing—I hate it, by the way," and here David offers me a sad smile, "and I know you don't like me going off to war. To be honest, I don't like it either, but I hope you will understand."

I understand, goddamn it. I do. David is doing to me what I did to him yesterday and now I understand his pain, his fear, his hurt.

"I don't want you to die," I say softly.

"I don't want you to live," David replies earnestly.

I burst out laughing. I know what he means, that he doesn't want me to suffer as a lab rat, but his words sound ridiculous and I can't stop myself. At first David looks wounded, like I'm mocking his sincerity until he seems to realize what he's said and he breaks out laughing, too. The tension between us disappears and our fate is decided: David will go off to war and I will go off to the research prison and we will both do what we can to make this fucked up world a better place.

"How about this?" I say. "If we do this war/lab rat thing, then let's make a pact."

"What kind of pact?"

"If I live, you live, okay?"

It takes him a moment to get my joke, but when he does, he lets out a deep, resonant laugh, that's so full of hope, I actually think I could believe my own deal.

We lapse into a warm, contented silence. I lean against his shoulder on the antique couch, again just the two of us and I know it won't last, I know the real world, the one neither of us wants to face waits for us just outside these walls, but I also know that's the way it has to be. It sucks, but didn't Jaz say we have to find the fun in the moments we have?

I hear a little cough and I glance up to the doorway. Hendricks is standing there, a broken man, looking old, rumpled, pale, his face wrinkled like linen. He seems unsurprised at my presence and I guess that David told him I was coming. I wonder how much more David explained about my purpose here.

I don't move from the couch, and neither does David who stays beside me, his arm wrapped protectively around my shoulder, as if we are the hosts and Hendricks is the guest.

"Did Ivy have antibodies?" I say without preamble. Hendricks deserves no courtesy from me.

Hendricks frowns, confused.

"Ivy died thirteen days after she got sick," I help him out.

I watch Hendricks's face closely, looking for signs that this information comes as no surprise, but he startles and I think it's genuine. I think he truly didn't know. That doesn't let him off the hook, though.

"How did you *not* know that?" I ask. "You treated Ivy."

Hendricks drops into an old, upholstered chair, rubbing his forehead. He looks tired, wrung out. Defeated. "It was chaotic back then," Hendricks begins. "We didn't know what we were dealing with. So many people, so many kids . . ." his voice fades.

"Cut the bullshit," I snap, unwilling to buy into his melancholic self-pity. "Tell me about Ivy."

Hendricks leans forward and drapes his elbows over his knee. "I honestly don't know much about Ivy. You were my focus, Lyra. You were our salvation. We were so convinced that you had the answer to a cure or a vaccine, that *you* had antibodies, so we didn't consider people who died from the disease. So yes, I treated Ivy, but only until I learned that her cells were nothing like yours. I was a researcher, remember, not a family doctor."

"You didn't care," I say bitterly.

Hendricks's head snaps up like I've slapped him. "Didn't care?" he repeats, his voice barbed. "Who I am—what I have become—is because I care. I care too much," he finishes heavily.

He drops his head, and with his hands still folded in his lap, he looks like he's praying. Maybe he is. Maybe he's seeking absolution, forgiveness. Let him try, the pathetic bastard. He won't find it from me.

"You said Jaz may have had antibodies because she lived longer than anyone else with the plague, but Ivy survived even longer than Jaz. *She* may have had antibodies." I pause, then, bitterly, I add, "You blew it."

I expect Hendricks to shrink from my accusation, but instead he seems surprisingly animated. He straightens in his chair, then pops out of it and starts pacing. He's muttering to himself and I look to David for answers, but he only shrugs in surprise.

Hendricks snaps his head up. "It's possible," he announces. He rushes toward the door.

"*What's* possible, George?" David calls to him.

Hendricks whips around, jittery with excitement. "That we may still have a sample of Ivy's blood."

I look up, surprised. "Really?"

"It's a long-shot," he admits. "Because we were so focused on phoenix cells as the answer, we dismissed everything else. And since your sister didn't have them . . ."

"But if you did have a sample of her blood, you could check for antibodies? Even after almost a decade?" I ask.

Hendricks nods. "You'd be surprised at how much researchers can extract from old blood. Investigators do it all the time, even if it's from a small stain on a piece of clothing."

But then he turns serious, as if reconsidering his initial enthusiasm. "As I say, it's a long shot that we kept any samples." He rushes out of the room, then pops his head back in. "Don't leave. I'll be back." A minute later I hear the front door open and click shut.

David and I look at each other.

Is it possible we're this close to a cure? If Hendricks finds Ivy's blood and if she had antibodies, could we finally beat the plague?

"Imagine if they'd examined Ivy's blood more closely back then," I say.

But David shakes his head. “Don’t do that, Lyra. You’ll drive yourself crazy trying to rewrite the past.”

“But your grandmother would still be alive, and Holly’s parents, and mine.”

“And you’d still have phoenix cells,” David reminds me. “They’d still be after you.”

David’s right. Whether I like it or not, my life seems to have a trajectory, like a speeding car. I can either control it in the direction it’s heading, or I can crash.

We sit in suspended animation, the future again unclear, and I think maybe this is the way it always is. My parents didn’t know what was to come—their capture or their deaths—and Hendricks didn’t either, not before he saw me at Mama Jua’s funeral. And just yesterday at this time David and I were making our way toward Canada with a little girl in tow, without an inkling that I was about to upend our lives. I guess the future truly is unwritten.

So when Hendricks returns an hour later, I’m prepared for his answer, whatever it is. Still, it stings when I see his crumpled features and I know he didn’t find it.

“If we had any of Ivy’s blood, it was destroyed a long time ago,” Hendricks explains. “And with your sister’s body embalmed and buried, we can’t get any more blood, so I guess we’ll never know. Unless,” he says wryly, “you and your parents happened to have kept anything stained with her blood?”

I laugh ruefully. A family on the run can’t be sentimental. The only thing of Ivy’s that my parents allowed me to keep was a ratty old stuffed bunny rabbit I kept shoved in the bottom of my backpack.

Then I stop. A sudden image bursts into my mind. Could it be . . . ?

David looks at me, alarmed. “Lyra, what is it?”

I turn to Hendricks. “She had a stuffed bunny. My parents

wanted to throw it out because it was so dirty and—" I pause. "Blood-stained."

Hendricks leans forward in his chair. "Tell me you still have it."

I picture the little gray stuffy as I shake my head no.

My parents never wanted me to keep the bunny.

"Throw it out, it's filthy," Mom would say whenever she saw me with it.

"But it's Ivy's," I'd protest.

"Yes, but *she* isn't here, is she?" Mom would snap.

For a long time, I thought Mom was a cruel, cold-hearted woman, not even letting me keep one thing from my little sister, but Mama Jua explained it to me.

"Your mama's still hurting, honey," she said, cradling the stuffed animal I'd brought to show her. "This little rabbit reminds her of the little girl she couldn't save. Why d'you think she's so fiercely protective of you? She just wants to keep you safe, that's all."

"But I can't even have it sitting in my room," I grumbled. "I have to keep it wrapped and hidden in the bottom of my backpack or Mom will throw it out."

"Well, then, how about you just keep it here with me?" Mama Jua offered. She got out of her chair, walked over to the end table crowded with pictures of her family and nestled the rabbit in between the frames. "There, now, she's like my family," Mama Jua smiled. "Anytime you want to see your sister's bunny, you just come right on in. You know not to knock."

"No," I say again to David and Hendricks, "I don't have the bunny. But I know where it is.

# CHAPTER 18

The next morning, David and I are walking along the railroad tracks behind my old Jamestown neighborhood where, just two weeks ago, I stood screaming wildly into the wind at the injustice in my life. Two weeks later, the injustices have mounted, yet I don't feel like I need to play chicken with a train to feel alive anymore. Instead, all I need is a purpose. Now I have that. Now I'm going to march up to Mama Jua's house, unrecognizable in a bright scarf, tailored coat and oversized sunglasses—hiding in plain sight—and I'm going to walk right through her door, into the living room, and scoop up that rabbit.

Hendricks doubts our plan will work. "The agents are watching your grandmother's house, too, David," he told us yesterday when we were still in Washington. "They know Lyra was friends with her."

"Then *I'll* go in and find the rabbit," David said.

"David, don't you get it?" Hendricks scoffed. "*Anyone* who goes near that house will be considered a suspect. You, me, your mom, anyone from the family, a stranger we hire off the street . . . They'll be immediately arrested and interrogated. They won't even come close to retrieving the rabbit."

"Then I'll *sneak* in," David insisted.

"Then you'll be shot and killed," Hendricks snapped back. "You know these agents don't mess around."

"But *I* won't be," I said. "I won't be killed."

"You'll be captured," Hendricks warned, "and sent back to the lab. Most likely *before* you get the rabbit."

Hendricks was right, I knew, but I also knew I had to try. It's better the agents find *me* than someone else.

"I'm doing it," I told Hendricks and David.

"Then I'll create a diversion so you can get in unseen," David said.

I think of Mo and his diversion, which ended with his bullet-ridden body bleeding into the ground, and my heart constricts. I strenuously objected to David's plan, since that *also* meant him getting caught—or worse—but David just smiled.

"You sacrifice, I sacrifice," he said.

My pace slows as we approach the hole in the fence beside my street, and I'm shaking. My stomach is in knots and my heart hammers in my chest. I feel like it skips a dozen beats, then speeds up, double-time.

"You okay?" David asks, turning toward me.

"Maybe?" I reply. I honestly don't know. I'm not okay that my parents died; I'm not okay that I'm working with Hendricks, my parents' murderer; I'm not okay that David is going off to war, yet I am okay because I feel like we're making the right choices. How does that make any sense?

David takes my hand and squeezes it.

"You should go back," I tell him. I'm jittery. My hands tremble, my body shudders.

David pulls me into a fierce hug. I cling to him, wishing he'd never let me go.

"You go back, I go back," David whispers in my ear. "You go forward, I go forward."

*You live, I live*, I think of our private joke.

I pull away and take a deep breath. I have to do this. "We go forward."

David draws his face close to mine and kisses me. His lips linger on mine and I lock away how it feels because this is it, our last kiss. From here on in, I'll have only my memories. Of the kiss, of him, of us.

Tears scald my eyes and burn my cheek as David steps back. He rests his palm on my face, wiping away a tear with his thumb.

When he speaks, his voice quivers. "I love you, Lyra."

I nod, my lips pressed together, because I can't talk. My throat closes up; I can barely breathe.

And there's nothing more to say, anyway. No "I'll see you soon," or "we'll be together again" because we both know better than to lie to each other. With David being sent off to war and me being sent off to science, we know we will never see each other again.

"Ready?" David asks.

*No! I'm not ready to leave you or have you leave me. I'm not ready to sacrifice myself or have you sacrifice yourself.* I try to steady my voice. "Ready."

David gives my hand one last squeeze—I grip it hard—then he bolts out from behind the bushes onto the road. I hear his feet pounding down the cracked pavement and I hear a wild yell.

"Where *is* she?" David screams, turning into a madman. "What have you done with her?"

I slink onto the street toward Mama Jua's house. Ahead, I see David flailing toward a pack of agents standing in my yard.

"Where is Lyra?" David demands.

One agent approaches him, his gun raised. "Stop," he orders.

*Don't go overboard, David*, I beg. I can't watch him get shot. I can't watch him die. Memories of Mo running out of the school, flinging himself into a hail of bullets crowd into my mind. I can't let that happen to David.

But David knows the plan. He stops and raises his hands, but still he yells, he screams. "Goddamn it, you have her! Let me *see* her!"

I notice the two agents in front of Mama Jua's house—just like Hendricks warned—look my way, and I forget to breathe. But I keep my chin up, my head held high and I continue walking purposefully.

I feel their eyes on me, even as David's rants fill the air. *Come on*, I think. *Turn away.* They don't though. They continue to glare, and I see their posture stiffen as I approach Mama Jua's house.

Oh God, David's distraction isn't working. My heart drums in my chest, and sweat pools at the back of my neck, underneath my scarf. I can't slip into Mama Jua's backyard with the agents' attention on me, so I have to change plans. Abruptly I stride up the path of Mama Jua's next-door neighbor and rap confidently on the door. *Please don't be home*, I think, because I can't come up an excuse for my presence on the spot and I can't afford any delays. I risk a sidelong glance at the agents and breathe with relief when I notice their attention is finally drawn toward my house. Quickly, I scurry around the side wall and sneak into Mama Jua's backyard. I can still hear David call out my name, but slowly his voice fades to a whimper.

My stomach flips with anxiety. What are they doing to him? I imagine him being handcuffed and then shoved into a car . . . No. I have to focus, concentrate. Just like with Mo, I can't let David's capture be for nothing. I hurry up the back porch. The door, as I expected, is unlocked. Thank God for Mama Jua's trust in people. I quickly slip inside, close the door, and step away from the window, listening hard. I wait for the sound of footsteps outside, or the rattle of the front door, but I hear nothing. There is only the quiet, comforting tick of Mama Jua's mantle clock coming from the living room. I scuttle forward, avoiding the windows.

I'm nervous now, but not because of the guards. I'm nervous that the bunny might not be there—maybe some family member did get by the agents and cleared out Mama Jua's stuff. If so, they would surely have thrown away an old, stained toy.

I sneak into the living room, but for a moment, I can't look up. I close my eyes. If the rabbit isn't there, all is lost. No blood, no antibodies, no cure. Or what if the bunny is there, but there are no bloodstains?

*No, stop second-guessing, Lyra.* I've come this far; I have to finish.

I snap open my eyes.

I look at the end table by the window.

*Oh thank God.*

There, snuggled among the frames, right where Mama Jua left him, is the bunny. In a flash I'm across the room and snatching the grey rabbit off the table. Quickly, I examine it and yes, yes, I'm right. Those dark patches around the bunny's nose and on the tips of its floppy ears look like dried blood—rust-colored and faded, but blood.

I turn to leave, but among the crowded frames on the table, I catch a glimpse of an image that looks familiar.

A picture of David.

It's a small picture set inside a thin silver frame, and it's a close up of his face. He's smiling, and now I am, too, because I know that smile. I love that smile. His black-pearl eyes crinkle as they stare beyond the camera's lens as if he's laughing. I don't remember the picture, but I must have seen it, probably a dozen times at least, every time I came to visit. Maybe Mama Jua even showed it to me when she was joking about setting us up.

I have to have it. It's all I've got left of David, now that he's gone from my life. I know Mama Jua wouldn't mind. If anything, she'd press it into my hand if she were here, chuckling the whole time over her matchmaking success.

I reach over to grab it, but my hand brushes against another, larger frame, and it collapses onto the picture in front, which, like dominos, knocks over another. My heart leaps into my throat. I lunge to catch the toppling pictures, but there are too many of them and they crash to the floor. For a moment I freeze, like a deer caught in headlights, because the smashing glass reverberates throughout the house.

*Run or hide? Run or hide?*

I hear the tread of footsteps on the front porch, then the front door slam open. I snatch up David's picture—I have to have David's picture—and I run. I'm not going to be caught like a sitting duck. I'd rather be taken down like a wild animal.

I flee through the dining room and into the kitchen.

The agents see me. They bark at me to stop—do they know it's me? Do they realize how close they are to their prey?

I lose momentum when I pull open the back door. An agent lunges for me; he grasps the edge of my coat and I'm yanked back. Instinctively, I thrash against him. My arms are loose; he can't pin me down. I kick out hard; my foot rams into his groin. He drops like stone and I shoot out of the house. I hear the squawk of a radio—the second agent, calling for back up. Then she's after me and I cringe, because I expect to feel a bullet in my back, but she doesn't shoot. Maybe she doesn't know who I am yet. Maybe they don't shoot everybody. Maybe they only shoot me.

I race through the neighbor's yard, but there's a fence in front of me. If I had my hands free, I could scramble over it, but I have the rabbit in one hand and David's picture in the other and I refuse to let them go.

I think about hiding in the old drainage pipe by the railroad tracks, like I tried to do the last time, but the agents are closer and the shrubs in the field will slow me down. I'm a fast runner and I only have to get a couple of blocks to the coffee shop where I'm supposed to meet Hendricks. I take off.

I veer right, through the neighbor's yard and back out onto the road. I don't look back toward my house. I don't see how many agents are after me, but I hear them. They thunder behind me and I pray that I'm lighter and faster than the herd. Pumping my arms harder, harder, harder, I fly over the pavement, my feet barely touching the ground. My lungs burn, my muscles are on fire, but I keep going. This is life or death.

A blast of wind pushes the scarf off the top of my head and my black curls come loose. Goddamn it, if the agents didn't already know it was me, they do now. My hair blows wildly around my face, into my eyes, and I try awkwardly to tug away the loose strands, but the distraction slows me down.

I see a black car up ahead. They're going to corner me. I won't make it. I won't get the rabbit to Hendricks.

I feel a sob escape my lips as I slow down, my energy spent. I have only a few seconds and then it's over. If I believed I could convince the agents to hand over the bunny to Hendricks, then maybe it would have been worth it, but I know I can't. They won't believe me that a worn old stuffed animal could stop the plague. They'd toss away the rabbit and toss me back into Moto's lab.

*I'm sorry,* I think, but I don't know what I'm sorry about or to whom I'm apologizing. David, because I couldn't convert his sacrifice to pay off? Ivy, because I couldn't ensure her legacy? My parents, for getting caught, again?

I hear the screech of tires, the crunch of metal, and my head snaps up. A huge silver car, as thick as a tank, clips the back corner of the agents' car, nudging it away. The silver car roars toward me.

I see the grim determination on the driver's face: Hendricks.

He shoots by me, then spins into a tight turn, barricading me from the agents running toward us.

He leans over and swings open the passenger's side door. "Get in," he shouts.

I dive into the car, clutching the stuffed rabbit and picture frame in a death grip, and slam the door shut. My breath comes short and quick, like I'm hyperventilating. I try to calm myself, inhaling and exhaling slowly.

The agents surround the car, their guns drawn. "Come out with your hands up," one of them calls out.

I hold Ivy's stuffed rabbit to my chest, thinking about what I said to her in the cemetery. It's time to move on.

"Goodbye, Ivy," I whisper.

Hendricks pulls out a plastic bag from his coat pocket and opens it. Gently, I place the rabbit inside.

"I won't lose it," Hendricks reassures me. "I can talk my way out of this." He waves at the agents as if they're pesky flies.

If only *I* could talk my way out of it . . .

Hendricks sees my face, and his expression softens. "I won't desert you, Lyra," he says.

I don't believe him—he's in this for himself, and always has been— but I don't really care, as long as he works on a cure. And if the rabbit isn't the answer, then maybe my phoenix cells are. That may take a lot longer and condemn more people to Hecate's curse, but either way, I'm not sorry I did what I did. In fact, I'm proud of it. I remember thinking, in my deepest moments of despair, that the real villain in my life was actually a meaningless, purposeless, restless, existence and I was right. But now I've vanquished it. I have meaning. I have purpose. Maybe I won't end up saving the world, but at least I'm taking a risk to make it better.

Clinging to that thought, clinging to the picture of David, I open the car door and climb out.

# CHAPTER 19

I keep my eyes shut as I step in front of the little mirror fastened to the bare wall. My shaking hands lift to my head; I try to stop them, but they will not obey. Instead, they land on my shorn head, the skin of my palms smooth against the exposed skin of my scalp.

Gone. All my thick, tangled curls, gone.

I can feel it, but I can't make myself open my eyes to see the damage.

I think about all I've had to endure in the three months I've been here. Needles and x-rays and MRIs and CAT scans; biopsies, bone marrow extraction, even exploratory surgeries. I think about the pain and how they're testing my tolerance for it. I thought last week, when they took to breaking my bones—first fingers, then toes—to see for themselves the level of my pain threshold, that the scientists could sink no lower.

I was wrong.

They shaved off my hair.

I feel a prick of hot tears behind my closed eyes, and I try again to tell myself it doesn't matter. It's only hair; it will grow back. It didn't even hurt.

But it did.

It hurt more than the scalpels and knives and broken bones.

I don't even know why they did it. I assume they're preparing for another medical procedure. Maybe they'll perform a lobotomy? Wouldn't that make it easier for them . . . To rid me of my personality, my intellect so they truly have a living, breathing, rag doll they can do with as they please.

I'm dying to know but I refuse to ask. I'm not going to break my vow of silence. I remember Hendricks telling Moto on the night he helped me escape that they needed me to talk about my history in order to fully understand how my cells work in real life. That's why they will never hear my voice. They will never hear an answer to a single question about my body, so I'm not about to ask one of my own—because Moto would use that against me. He would say he'll only answer my question if I answer his. But I won't do it. I won't tell the intrusive bastards when I hit puberty or how regular my menstrual cycles were when I was on the run. As it is, they've measured every ounce of blood from my periods since I've been here—they wouldn't even give me tampons. They also had the temerity to ask about my sex life—after they did a full gynecological exam.

"Tell me, Lyra," Dr. Moto said, coming into the exam room after his minions had violated me, then left me to get dressed. "How old were you when you first had penetrative sexual intercourse?" Moto settled himself on the doctor's stool in front of me, a thick chart open in his lap. He scanned the file—he never looks at me—then launched into his questions. "Your hymen is broken, and yes, yes, yes, it's not an accurate indicator of virginity, but with two boyfriends . . . let's see . . ." he searches the page, "Jonah Peterson and David Jua . . . I expect you were sexually active."

My stomach knots up in anger. How *dare* he . . . But I work to smooth out my expression so he can read nothing from my face. If I'm not going to speak verbally, I'm also not going to communicate with body language, either. I'll be damned if he learns anything about my sex life, like me losing my virginity to Jonah. *Never* will Moto know about our tryst on the beach, our awkward, passionate, crazy fun night under the stars. We had it all planned out—the rough wool blanket, the pilfered wine, the condoms. I remember how nervous we were, how shy, and I remember how I flinched when it hurt, although it was nothing like pain I've been used to, but Jonah didn't believe me when I told him I was okay, so he wouldn't stop apologizing until I kissed him hard to shut him up and that broke the tension and we laughed and laughed and rolled around in the sand and washed ourselves off in the ocean . . .

No, *never* will I let Moto use that memory—or any memory—against me.

I love denying them information they so desperately want. I love driving them crazy—just like the agents did to me when they first picked me up and refused to speak to me. But most of all, I love the control. My silence is my own. No matter what they do to me, they can't take it away.

I feel better now, thinking of Moto's overall frustration with me, so I decide I *can* look at my bald reflection. I drop my hands, take a deep breath, and open my eyes. I can't see my whole face in the too-small mirror, so the first thing I notice is my eyes. Bright, crystal blue spheres pop out at me, stark against my pale skin.

I feel a welcome rush of relief. They're *my* eyes. I step back, bumping against the end of my bed, and slowly turn my head from side to side. I'm now aware of the lightness around my shoulders; I never realized how much my long hair weighed me down. I jiggle my head, like a dog shaking off water, and I feel a rush of cool air across my neck.

I crawl on the edge of the bed and kneel back to get more distance from the mirror. Now I see my whole face, my whole head.

And still, I see only *me*.

Then I laugh, and it comes out like a witch's cackle and that makes me laugh even more and that gets me thinking of Mama Jua who always wanted me to laugh and laugh some more.

They haven't done it. *Moto, et al.* They haven't broken me. They haven't erased me. They can siphon off every bodily fluid I have, shave every hair off my head, but they can't drain my resilience.

And with a sudden, unexpected, triumphant thought, I realize that's what my parents gave me. Resiliency. Adaptability. Perseverance. Their legacy wasn't just a lifetime of loneliness and isolation, after all. They also taught me how to be strong in the face of cruel circumstances. They taught me what I needed to know to live the life I chose for myself.

I lie back on my pillow; the pillowcase feels strange on my bald head, cool and crisp, but surprisingly refreshing and I think about Mom and Dad for the first time without the stabbing pain of a serrated knife carving up my heart. I don't think they would agree with my choices, not after all their sacrifices to protect me, but then again, I didn't agree with all of theirs. They should have listened to me better, and yes, maybe I should have listened to them better, but finally, all these months later, I've let go of my anger. The lava beast, my constant companion for years, has disappeared.

And that brings me an overwhelming sense of relief. Tears pool in the corners of my eyes. The floodgates of warm, welcome memories spill open, and I smile.

I remember when I was about ten or eleven and we were living in Utah, there was a total eclipse of the sun. Dad bought us three pairs of eclipse glasses—a luxury we could barely afford, but Dad insisted. He said this once-in-a-lifetime experience would be as valuable to me as food.

"We're not made of cells—phoenix or otherwise," he said to me with a wink. "We're made of memories and I want to give you as many extraordinary memories as I can."

I remember sitting in our backyard, on plastic lawn chairs, watching the moon slide across the face of the sun, and for a while, I was utterly bored. The sky darkened, yes, but it seemed more like the normal gray of cloudy skies than the start of an exciting astronomical event. Then, then . . . The moon crossed paths with the sun and the world turned a grayish purple and then black and then we, all three of us sitting there, our heads tilted to the heavens, turned to shadows, and I was awed.

Dad leaned over to me and whispered, "Just because something can be explained by science doesn't mean it's not magic."

And I remember another memory about magic. In my head, I hear my mom's voice from another night, another lifetime. "*Star light, star bright, first star I see tonight, I wish I may, I wish I might, have this wish I wish tonight.*"

Mom is tucking me into my new bed—which move was that? The fifth or the sixth? I don't remember. How old was I? No idea. But I remember Mom's rhyme and my wish.

"I wish we could go home," I said, whimpering.

Mom smoothed my hair and kissed my forehead. She tapped the cover of the fairy tale book we'd been reading. "You know that Snow White was on the run, too, right?" she asked. "And Sleeping Beauty had to be hidden away, just like you. But they got to live happily ever after; they just had to be patient. Like you have to be."

I remember pulling the blankets up to my chin, muffling my voice. "Will I live happily ever after, too, Mommy?"

Mom tugged the covers off my face and wiped away my tears. "I promise."

The rattle of keys in the lock startles me out of my reverie. I sit up, scowling, alert and on guard. I hate being summoned at their whim.

Dr. Hendricks—George, he insisted I call him—opens the door and walks in, precariously balancing a tottering stack of old books.

I'm a little surprised to see him—Moto has restricted his access to next-to-nothing—but I have to admit that so far, George has kept his word. In all the time I've been here, he hasn't yet deserted me.

"I thought I already read everything you had in your house," I say, plucking a few volumes off the top.

George dumps the rest of them on my bed. "I love what you've done with your hair."

I'm about to snap at him until I realize his sarcasm is sympathetic. "Moto didn't warn you?" I ask.

George sighs. "You know Dr. Moto chooses not to share his research strategies with me anymore. For some reason, after my little stunt trying to protect you in Jamestown, he no longer trusts me." Here George leans closer and fake whispers, as if Moto will hear. "He thinks I'll divulge all of his secrets to you and that will somehow undermine his evidence."

"You did remind him that I'm not *actually* a lab rat, right?" I say.

"Every day, my dear Lyra, every day. In fact, just yesterday, I begged him to move you to a dorm on campus—or at least let you go outside."

My heart leaps ahead of my head. Outside! Yes! I can already feel the hot sun on my face and the cool breeze on my skin. I smell the fresh grass, the summer flowers, maybe even an amaranth plant, like Mama Jua grew in her front garden. I see the night falling. I see the stars, my stars, Vega and the constellation Lyra, sparkling.

George continues wryly. "But Dr. Moto somehow believes you are a significant flight risk, should you leave the confines of these chambers. I do believe he thinks you'll clock me over the head again."

"I just might," I grumble.

"Yes, well, that's the problem, isn't it?"

"Come on, George. You sprung me from here twice before. Do it again."

George looks at me, his hangdog face falling. "Which is why they won't let me near you without a platoon of guards on my tail." He shakes his head backward beyond the closed door where the security detail, the ones who always tail him when he visits me, are lurking.

"But at least you convinced Moto to give me a TV, right? Or a computer or a cell phone, *something*, so I can communicate with the outside world?"

"According to Dr. Moto, you're not supposed to belong to the outside world anymore," George replies. "So, no, I haven't yet convinced him to treat you like a human being instead of an animal. He thinks that if you know what's going on in the world, you'll somehow use that information to escape."

"He's right."

"Yes, Lyra," George says impatiently, "I know, which is why you're not doing yourself any favors by refusing to cooperate."

I think of what he told Moto the night he helped me escape, that to get a little, Moto had to give a little. I raise my eyebrow at George, readying for a fight. Does he think now *I* have to give a little? That I'm going to *try* to curry favors with my captors?

"I found those books in my attic," George quickly changes the topic. "They're old and musty but they're all I've got left. Otherwise, you've read me out of house and home." He smiles and flicks his wrist toward the stack of books already on my metal night table.

I flop down on the bed, dejected. I know George can't do anything more for me; I heard it was a fight just to allow him to bring me books, but still, he *owes* me . . .

I rifle half-heartedly through the books, and I toss aside a dusty tomb on ancient civilizations, a hardcover horticultural encyclopedia, and a faded book of children's tales, among others. I'll read whatever George brings me, whether I like it or not, because it's better than the insanity from boredom, but I really wish he had better taste in books.

"I recommend the leather-bound volume there," George says, nudging it toward me.

It's a century-old philosophical treatise—*No thanks,* I'm about to retort—when I suddenly realize what George means.

Contraband. Oh my God, how long has it been? A month? Six weeks since he slipped me anything in a book? I'd almost given up hope he ever would again.

I flip the book over and shake it open. A thin page of crisp newsprint flutters to my bed. I snatch it up.

"It's from today's paper," George whispers. Eagerly, my eyes drop to the black print and the headline blares at me. *Thirty-Five Days Plague-Free Across the Country: Outbreak Officially Over.*

"Really?" I scan the article, excited and so, so, profoundly relieved. "Ivy's cure is still working?"

He nods, and suddenly I feel tired, bone-weary, near-collapse exhausted. I think back on how upbeat George was in those first few weeks when he insisted I keep the faith, but how could I believe he'd succeed in creating a cure? When my parents were sick, he told me he could have a cure ready within a day. Now it was taking weeks. George tried to explain the complexity of the degraded antibodies—ten-year-old splotches of poorly-stored dried blood from a stuffed animal were extraordinarily hard to work with—but I didn't care. I'd given up everything for this cause. I was desperate to see results.

I skim read the article, my eyes scanning, jumping for key words. "What about the quarantine camps?"

"All closed," George says and his smile widens.

Closed. Shut down. The government-sanctioned death houses are finally out of business. About fucking time.

"And the vaccine?"

"The manufacturer ran out," George explains. "They're making more, but I think we've done enough mass immunization for herd immunity to take effect and ward off another outbreak."

"Do you think Holly got vaccinated?" I ask suddenly. "Didn't you say children were supposed to be prioritized?"

George's eyes always soften when I talk about Holly—almost like he cares about us. "Yes, I assume she did," he answers. "Most schools have reopened, so they've vaccinated every child. Didn't you tell me Holly's now enrolled in kindergarten?"

I nod, thinking of the last letter George smuggled in for me from Alexis, the orphanage's director. I picture Holly running around the play yard, climbing on the monkey bars, chasing her friends. It's the way her life should be.

"Lyra," George says, his tone serious.

I look up, my eyes narrowing, annoyed at his shift in tone. He just gave me good news; I don't want to hear anything bad. "What?" I say, my voice cooling.

"The experiments on your phoenix cells," he says, and pauses. "They're not going well."

"Good," I say, but a coil of anxiety tightens in my chest, choking out my initial relief. George may not be a part of the cloning research team, but he knows enough.

"Not good," George frowns. "It took me months to discover I couldn't use your phoenix cells to find a cure for the plague when you were a kid; I'm afraid it will take them years before they realize they can't create their super soldiers."

My head shoots up, amazed. "You think it's really not possible to clone me?"

George laughs. "You are unclonable, Lyra. You're an original."

I scoff, and brush aside the compliment. "Seriously."

George's smile fades. "Seriously, cloning is possible. Moto is right about that. It's just not practical. Or ethical, for that matter."

"That hasn't stopped them in nine years."

George nods solemnly. "That's what I'm trying to tell you. I'm afraid Moto won't stop. I thought maybe once they met you, they'd see . . ." his voice trails off. Then he takes a deep breath. "I thought I could get you out of here again, but I'm afraid they'll keep you here forever." My stomach sinks, even though I knew that had always been Moto's plan. Why release the goose that lays the golden egg into the hands of potential enemies? No, George was naive to think they'd let me go. I am a top-secret weapon; Moto will ensure I'll never actually see the light of day again. George exhales slowly and a heavy silence descends. What more is there to say? He reaches behind him, his hand twisting the doorknob. "Do you need anything else?" he asks.

"My freedom," I snap.

George looks at me sadly. "Anything else I can actually get for you, like a new mattress or more new clothes? More answers to how your phoenix cells work?"

I shake my bald, shorn, cold head. I'm not up for a science lesson today, although I usually like hearing George's explanations about my physiology. I've already learned so much about my immune system and gene mutations and my hematopoietic stem cells—self-renewing cells found in my bone marrow—as well as George's theory that Ivy had only a minor gene mutation which is why she lived longer than most with Hecate's Plague, but not enough to survive it. George has promised to answer as many of my questions as he can—why has no one seen this mutation before? What will happen to *my* children, if I choose to have them? Will the protection of my phoenix cells ever "run out"?—but he constantly warns me he's often working only on theories. "Honestly Lyra," he keeps saying, "we're just getting to know you." In truth, I think he likes educating me as much to enlighten me as to defy Moto, but I'm not complaining.

George walks to the door, his hand on the handle. "I'll be back as soon as I can," he says. "And Lyra . . ."

I don't look at him. I know what's coming, his ritual. "I'm sorry."

I don't care. I don't care that he's sorry for killing my parents, or for putting me here or for his own guilt. No matter how many answers he gives me, how much information he provides, he won't get the forgiveness he seeks, not from me, and he should know better. He knows I tolerate his visits only because I need him.

"Check out the plant book first," he says quietly, with a nod toward the pile on my bed. "Then I'd recommend the fairy princess book."

I look up at him for a moment and then I snatch the heavy floral encyclopedia from the pile, and flip it open. The door clicks softly behind him as I thumb through the pages, searching for the contraband. What is it, what is it? More newspapers? I fan through the pages, catching glimpses of colorful flowers as if they all belonged to the same elaborate garden until—there! Stuck in the back. A thin white envelope. I set the book down and tear open the letter. Inside is a small photo and I smile at the young man grinning back at me.

David.

He looks good. It's strange to see him in dust-colored camos, but he wears the uniform with an easy confidence. My smile widens to a grin. A sheep in wolf's clothing, I think. Fighting from the inside.

I jump to his letter.

*Hey Lyra,*

*Just wanted to let you know I'm being deployed overseas now that basic training is over; I'll be training for a few weeks at the Interpreter's base and then, well, then who knows where I'll be sent. But if I can save one life, right? That's what we decided. You and me. Saving the world one life at a time (or thousands, in your case).*

*Write me when you can. Hang in there. My mom and Ahimsa haven't given up on getting you out (but don't tell George, okay?).*

*Miss you and love you always,*

*David*

*p.s. Don't forget our deal: you live, I live. I will see you again. Xoxo*

You live, I live. Our inside joke.

My heart pounds at the thought of him fighting in the desert. Mom said it had been hot and dry and dusty when she served ten years ago; what are the conditions like now? Will David be okay? I hate not knowing what's going on. I never thought I'd miss the state-run news until I was barred from even that and it makes me feel nervous, anxious, and scared for David, but then I reread the last line.

*I* will *see you again.*

David's out there, literally stepping into a battle zone and I'm in here, fighting off the enemy, so all logic dictates, all the odds prove, that David is wrong. Yet my breath still catches with a surge of his confidence. Maybe he's right. Maybe we can *make* him right. Somehow. I tuck the letter carefully back into its envelope and place it next to the picture of David in a thin silver frame, the one I took from Mama Jua. Moto wasn't going to let me keep it until George intervened. I still hate George; I hate how he ruined my life, how cold he was, how calculating, but he's my lifeline so I hold a sliver of gratitude him for that.

George said to check two books, and if he put David's letter into the encyclopedia, then whatever's hidden in the pages of the children's stories must be from Holly.

I find the envelope jammed in the middle of the book. It has my named scrawled across the front in thick red crayon. I'm so excited. I've never gotten two letters at a time, but I force myself to open the envelope slowly so I don't rip what's inside. I can't afford to ruin anything Holly sends me. They're my talismans, her notes and drawings and letters. They protect me against despair.

I unfold a simple, hand-drawn picture of Holly and me, and my heart melts. We're stick figures, me in blue crayon and Holly in green. We're standing on top of a brown castle, decorated with red flowers, like in the fairy tales. Above the castle, in the streaks of a black night sky, beside a lopsided yellow star, is one chunky word, its first letter spelled backwards: Sisters.

I start to cry.

I don't have Ivy; I don't have my parents. But I have David and I have Holly.

And I have hope that I'll see them both again. I'm not yet sure how or when, but I'll find a way. I know I will.

I think about the magic that Dad believed existed in this world, and Mom's promise that everything will turn out all right. I think about David's letter and then Holly's picture, and suddenly I'm reminded of something.

I snatch up the plant encyclopedia, and flip to the *A*s.

There: the deep, garnet-red flower.

An amaranth.

The flower Mama Jua gave me, the one she said reminded her of me.

I scan the caption, and when I do, tears burn my eyes.

"Culturally, the amaranth flower has been used as a symbol of immortality since ancient Greece. Its name derives from 'amarantos', which means 'unfading', or 'one that does not wither'. Ancient indigenous people thought of it as a plant that never dies. Like the phoenix bird, it always rises from its ashes."

"They remind me of you," Mama Jua had said when she gave the amaranth flowers to me last fall. "They are beautiful and vibrant and strong and they thrive longer than most."

The words on the page in front of me blur, but I'm smiling. Mama Jua knew. All along, she knew about me. About who I am, what I am, and still she treated me like me. Like Lyra. And even though she must have known what my future would hold, still, she gave me hope I could make my life my own.

She was right.

# ABOUT THE AUTHOR

Jen Braaksma is an author and book coach. Her debut YA fantasy novel, Evangeline's Heaven, was published in 2022. She started her career as a journalist, then veered into the classroom as a high school English teacher for almost two decades. Now a book coach, she helps other writers develop and share their stories. She lives in Ottawa, Canada, with her husband (soulmates do exist!) and two daughters (Best. Kids. Ever.).

*Author photo © Annemarie Grudën*

# SELECTED TITLES FROM SPARKPRESS

SparkPress is an independent boutique publisher delivering high-quality, entertaining, and engaging content that enhances readers' lives, with a special focus on female-driven work. www.gosparkpress.com

***Evangeline's Heaven: A Novel***, Jen Braaksma. $17.95, 978-1-684631-53-7. When war ravages the Seven Heavens, Evangeline, daughter of the rebel angel leader Lucifer, learns how far her father will go to claim power—and has a crisis of faith. With the fate of the Heavens hanging in the balance, she must decide who she's going to be: her father's daughter, or her own person.

***Within Reach: A Novel***, Jessica Stevens. $17, 978-1-940716-69-5. When 17-year-old Xander Hemlock dies, he finds himself trapped in a realm of darkness with thirty days to convince his girlfriend, Lila, that he's not completely dead—even as Lila struggles with a host of issues of her own.

***Beautiful Girl: A Novel***, Fleur Philips. $15, 978-1-94071-647-3. When a freak car accident leaves the 17-year-old model, Melanie, with facial lacerations, her mother whisks her away to live in Montana for the summer until she makes a full recovery.

***Serenade: A Novel***, Emily Kiebel. $15, 978-1-94071-604-6. After moving to Cape Cod after her father's death, Lorelei discovers her great-aunt and nieces are sirens, terrifying mythical creatures responsible for singing doomed sailors to their deaths. When she rescues a handsome sailor who was supposed to die at sea, the sirens vow that she must finish the job or faced grave consequences.

***Running for Water and Sky: A Novel***, Sandra Kring. $17, 978-1-940716-93-0. When 17-year-old Bless Adler visits a local psychic, the woman describes a vision of Bless's boyfriend, Liam, lying in a pool of blood—sending Bless on a 14-block sprint to reach Liam before she loses the only person she's ever opened her heart to.

***But Not Forever: A Novel***, Jan Von Schleh. $16.95, 978-1-943006-58-8. When identical fifteen-year-old girls are mysteriously switched in time, they discover the love that's been missing in their lives. Torn, both want to go home, but neither wants to give up what they now have.